THE WATCHER'S PREY

Ruth May

Copyright © 2026 Ruth May

All rights reserved.

No part of this book may be reproduced, stored in a retrieval system, or transmitted in any form or by any means, electronic, mechanical, photocopying, recording, or otherwise, without prior written permission of the copyright holder, except for brief quotations used in reviews or certain other non-commercial uses permitted by copyright law.

This is a work of fiction. Names, characters, events, and incidents are either the product of the author's imagination or used fictitiously. Any resemblance to actual persons or actual events is entirely coincidental.

This work was authored by a human. Artificial intelligence tools were used solely for grammar and spell-checking and did not generate or contribute to the creative content.

ISBN-13.970-1-7643997 1-5

Cover design by Ruth May using an image sourced and licensed from https://www.shutterstock.com/g/nikolavukojevic (Cafe Racer)

Prologue

She takes a long draw of her cigarette as she leans her back against the cold brick wall. The alley cuts between two city centre buildings, the one behind her casting enough muted light from those still working on the seventeenth floor to pierce the blackness. She needs a break. She's struggling to find the motivation to head back inside.

Slowly she exhales, creating a plume of fumes dissipating into the ether. Traffic is light at this time of night with only the occasional sound of a car or motorbike passing along the main road, interspersed with the chatter of people heading to the pub nearby.

Peace at last.

She stubs her cigarette out on the ground, grinding it with the sole of her high heel shoe and she notices hers is not the only one. There's a collection around her feet, a multitude of filters, some stained with lipstick. She recognises her own favourite shade on many, too many. The butt bin, provided to avoid littering, tucked against the wall, sits practically empty.

She takes the packet from her jacket pocket and pulls out another. She debates with herself whether or not to light it. She's going through more of these than she would like and she notices that it's her last one. Does she light it now and find somewhere to buy more on the way home, whatever time that will be, or does she hold off and make sure she has at least one to get her home.

She pulls the lighter from her pocket and lights it; the flame illuminates her face.

A motorbike pulls up close by, the engine shuts off, and then boots clumping against the pavement, heavy and solid. They're getting closer. She looks to the end of the alley as a shadow appears. A man steps out of the darkness. Tall. Broad-shouldered. Eyes hard, fixed on her.

'Stay the hell away from Marcus,' he says, voice low and urgent, each word a strike. 'Do you understand? Stay the hell away from him.'

She frowns, flicking ash to the ground. She doesn't know him. She doesn't care. She takes another drag of her cigarette, but the knot in her stomach tightens anyway.

He takes a step closer, urgency radiating from every line of his body. 'I said stay away.'

She shakes her head, exhaling slowly. 'I'm not...'

A roar cuts through the night before she can finish the sentence. Tyres scream as they cut a ninety-degree angle from the road straight into the alley. The headlights blind them both, and she holds her hands up to shield her eyes. The bike charges toward them, fast, too fast for the confines of the alley. Something's not right. This is not some kid out for a joyride; they're coming straight for them, and she steps back as far as the wall will allow. The bike slows as it comes up to them. Now she can see that there's not one rider but two. Black head to toe, including their visors. The passenger lifts his arm and too late she realises what they're holding.

A gun.

Time slows.

The man shouting at her seconds earlier pushes her, but it's already too late.

The shot cracks, sharp and final.

He jerks back, blood blossoming across his chest, warm and dark. A strangled sound escapes him as he crumples to the ground. Her cigarette drops from her fingers, forgotten. She races forward, knees hitting the wet concrete, hands pressed to his wound, fingers trembling as crimson seeps through.

'Oh my God!' she screams, panic shattering her voice.

She expects the motorbike will disappear out of the alley at the other end before she even has time to raise the alarm. Only when she looks up, searching for anyone to help, does she see the bike's brake lights. The rider puts out his leg as he balances himself while turning the bike around.

They're coming back towards her.

She gasps as she realises the danger she's in. She scrambles to her feet and tries to run in her heels. As the bike comes level with her, she turns to the wall; she doesn't want to see what's coming. The sound of the gun ricochets off the walls, and a piercing white heat scorches her back.

Chapter One

She squints as the late afternoon sun filters through the grimy window. The high-pitched reproof of her mother's voice echoes through the cramped space. 'For god's sake, Anna, this place is a pigsty.' As if to prove her point, she bangs and clatters her way back to the kitchen.

Anna sits up and rubs at her eyes, pushing back a tangle of dirty blonde hair from across her forehead, trying to remember when her parents arrived. It wouldn't have mattered anyway; they have their own key, and her mother is not afraid to use it.

She can't say her mother's description of the place she currently calls home is wrong. She can't remember the last time she cleaned up. It's a far cry from the place she used to have. Marble countertops, skyline views, state-of-the-art kitchen. She loved keeping the place clean; she could even have been described as fastidious.

This place is falling apart.

One hob on the stove, which must be older than she is, doesn't work. The chipped countertops are stained with God knows what, and the lounge room carpet still looks like a crime scene even after she had it professionally cleaned. They had announced afterwards, when she complained about the quality of the outcome, 'That's as good as it's gonna get.'

She sinks further into the couch, pulling the blanket tighter around her shoulders and tucking her feet beneath her. Her mouth is dry, and her tongue feels like it's sticking to the roof of her mouth. She spots a half-empty glass of water on the coffee table and reaches for it. She has no idea how long it's been there, but as she lives alone, there's no danger it belongs to anyone else. She chugs it down and puts the glass back on the table, using its base to clear a space among the clutter. She reaches for the packet of cigarettes only to be disappointed to find it empty.

Her mother, dressed in her uniform of a white blouse and beige slacks, stands in the space between the kitchen and the lounge that Anna suspects at one time was a double set of doors. Anna considers her mother's wardrobe an exercise in neutrality; she can't remember when she ever saw her mother wearing a real colour. The only exception being her mother's nails, long red talons reaching out to destroy whatever offends her.

The sound of table legs scraping on the balcony tiles screams as Anna's father moves it inside the apartment. The impending storm fills the room with a howling warning from the window.

'There's a cyclone coming, heard it on the drive down,' his voice muffled by the weather. His presence is less of a storm and more of a steady drizzle. He steps outside to examine the sky; his tanned hands gripping the balcony railing as he leans out. The wind ruffles what's left of his hair.

Anna sighs. She has little room inside for the few sticks of furniture she still owns, let alone the outdoor furniture as well.

Her parents had suffered, as they describe it, through the university years, hoping she would grow out of the idea of being a writer and refocus on a more practical career path. Now they relieve their frustration by judging her housekeeping skills as though the two are related.

The clatter of stacking dishes. The swish of a cloth scrubbing the counter. An orchestra of disapproval. Her mother's frustration shows. Her lips pressed into a thin, disapproving line. Her dark eyes sweep over the room with disdain as she continues her aggressive cleaning.

Her mother picks up a pile of picture frames from a kitchen chair. 'What do you want to do with these?' she asks. She holds one up as if Anna doesn't know what it is. It's the first front-page story she wrote for the Courier Mail. Her mother's lip curls as she wipes over one and then returns it none too carefully back on the chair. A process she repeats with each frame until the pile wobbles precariously with the last one.

'What are you doing here?' Anna mumbles, the taste of caustic cleaning products biting at the back of her throat. Her mother must have come prepared because she's sure she didn't have any cleaning products under her sink. The pounding at the back of her eyeballs and the shooting pains through her back remind her that she and any kind of movement are not friends.

'What am I doing here?' Her mother scoffs, spraying yet more cleaning products into the already saturated environment. 'What are you doing here? You were supposed to be in rehab for another two weeks, and yet here you are wallowing in self-pity and filth.'

She's not sure what upsets her mother the most. That the rehab hadn't worked or the money, good and bad, they've thrown at her problem. Wanting to 'fix' her when, in truth, there is no 'fixing' her. Anna wants to quip back with the definition of madness, about doing the same thing the same way every time and still expecting a different result.

The pain is real, despite her parents consulting with a slew of specialists who are happy, on her mother's dime, to tell her otherwise. They throw mindfulness techniques and other mumbo jumbo at her to help her deal with the pain shooting through her spine every time she moves. None of it works, but they persist anyway. This time it all came to a head very publicly when, five months ago, she humiliated herself. By the time they'd carted her off to rehab, she could scarcely string together a coherent thought, let alone actual words.

As if on cue, a sharp pain grips Anna's lower back, and she arches away from it. She presses her palm against the scar tissue as a memory assails her.

The hospital bed had been cold beneath her. The fluorescent lights hummed. Too bright, too sterile. The doctor, a man with tired eyes and a voice softened to deliver unwelcome news, standing at the foot of her bed.

'You're lucky,' he said. 'The bullet didn't hit anything vital. No nerve damage that we can see, no spinal trauma. There is pain for now and we're giving you something for that, but it should abate as the swelling goes down.'

The weight of what had happened pressed against her chest. The man standing next to her, Marcus' brother, Jonas, had taken the bullet she was sure was meant for her.

She shakes herself free of the memory and grabs her mobile phone to check the time. 'I left early,' she says as she notes the day of the week, Thursday. She wonders what happened to Wednesday.

'I can see that,' her mother picks at the mess covering the dining table and scowls as she tries to discern rubbish from anything useful. She holds up each item and waits for Anna's shake or nod to confirm its status.

'I put your things in storage,' her mother continues, voice clipped, referring to the fact that she lost her apartment because she couldn't pay the rent. 'I've left the paperwork on your desk. When you eventually get around to unpacking it, assuming you do at some point, don't get snippy with me if you can't find anything. I boxed everything up and got it out of there. Such a lovely place.'

Anyone would think she was the one who got evicted. The curl of her nostrils conveys what she thinks of Anna's new living situation. If she's honest, she might have to concede this point to her mother as well.

Her fingers fly through the debris of the coffee table, glancing up at her mother to see if she's watching. She knows what she's looking for, and she hopes her mother hasn't already found them and thrown them away. She grabs the bin from the side of the couch and puts the rubbish in it. The hope being that her mother will think she's helping her clean. Plus, she can't find anything among all the crap, and she's likely to overlook them if she's not methodical. Finally, she finds it. A sleeve of painkillers. Contraband. Surreptitiously she slides the last two pills into her mouth. With nothing to drink at hand, she has no choice but to swallow them dry. Not pleasant but this way she avoids her mother asking what she's doing if she gets up for water. The issue of where to replenish her stock being a later problem.

'You had a career,' the tone reinforces her mother's opinion of her chosen profession, but over the years even she has conceded it's better than no job at all. Her mother's onslaught continues, 'Now what are you going to do?'

'I'm working,' she mutters. A half-truth. Jasper's latest email is unread, but she suspects she knows the contents. More of the same poor quality of her work, inability to meet a deadline, missing editorial meetings, blah blah blah.

Her mother picks up the empty painkiller packet and holds it up in front of her. 'You're using again.' It's not even a question at this point. 'You're going to end up back in rehab.'

Anna exhales. What can she say that hasn't already been said?

Her mother returns to the kitchen, hands full of dirty cups and glasses and puts them in the sink with so much force Anna's stunned one doesn't break. 'You can't keep living like this, it's not fair on us.' Her mother's statement is as if Anna asks for the regular intrusions and lectures.

Anna shuffles to the kitchen. Her bare feet stick to the linoleum floor. She recalls spilling a soft drink that she didn't bother to clean up. No doubt her mother will have the mop out soon enough. She shakes the kettle and tops it up in the sink. She turns it on and then reaches on her tiptoes and fumbles to find a clean mug from the cupboard above the kitchen bench. There are none. They're all stacked with soap suds collecting in the creases of the draining board.

Her father clears his throat from the doorway, and her mother changes the subject. Anna suspects it's a prearranged cue between them. She can imagine them in the car. Planning attacks, countermoves, and various other strategies to manage their wayward daughter.

'We missed you this weekend. Of course, it went off without a hitch and Cousin Robbie looked fantastic.'

'Of course he did,' Anna replies absently as she grabs a cup and dries it before making her coffee. The fridge holds only expired milk. She gives it a sniff anyway to see if it's worth the risk. It's not. She tips the curdled milk down the sink, turns on the tap to wash the lumps and stench away and throws the empty carton in the under-sink bin.

'The bride did too of course.' Mother valiantly tries to keep to the script.

'She's a fucking model mum, of course she did.' She pulls a teaspoon from the cutlery drawer. The sound of wood-on-wood screams as it opens and grates on her already frayed nerves. Her mother flinches and eyes the offending drawer, and glances at father. He nods, acknowledging that he will add fixing the squeaky drawer to his to-do list for his next visit.

'Robbie always looks smart,' her mother continues.

'You mean clean and sober.'

'Could carry off a Hessian sack that boy.' Anna's mother refuses to rise to the barbs Anna throws, spoiling for a fight so her parents will leave.

'Like he'd be caught dead in anything that doesn't have a designer label.' Anna grabs her coffee and returns to the couch. She remembers a pack of cigarettes in the coffee table drawer and retrieves them. She slides a cigarette between her lips and picks up her lighter. She flicks it once, twice, before she's able to suck back the nicotine fix she needs. A knock at the door interrupts the moment, saving her from the lecture her mother's frown and glance at the cigarette signal as a precursor.

Her mother huffs with relief as she opens the door to find Jasper standing there, ready to take his turn with the Anna baton and the relay of managing her. Her mother strides across the room, retrieves her handbag and gives her father the look. The one to say it's time to go. She adjusts the strap as she pulls it over her shoulder and steps up towards the door and Jasper. 'Well, since you're here, and there's certainly not enough room for a crowd,' she steps closer to the door.

Jasper steps inside and shakes the rain off his jacket, the same one she's seen him wear for as long as she's known him. He has always looked tired and smelt of coffee and cigarettes. He embodies the stereotype of an editor. She doesn't think it's intentional; it's who he is. His salt and pepper hair, deep lines etched into his forehead, and dark bags under his eyes all tell a story of a life well lived. Lived hard is probably more accurate. A cigarette dangles from his fingers in one hand, and a takeaway coffee in the other. 'Morning Anna,' he says, his voice gravelly and his eyes judging the new place.

Anna's father pats her shoulder on his way out. Her mother lingers a beat longer, eyes scanning her daughter's face for something, perhaps hope. 'We'll talk soon,' her mother says before closing the door behind her.

Jasper exhales and drops onto the couch next to her. He looks around, and even her mother's thorough cleaning cannot disguise the squalor. 'Did you get my email?'

Chapter Two

The rough fabric of the couch digs into Anna's skin as she settles back against it. The air smells of stale cigarettes and greasy takeout, battling against the sharp sweetness of floral-scented cleaning products. Jasper drops onto the couch beside her, his arms resting on his knees. The look equal parts exasperation and concern.

'Jesus Anna.'

He rubs his temples. A tired sigh escapes him. 'Look, here's the deal, and I hate to do this, but you have got to pull yourself together. I've held the brass back for as long as I can, but I've got junior reporters snapping at your heels and I can't hold them off for much longer.'

'You mean Veronica?'

'Among others, yes.' He waits and lets the moment sink in. 'They pay you too much for your stories to be middle of the paper fodder. They can get those much cheaper, easier and without the drama.'

Anna gives him the side-eye. 'Drama, is that a euphemism for something? I was shot Jasper. You do remember that don't you.'

He nods; he's all too aware. 'That's why they haven't let you go before now; but you are on your very last life. I have no favours left to call in.'

She's tired, hungover and in pain. Common sense tells her she should shut up and take her lumps. But she never did well when it came to common sense. 'Do you have any idea of the pain I'm in most days? I'm damn sure Veronica's father doesn't. If they're in profit, who gives a shit about where the stories come from or the cost to make them happen. All he cares about are headlines, and Veronica wants her byline on the front page. No one seems to give a shit that she's not even good enough to write greeting cards. '

'Her writing is better than yours these days.' He reaches into his jacket and pulls out a packet of cigarettes, offers Anna one, which she snaps away from him, and then he lights them both.

'I can't keep fighting for them to keep you on staff when the work you're producing is ...' She watches as he struggles for a kinder word than what he's obviously thinking.

'Shit,' she says, saving him. She takes a long drag on the cigarette. The red glow lasts for a few seconds and crackles as it burns down. She holds the nicotine in her lungs, savouring it, then slowly exhales.

He nods, 'frankly, yes.'

'So, this is an ultimatum?'

'Yeah, I guess it is.'

'Let me have it then.' She straightens, shoulders tightening, bracing for what she knows is coming.

'Freelance.'

She remembers the constant struggle before she became a staff writer. It's even harder now. Scratching around for scraps of stories. Pitching ideas and hoping someone will buy them. She doubts she has it in her. She swallows hard; the panic rises in her chest, but she pushes it down. 'How long?'

'To get your shit together and deliver something worthy of the front page?'

She suspects he's leveraged his own political capital to have the option to make this determination himself, but political and relationship capital only goes so far, and over the last five years she knows he's used most of his to help her. 'Not long,' he says.

She takes a deep breath to quell the frustration. 'Days, weeks, months. Give me a clue here,' She didn't intend to be as brusque as the words sounded.

'I can probably hold them off for a couple more weeks, but that's the absolute best I can do.' His expression softens, but his voice remains steady as he reaches out and holds her hand. 'You know you can do this. You can beat it and get back on track.'

'Can I?' the pain screams from her voice. She crushes the cigarette out in the nearest ashtray. A slight smirk of satisfaction as she grinds the butt and ash into the gleaming clear crystal, imagining her mother's disapproving look.

Jasper stands and moves toward the door.

'Going so soon,' she snipes at him, when what she really wants to do is beg him for help.

'You've worked too hard to throw everything away, don't let what happened break you.'

'But that's exactly what it has done Jasper, I'm broken, I'm in pain and I'm so sick of everyone telling me it's in my head, or how I should pick myself up and dust myself off. You all make it sound like I'm choosing this.'

She drops her head into her hands, too exhausted to fight anymore. She can still hear him breathing. The heavy in and out with a low rattle of a smoker's cough threatening to explode at any second.

'That's my point Anna. You can choose to let what happened break you, your words not mine. Or you can rise above. So yes, in some respects I do think you have a choice. One is easy. One is hard. Both, however, are still choices.'

His words linger heavily in the air. Only when she hears the soft click of the front door closing behind him does she look up.

The silence settles back in, thick and suffocating. The wind howls outside. Trees dance at the side of the road like those crazy inflatable people designed to catch passing motorists' attention and entice them to look. The rain pelts at the window faster and heavier, but she's lived through enough of these storms to know what's going on outside her window is only the opening act.

You don't get to quit because it's hard. Life is hard. She decides she needs a talking to and who better than her to do it. If her mother is to be believed, she never listens to anyone else anyway. So, you got hurt. People get hurt all the time. But getting shot is not in the same league as falling out of a tree and breaking your arm. She rubs her arm unconsciously, relating to an earlier memory. You move on, or get on, but do something. She stares at her laptop, balanced on the edge of the coffee table. She brushes off a layer of dust as she opens it, wondering to herself if her mother had deliberately not touched it in her whirlwind of cleaning.

Come on, Anna, type something, anything. Your grocery list, if you have to. Or your obituary, career-wise at least. Your choice.

Jasper's words echo in her head. It's a choice.

It's not a choice, she argues with herself. You don't choose to be in pain; you either are or you aren't. There's no in-between. How am I supposed to function when every nerve ending is on fire? How am I supposed to write anything, let alone something worthy of the front page, in less than a couple of weeks, when I can't think straight? justifying her own weakness.

Giving up is a choice too. She can always get a job at the local supermarket.

She shudders. Reminded of her first job as a check-out-chick, the long hours, the rude customers, the creepy boss with wandering hands. They wouldn't re-hire her anyway, given her first paid story exposed their significant culture issues stemming from short wages and bullying to sexual harassment and everything in between.

She powers on the laptop and waits for it to run through the usual setup. She hasn't used it for so long, and it's doing updates, lots of them. While she waits, she thinks about the potential stories she can remember. She kept them all in a folder labelled potential until she was ready to tackle them. Sometimes it would be something timely, like Christmas, or the anniversary of a brutal crime that was never solved. Sometimes it was just snippets of something overheard in a coffee shop or on the bus.

One of her best stories came from an overheard conversation on the bus. Two public servants talking about how their boss was sexually harassing a younger colleague. A little digging uncovered that the boss in question was a high-ranking public servant, married with a couple of kids and a promising career, if only he could have kept his hands to himself.

Another time, a woman sat in front of her with her laptop open, and she was so oblivious to everyone around that she didn't even notice when Anna leaned forward to get a better look at her screen.

She looks across at the pile of framed front pages teetering on the chair from her mother's earlier polishing and allows herself a smile.

The laptop finishes its updates, and she uses the trackpad to navigate to the folder. Inside a cluster of topics, some are only one word, some more descriptive. All of them at this point represent a false start, bad timing, or someone with a vendetta looking to use her as their weapon because they didn't have the guts to confront whatever problem they wanted her to solve for them.

One folder stands out. WATCHER, all caps, shouting at her. Delete it, do it fast before you start thinking you can handle it; you can't. She hovers for a beat, then drags it into the trash. You did your best and got a bullet for your troubles. Someone else's story if they want it badly enough.

One by one, she sifts through the rest. Half-formed ideas and dried-up leads. Whispers leading nowhere. Her fingers slow on the trackpad, then stop. She hasn't spoken to any of her sources for months, sometimes years. With a snap, she slams the laptop shut. Frustration prickles beneath her skin. She reaches for a cigarette, but the pack is empty.

Swearing under her breath, she stands and grabs her phone, ready to make a dash to the corner store with a hope and a prayer that she has enough money left on her credit card. A loud crack splits the moment, followed by a thud as a large tree branch crashes into the sliding door. The glass doesn't break, but as the wind keeps whipping the branch across the balcony and against the glass, it's only a matter of time.

She slides her phone into her jeans pocket and steps outside. The wind lashes her hair, rain stinging her cheeks as she wrestles the branch. For a moment, she considers tossing it over the edge. Let it be someone else's problem.

Perhaps she could write about how everyone these days is only out for themselves. Hardly front-page news, barely news at all. With a grunt, she wrangles the branch so that it's contained within her balcony, and she uses cable ties to secure it to the railings. She prays the wind won't get under it and take out her balcony with it. She grabs the tape and starts from one corner of the glass diagonally to the other and then mirrors the look, followed by top to bottom, then side to side. She has to stretch to reach the corners, but at least if the glass breaks, it shouldn't shower her with shards.

She steps back inside and pushes her rain-soaked hair back from her face. She grabs a hair tie from the table and secures her hair in a messy bun as she sinks onto the couch and, after catching her breath, pulls her phone from her pocket. She's not so desperate for a cigarette to face the winds and rain, not yet anyway. She scrolls through her contacts, eyes skimming over names, sources, friends, people who used to take her calls. A change in government means all the chiefs of staff and ministerial advisors have changed. They've all moved on; perhaps I should take the hint.

She puts the phone back on the coffee table, then picks it up again. She does this three times before she finally plucks up the courage to tap a number.

Two rings. Then a sharp, impatient voice.

'Hello?'

She hesitates, throat dry. 'Hi, it's Anna Levesque--'

'Fuck off.'

Click.

She repeats the process with several other numbers; hopeful one will take her call. But none of them has any desire to talk to her. There's probably no one in her contacts she hasn't leveraged either for a story or, more recently, her addiction. Yup, should've known none of them would piss on me if I was on fire. Sure, they were happy to talk when it suited them, but now, where are they all?

She stares at the screen. Her thumb drags down the list again.

One by one, she tries them. One by one, they shut her down until there's only one name left. Marcus, Jonas' younger brother.

Her thumb hovers over the call icon as she looks at the number. She takes a deep breath before putting the phone down and leaning back in her chair. She can't make the call and even if she could, what would she say. She steeples her fingers and wraps them around her forehead, then closes her eyes.

She can't believe she's considering it as she leans forward towards the laptop. She opens the trash folder and drags the Watcher folder back onto her desktop. Her fingers hover for a moment before she clicks it open. Notes spill across the screen, fragments of interviews, scraps of timelines, threads of conspiracies half-formed and abandoned.

The photo gallery.

Images of shattered bodies and blood-soaked crime scenes flash before her eyes. Traffic accidents and suicides. She skims through them until she reaches the last one.

It's a grainy still from a CCTV camera. She's kneeling on the pavement, hands soaked in blood, pressing them against a man's chest. Jonas. Oblivious to the gunman on a bike doing a U-turn and coming back for her.

The memory assaults her senses, and her breath hitches with the vivid recall. She hasn't spoken to Marcus for years. He blames her. She blames herself. If anyone will understand, it's him, but even she admits she's not very convincing. She presses the dial button. It rings once, twice, three times.

'Hello?'

His voice is familiar, but distant. She can almost feel the space between them, heavy, but she pushes past it. 'Marcus?' she whispers almost as if she's afraid saying his name will conjure up past demons for them both.

'It's Anna, don't hang up,' she adds desperately, 'please don't hang up.'

There's a long pause. She imagines him on the other end of the line, weighing up whether to speak to her. Her pulse quickens. She grips the phone as the memory of their last conversation rushes over her.

Marcus standing rigid at the foot of Anna's hospital bed, his eyes bloodshot, his face stamped with fury.

'What was he doing there, Anna?'

She tried to sit up straighter, but the pain stopped her. Sharp and unforgiving, radiating from her lower back and curling around her spine. She winced and shook her head, her throat too tight to speak.

'I don't know,' she said at last, her voice barely above a whisper.

'Why?' Marcus snapped.

'I don't know.'

He stepped closer, and his shadow crawled over her, settling on her shoulders until she could barely draw breath. The air pressing against her ribs, squeezing the truth out of her even though he hadn't touched her at all. 'He's dead because of you.'

The words hit harder than the pain radiating from the site of the surgery. 'That's not fair.'

Marcus's hands curled into fists at his sides. His voice cracking under pressure. 'I told you how dangerous it was.'

'I swear...' The words hung in the air between them, useless. She could see it on his face. Nothing she could say would make him believe her. She had wanted to tell him that she had no idea what Jonas was doing there other than to tell her to stay away from Marcus. To tell him she hadn't called him, he ambushed her when she went out for a cigarette. The paper's smokers' spot was hardly a secret. She didn't say any of it. She lay there, feeling sorry for herself and for Marcus, and feeling more helpless than she had ever known.

'What do you want?' Marcus asks, snapping her back to the present. Her heart races, and for a moment, she struggles to find her voice.

'I need your help,' she says, her words trembling. 'There's no one else I can ask.'

She might have thought they'd been cut off if she couldn't hear him breathing. The silence is heavy. It's human nature to fill the void silence leaves; it makes people uncomfortable. She knows because she's used it to her advantage many times. Some of her best stories have come from people who are too uncomfortable with silence to let it be and instead tell her things they hadn't intended. Not Marcus. He's always been comfortable with silence. She counsels herself to be patient.

'I was on my way to work,' he replies, his tone flat and giving nothing away, 'but I'm on a split shift. I can meet you at twelve, usual place.'

By the time she says, 'I'll be there,' he's already hung up.

Chapter Three

Marcus pushes the wheelchair down the long, sterile corridor, wheels squeaking on the linoleum. His skin tanned from long hours outdoors, and a tattoo on his neck peeks out from under his collar, a memorial to his brother, Jonas.

He leans forward to his patient, wearing a white tee shirt and grey jogging pants. Comfortable clothing with the advantage of no zips, buttons and especially no drawstrings. 'You OK there Thomas?' he asks. Thomas is catatonic, but Marcus knows he's in there somewhere.

The fluorescent lights buzz overhead, casting a cold, harsh glow and throwing sharp shadows across the scuffed, yellow walls. Surrounded by the sterile scent of antiseptic, the sound of the distant echo of footsteps and soft murmurs from the nurse's station.

Lucy steps into the hallway from another patient's room ahead of him. Her faded blue scrub top clings to her slight frame; her dark hair pulled back into a ponytail with unruly wisps escaping. With a practiced snap, she pulls off her gloves. Their eyes meet, and her lips twitch into a small smile. He scratches the rough stubble on his jaw, trying and failing to hide his own grin.

Her expression softens, as it always does when she sees him. She falls into step beside him. 'You've been quiet today. Is everything all right?' she mumbles and looks around to make sure no one hears, then touches her fingers lightly to his.

'Long shift,' he mutters, his voice low with a small smile all the same.

She cocks her head to one side, and her eyes tell him she doesn't believe him. There's something else; something in his tone has her on alert. She watches him, eyes narrowing, the tension in his shoulders, the way his grip tightens on the wheelchair handles. No matter how hard he tries to hide it, she's been able to read him since the day they met. The day Jonas was killed.

The drive was a blur. Red lights he blew through; the sharp twist of the steering wheel; the way his hands were shaking. The phone call, *your brother's been shot,* and nothing afterward makes sense. By the time he shoved through the sliding doors of the ER, he was frantic.

'Where is he?' he demands at the triage counter, his voice cracking, ignoring the groans and complaints of the people he's pushed past. 'My brother, he was brought in, gunshot wound, where is he?'

She doesn't answer him fast enough, doesn't understand the panic threatening to consume him. The secure doors between the waiting area and the treatment rooms swish open as a nurse comes out. He's moving through the doors as she calls out, 'Sir, wait…'

He pushes past patients and nurses, a man carrying a cup of coffee that spills across the floor. He scans every curtained bay, every open door, searching for his brother's face.

Then he hears the urgent voices of a trauma team. He follows the sound only to freeze when he gets there. His brother is on the bed, unmoving, surrounded. Blood everywhere, on Jonas, on the doctors and nurses, and soaked bandages discarded on the floor. The heart monitor screaming out the monotone song of death. A nurse performing CPR.

A hand grabs his arm. Not the grip of a security guard, something softer, gentler, yet steady. 'Sir, you can't be here,' she said. He doesn't even look at her. All he can see is Jonas.

'That's my brother,' he says, breath hitching. 'That's my …. Just let me …'

He takes another step, but she holds him back. 'They're doing everything they can,' she says softly, as she tries to guide him away while holding up a hand to the fast-approaching security guard.

The rhythm in the treatment bay falters; compressions stopped, hands pulled away. The doctor leans over his brother, head bowed, then checks his watch and announces the time of death.

He watches it all. The doctor's tense shoulders, someone reaching up to turn off the monitor's alarm.

He can't breathe.

'No...' His knees buckle. She catches him before he hits the floor. She doesn't say anything. No platitudes, choosing instead to let him be present in the moment.

He went back to the hospital the day after the funeral. To apologise, to the staff and to find her. To thank her. They were married within a few months, but she kept her own name, which is why, when she took this job, no-one at Greenwood realised they even knew each other. He had told her then that they should keep it that way. She had been confused at first, but now she knows why.

'What is it?' she asks, keeping her voice soft as they approach the nurse's station. A glance at the patient confirms he's still too out of it to notice them. Marcus adjusts his grip on the wheelchair and looks at her. His hesitation gives him away, and he knows there's no point in trying to keep it from her.

'Anna called,' he says quietly, guiltily.

Lucy's brow furrows. 'Who?'

'Anna.' His tone implies she should know exactly who Anna is and seems incredulous that she doesn't.

Her face stays neutral for a beat as she sorts through a mental list of patients and staff. Then it clicks. Her eyes widen. 'You mean that Anna?'

Marcus nods, shifting his weight from one foot to the other. Hypervigilant to anyone who might overhear them.

'What does she want?' Lucy asks, folding her arms.

'She wants to talk. Meet.'

A muscle in her jaw twitches. 'Right. And you're considering this?' She stands, eyes fixed on him, leaving nowhere for him to escape. Her feet are far enough apart that he can't slip past without bumping her.

He drags a hand across his face. 'Lucy...' his tone begs her to understand.

'No,' she shakes her head. 'I thought you were done with all that.'

'So did I,' he mutters. His voice strained. He really had believed it too until he heard her voice, and then it all came flooding back.

She studies him, her stare sharpening. 'But you're not.'

Marcus swallows, gripping the wheelchair even tighter. 'It's been five years, Lucy, and I still don't have answers.' His eyes plead with hers.

Lucy makes a noise in the back of her throat as she swallows down her frustration and fear. She glances down the corridor, then looks back at him. The worry is there in her eyes, and he can feel it in his gut. 'What happens if you pull at that thread again?' she asks, her voice low. 'You think all she wants is to catch up? Why now? Does she know?' She nods down at the catatonic patient in Marcus' care.

'I don't know,' his voice is harder than he meant it to be. 'But if I don't go, I never will. And I think...'

She steps closer, her expression hardening. 'And if you do, she might get you killed, like she did Jonas.'

The words take his breath away. He flinches, his jaw tightening, but he doesn't look away. 'We don't know that, not for sure.'

Lucy's face softens with regret the moment she sees the effect her words have. 'I'm not telling you what to do,' she says, her voice steadier now. 'But I don't want you pulled back into something that almost destroyed you.' Her voice trembles as she exhales. 'You know chasing this won't bring him back.'

A crackling sound breaks through the tension. The speakers boom as an intercom announces Lucy is needed elsewhere. Lucy glances at it, then back at Marcus. She reaches out, her hand squeezing his forearm with tenderness. His chest tightens. 'I won't tell you not to if that's what you're hoping. I don't like it, but if you do this,' she murmurs, her voice low but earnest, 'please be careful.'

Chapter Four

The afternoon heat radiates off the asphalt of the old Queensland Parliament House car park, shimmering in waves. The wind has died down, and some are predicting the path of the storm will miss the city entirely. Veronica Stone leans against a black sedan in her cream pantsuit. Her red hair weaves across her shoulders. Around her, the air hums with the distant chatter of tourists and the occasional chirp of cicadas, a reminder of the vibrant life outside the political facade. She adjusts her sunglasses, scanning the crowd for a familiar face. Her phone close to her ear.

'She's in an Uber.' The distorted voice tells her. The same one he's used ever since their first phone call soon after she graduated university and her father put her on the paper's writing staff. She had rankled at the title of 'junior staff writer' but her father had explained how anything more senior would simply piss off the more seasoned writers. She had to earn her spot and their respect.

The first time the distorted voice called, she had almost laughed out loud when she asked him his name, and he told her to call him Watcher. She had thought it ridiculous and asked if he wouldn't prefer *Deep Throat.* He hung up. It was months before he called again, and then she listened. She's been listening ever since. Something about him scares her, and if he is who she suspects, her fears are well-founded. Not from his reputation, not his public one at least, but in dark corners and whispered tones.

At first, the leads he gave her were small and inconsequential. Far from the front-page covers she craved and still does. No, Watcher was more concerned about the stories Anna was working on. He had instructed her to find a way into Anna's graces. Keep close to her. She had found it harder than she had imagined. Her father's power and influence had always opened doors for her in the past, not with Anna.

'She's not here yet,' she tells him as she looks around her.

'I know that,' he snaps back. 'She's close.'

She's not surprised that he knows where she is. She also suspects she's not the only person he has keeping tabs on Anna.

'I don't know why you're so obsessed with her. She hasn't worked on anything half decent for years, and since that thing at the Awards show...'

'I don't pay you to have an opinion. I pay you to do as you're told.'

And pay he does; she could never accuse him of not being generous. Nothing traceable; envelopes with wads of cash left on her doorstep. When she told her father, his only advice was to be careful. In the early years of her career, Anna hogged all the front pages. Her stories ended careers and sent people to jail. Veronica couldn't compete with her back then, but now Anna's career is spinning out of control. Even with Anna out of the way and most of Anna's stories relegated to the middle pages of the paper, Veronica still can't get the front pages.

She's never concerned herself with the morality of what he's ever asked of her either, although her conscience pricks her more these days.

She never really thought about what it all meant, but there had been some tasks which left her feeling like she was part of something she wouldn't be proud of. Borderline illegal, but when she expressed these concerns to her father, he had warned her, 'don't try to work it out, don't ask questions, just do what he asks.'

She lets her jealousy and frustration get the better of her anyway. 'I get that, I'm just saying, even Jasper's ran out of patience with her.'

'You assume too much and know too little.'

She knows more than he thinks. She's getting closer to the day when he won't be able to speak to her with such condescension. He doesn't realise she's been keeping an eye on all the little tasks he's asked of her. Asking herself, who benefits from each seemingly inconsequential task? One name is almost always on the periphery but removed enough to be coincidence, not hard proof. One day she'll have enough to expose him, and when she does, then she'll have her front-page cover. In the meantime, she's at his beck and call, and if he wants to know what Anna's up to, so be it. If it helps Anna further down a path of self-destruction, she's more than happy to do her part.

'Find out who she's meeting with.' With that, Watcher hangs up.

She slips her phone into her pocket and straightens, eyes flicking towards the car park as Anna's Uber pulls in. Veronica has strategically moved away from the car and placed herself among a group of tourists taking pictures. She turns her back and uses her phone camera to watch Anna.

The Uber door swings open and Anna steps out. Her once vibrant aura dimmed but still unmistakable. She's wearing track pants and an oversized hoodie. Her clothing choices are all wrong for the Queensland heat. The baseball cap sitting low over her sunglasses.

She watches as Anna scans the car park, her eyes flitting from the building on one side to the steps to the park on the other. Only when she seems satisfied does she head for the park steps. Veronica turns and steps forward, placing herself right in Anna's path.

'Anna,' she calls out, feigning surprise and heading straight for her like a long-lost friend.

Anna freezes, then ducks her head down and pretends she hasn't seen or heard her.

'Anna, hi,' Veronica jogs into Anna's path.

'Veronica,' Anna's eyes flick towards the gardens, then away, searching for an escape route. There is none.

Veronica steps up, closing the gap. A subtle smirk tugs at her lips. 'How've you been, you know, since...'

At the Walkley's Anna was so drunk, or high, or both, she fell gloriously as she ascended the stairs to the podium to present an award. An award she'd won many times before, but not this year, not even a nomination.

She banged her head on the way down and landed with the skirt of her dress around her neck. She then stumbled and tripped on her way to the Dais only to express how unworthy, in her opinion, the winner of the award was. So many cuss words littered throughout her speech, the official live stream beeped out most of what she said, but the uncensored version went viral. Veronica had argued with her father deep into the night about how the story might not be front-page news, but it's news, and they can hardly say they are being impartial if they censor themselves. He let her run with the story but insisted she take an empathetic view, the perils of success and how the paper will stand behind Anna while she recovers.

Anna's chin dips lower, as though shrinking into herself. Her hands clenched at her sides. She forces herself to keep her eyes averted, though Veronica can see the tension in every movement.

'Yeah,' Anna shrugs, 'Been busy.' The words are too tight. Her eyes dart around, and her posture falters for a minute. There's a flicker of something Veronica recognises, a flash of fear, or guilt, buried beneath what appears to be total exhaustion.

Veronica tilts her head, noting every subtle shift. 'I'm sure you have.' Her voice is syrupy sweet, a taunt veiled in politeness. 'I meant to ask; will you be going to the awards again next year?' Without waiting for an answer, she plows on. 'You know the videos from this year are still making the rounds on-line.'

Veronica catches the quick movement and discomfort as Anna swallows hard and tries to recover. She knows she shouldn't be enjoying it, but she can't help herself. When Anna tries to step around her, Veronica moves with her, making it impossible.

Anna's eyes flick to the side, and Veronica follows her look. All she can see are the steps to the park, and no one appears to be waiting or watching. All the same, she feels hostility building in Anna. The clenched hands, the way she can't seem to stand still. 'Oh, come on,' Veronica laughs as if she's told some kind of joke. 'Someone tagged me in it again last week.' Of course, as far as Veronica is concerned, Anna is the joke.

Veronica sees the way Anna recoils but quickly regains her composure. The silence stretches as Veronica watches Anna squirm. She doesn't let up. 'So, what are you up to these days?' she presses; her voice cuts through the air with subtle malice. 'I'm sure you've got something big cooking?'

Anna's focus snaps to Veronica. She struck a nerve. She is working on something, but it could be nothing. What Anna's written lately has not even been worth the paper, so the lie she senses behind Anna's eyes tells her the Watcher might be onto something. Then he's usually one step ahead of everyone else, so it's not really a surprise.

'A few ideas,' Anna mutters, unable to meet Veronica's eye.

Liar. Whatever she's working on, Veronica now knows it's

important enough for Anna to lie about it and for Watcher to want her to find out what it is. Anna makes him nervous, although God knows why. She's been practically irrelevant for the last five years, and yet he always wants to know where she is and what she's working on. Veronica takes a step closer, her curiosity piqued.

'You know you can trust me, right?' She says, hoping to coax out the truth. Anna's look flickers, revealing vulnerability before she masks it with a forced smile. 'Of course I trust you, but this is the game right,' Anna replies, her voice barely above a whisper. 'First one to break the story gets the glory.'

Veronica takes a beat and then steps back, offering Anna enough space to pass. She waits long enough for Anna to move off, then follows her to a small café in the gardens.

Chapter Five

Daylight filters through the café's wide glass windows, casting shifting patterns of gold and green across polished tabletops. The Brisbane Botanical Garden Club hums with warmth and life. The rhythmic hiss of the espresso machine, the cheerful clink of cutlery, and the comforting chatter of lunchtime conversations.

With every room she walks into, Anna is always looking for the exits, where to head in an emergency and any other threat. A habit she's picked up over the years. She's learned how to scan a room and work out the best place to sit to give maximum coverage of the room and the least opportunity to creep up on her. She does that now, settling for a table in the corner. The only thing at her back is the window and beyond the window, tall, gangly shrubs.

She scans the surrounding room, noting who is doing what. Looking for signs that someone is watching her. Not just those who make eye contact and glance away, but a camera phone at an odd angle, reflective surfaces. She tells herself she's being paranoid but the hairs on the back of her neck prickle in warning. A shadow outside crosses over her table, but when she turns around, there's no one there. *You're being paranoid,* she chides herself.

Anna sits at a corner table, her fingers drumming an anxious rhythm against her coffee cup. The bell over the door chimes to announce someone new. Her eyes dart to the sound, hopeful it's Marcus', disappointed when it's not. She checks her phone. Her mind races with her thoughts. Wondering whether he'll show up, and if he does, how will he be with her?

These thoughts, and many others, gnaw at her. She'd hoped the familiarity of the café would make this easier, not harder. The place hasn't changed at all except in its wear and tear. The colours are not as vivid as they once were. The scuffed deck is evidence of the tramping of what she imagines, even with the close-downs for COVID, were many feet.

The last time she was here was with Marcus, before Jonas was killed. She wonders whether she's avoided the place consciously or whether guilt has something to do with it. She already knows the answer, guilt.

Bumping into Veronica has rattled her more than she wants to admit. It's unusual for Veronica to be hanging around Parliament House. By her own admission, it's full of doddering old farts, and she's shown no interest in politics before. But that was a long time ago. She hasn't really been keeping an eye on what Veronica has been doing. She's only just managing to keep her own spot, but if what Jasper says is true, Veronica is the one snapping at her heels the loudest.

Anna's not worried about being out-written; as far as she's concerned, Veronica's writing is trite at best. Leave her to the sparkling glitz and glamour; after all, she's grown up surrounded by it. Perhaps she should take more notice of Veronica and what she's writing these days. After all, she doesn't need to be good; all she needs is to be good enough to justify her father pushing someone else out. She had never thought she would see the day when she would feel threatened by Veronica, and she decides it won't be today either. She forces the niggling doubts creeping in from the darkest recesses of her mind, scrambling for light and attention, back down where they belong.

She sips her coffee, feeling the warmth of the cup in her hands. The bitter taste lingers at the back of her throat, a familiar comfort. The steam rises in delicate wisps. The sunlight filters through the windows, casting a warm glow on her face. She closes her eyes for a moment, savouring the solitude.

The door chimes. She opens her eyes and glances at the sound. Anticipation fills her with hope, only to sink again when she sees it's a couple chatting and laughing as they come through the door. She watches them find a table, their laughter blending with the soft background music. The gentle touch of her hand on his shoulder. He pulls out a chair for her and waits for her to sit before he takes his own.

Anna takes a deep breath and embraces the stillness. Peace is not an emotion she gets to feel these days without chemical inducement; the inducement required more frequently than she would like to admit. She blames anything and everyone but herself for her decline, especially the shooting. Her parents refer to the shooting as *her accident*, as if her survival of someone sent to kill her was anything but intentional. The police are no closer to finding out who he was and, more importantly, who sent him. She has her suspicions, which, of course, is even more reason to leave this story alone.

The door chimes again.

She looks up.

Marcus. She swallows and her breath hitches. She gives him an awkward wave, but his scowl makes her lower her hand. His eyes sweep the room, posture tight, shoulders back. He's not the same man she remembers. Time has weathered him; he's more guarded. He wears a biker jacket over blue scrubs. The jacket she recognises, Jonas's, but the scrubs are a surprise. He makes his way to her table, stopping only to order his drink from the counter on the way and grabs a table number to bring with him.

She considers getting up to greet him with a hug but thinks better of it. His face is not giving off warm or inviting vibes. Besides, they've never hugged before so why start now. It feels awkward for a second before he takes the seat next to her, the one that gives him the second-best view of the café.

'Anna,' he says, his voice low and cautious. She musters a tight-lipped smile, masking the flood of memories rushing back at the sound of his voice. 'Marcus, been a minute,' she replies.

Silence hangs between them. In the Uber, she had thought about what she would say to him, and now he's in front of her, all those words elude her. They sit in silence until his coffee arrives. The café buzzes around them. Both are wary, afraid of saying anything to break this fragile moment. It's awkward, and she's relieved when he speaks.

'I was surprised you called,' his voice tinged with uncertainty. Anna studies him, noticing the lines etched on his face and the weariness in his eyes. He looks tired, and what she's about to ask is hardly likely to improve his sleep habits.

'I didn't want to. I figure I've cost you enough and should leave you alone, but...' her tone betraying a mix of emotions.

'You called anyway. I'm assuming you want something.' The coldness as sharp as an early frost. Unpleasant and unexpected, but it is exactly what she deserves.

'I'm sorry,' she says. She makes sure he sees her. She wants to scream at the top of her lungs how sorry she is, but this will have to do, although the words feel woefully inadequate as they leave her mouth.

'For what, you didn't kill him, if that's what you're apologising for. Or are you apologising for something else?' Suspicion laces his words, and he's every right to feel that way.

She looks away. Shame colours her cheeks. She abandoned him when he needed her most. He was the source for a story, nothing more, she had told herself whenever he came to mind. They had been close once. Sometimes she wondered if they would have ended up together if things had been different. The attraction was there for her at any rate. She allows herself to wonder. He still looks handsome. Then she notices the gold band on his finger.

'You got married?' she sounds more shocked than she had meant to. She purses her lips and looks down at her coffee cup, attempting to hide her embarrassment.

He looks down at his hand and turns the band around on his finger. 'Yeah, last year.' A smile crosses his face, but it's gone as quickly as it came.

She waits for him to share more, but it's not forthcoming. 'I'm very happy for you,' she says. It sounds trite. It feels trite. She picks up her coffee and takes a sip as she wonders again how unfair what she's about to ask of him is. She knows finding out he's married should change everything. It's not just Marcus anymore. The danger she could expose him to, and for what? To save her sorry ass. She thinks about how she has no right to drag him back into this story. She's thought of nothing else since he agreed to meet her, and now there's a wife. She wonders what kind of woman finally tamed the man she always thought couldn't be.

Marcus looks at Anna and says, 'I don't have long, so if you could get to what it is you want.'

She's taken aback by his brusqueness, but she nods as she bolsters her courage. 'It's about Greer,' He doesn't look surprised, quite the opposite. Has he been expecting her to come back, wanting to finish this story? He had told her he wanted nothing more to do with her, and she kept her distance, telling herself she was respecting his wishes when, really, she was simply too scared.

'Last time we talked about Greer, Jonas ended up dead.' The pain of losing his brother carries through his voice.

She nods, acknowledging the gravity of the situation. 'I know, and I am sorry, and if I had anyone else, I could turn to.' She can hear the pleading in her voice, and she sounds pathetic.

'Why now?' He's watching her closely, reading her. Searching her face for something, but what is it he expects to find? Remorse? Of course, there's remorse by the bucket load, but she tells herself she has no choice.

'I need a story, a front page one, otherwise I'm going to get fired.' She sounds selfish. She is being selfish. As if her keeping her job can justify what happened last time.

He shakes his head and snorts with derision. 'Same old Anna, always about the story.'

'It's not like that, I just,' she shakes her head and tries to compose herself. 'My life has turned to shit.' *The understatement of the year*, she thinks, tears welling in her eyes. She places her hands flat on the table so he won't see them shaking. 'And I don't mean a little, I mean a lot.'

'Got anything to do with that Award show?'

She gasps, but of course he would have seen it. Everyone with a pulse has probably seen it. A man at a nearby table clears his throat, and Marcus' shoulders jerk slightly. His eyes narrow as he checks him out, and only when he's satisfied does he look back at Anna.

'You think I've been living under a rock for the last five years, of course I saw it, everyone's seen it. Spec...tac...ular, Anna.' There's a slight chuckle in his voice. A shared moment of light laughter passes between them, and she feels the tension ease a little. If she can get the banter they had back, there's hope.

'Geez thanks, glad the worst moment of my career, my life, amuses you.'

'The papers said you were in rehab.' His voice is sombre.

'Yeah,' she shrugs. 'Didn't take.'

'They said it wasn't the first time.' He watches her closely. Is he trying to catch her in a lie? An excuse to leave indignantly with his conscience salved for the story they both walked away from.

'No, it wasn't.' She looks him dead in the eye to warn him he's the one on thin ice now. She's already had a lecture from her mother today. She doesn't need one from him.

'Pills?'

She nods.

'Because of what happened?'

She looks at him and swallows hard, then nods, slower this time. They both lose themselves in their own thoughts for a moment.

'They thought he was me,' Marcus says and looks at Anna. 'I guess to them it doesn't matter. They got the result they wanted.' She can see and hear the guilt he clearly feels. The downcast eyes. The deep sigh. The tone of his voice.

Anna takes a deep breath and asks what she really wants to know. 'You want me to leave this alone?' she prays for him not to say no, but the longer he takes to answer, the more she's convinced he's going to walk away. He came only to show her the decency and respect of telling her to her face.

'No,' he's emphatic. 'I want to nail these bastards.'

Has he been waiting all this time for her to come back? Is it finally their time to get revenge for what happened? She dares to hope.

He leans in closer, his voice quieter. 'But there's been changes since you and I last spoke.'

She stares incredulously. *The story couldn't have changed that much*, she thinks, but something in the way he looks at her makes her wonder. There had always been a sense that there was something more to it. You don't go around shooting people on the street, even if it was late at night, for a story about patient neglect, no matter how significant the neglect might be.

The tension in his body. The furtiveness and guarding heightened. She had thought she had mis-remembered his mannerisms and body language, but now she realises he's more on edge than before. A sense of foreboding seeps into her pores, but she can't walk away again. Judging by the look on Marcus' face, she suspects he won't let her, and if she does, he might hand the story, whatever it has become, to someone else. Veronica instantly comes to mind.

'What kind of changes?' she leans in. She can smell the notes of his aftershave, musky and masculine.

He reaches into his pocket and pulls out a piece of paper. He places it face down on the table and slides it across to her as he looks around, hypervigilant. Anna hesitates before she turns it over. Greer's face stares back at her, but it's not the face she remembers. His eyes are hollow with dark black circles under them, his face gaunt, head lolling to the side and drool spilling from his slack lips.

She looks up at Marcus. 'What the hell?'

'That's Greer now. What they turned him into. They used him to test some innovative technology and who's around to object? His daughter? She hates him. Has never visited.'

'And you think this is what it's all about?' Anna asks.

'I think it's part of it.'

Chapter Six

Marcy stands at the edge of the graveside, her hands resting lightly on the swell of her belly. The air bites at her cheeks, but the numbness inside her dulls the sensation. The surrounding mourners, dressed in muted shades of black and grey, blur into a sea of sorrow. Words of condolence float around her like smoke, insubstantial and empty. Even her baby, normally restless at this time of day, doesn't move.

The officiant, who had never met Nathaniel, talks about her husband as if he were a long-lost friend. About his passion for the planet. His unrelenting fight against corporate greed. His untimely death and how he leaves Marcy and their unborn child, a daughter, behind.

They said it was an accident. How he must have fallen asleep at the wheel on an outback road kilometres from anywhere. She didn't believe them. He wasn't supposed to be there. He told her he was going to sleep in the motel and drive home in the morning. Nathaniel took risks. She knew that. But they were always calculated, never careless. He simply wouldn't drive tired, even before he found out he was going to be a father.

Her hands won't stop shaking. Three pregnancy sticks lined up with military precision on the bathroom counter. Each one with the same result. She rearranges them as if a new pattern might change the results. It doesn't. They are all positive.

She sinks onto the cool tiles. Her legs folded beneath her. Thoughts spiral until she hears the front door open. He calls out her name, and she can hear his boots on the timber stairs clomping toward her.

'There you are,' he says as he steps inside with the dust still clinging to his boots and his shirt marked with sweat stains. He looks exhausted, but when he sees her, he smiles, but only for a second. Instantly he's on the floor next to her.

'Hey, Marce,' he says, his voice soft. 'You, OK?'

She stands too fast, her legs unsteady, her balance off-kilter. 'I need to tell you something.'

He's on his feet next to her, concern etched across his face. 'What?'

She can't get the words out. If she says it, then it's real. Instead, she lifts the three sticks, her hands trembling as she hands them to him. He looks at the tests, then at her, then back at the tests.

Time stops. His eyes widen, breath catches, until slowly a smile curls at the corner of his mouth.

'You serious?' he asks as he reaches toward her.

She nods, tears already blurring her vision.

He laughs, soft, breathlessly. She expected fear, stress, anger; they hadn't been more careful. This was not part of the plan, not while his work took him away from home so much. He cups her face, using his thumbs to wipe away her tears. His smile reminds him of when she accepted his proposal. Pure joy.

When the service is over, she stands to the side, reluctant to leave but aware of the expectations of the surrounding people. Family, friends, colleagues. All recycling the same comments, a variation of the same theme, sorry. They want to be helpful. She wants to be left alone.

A hand touches her elbow, and she turns to see Tristan standing there, his expression uneasy. Beside him, Quentin watches her with his usual impassive gaze, his posture as stiff as ever. They had ended up at the same organisation through the same graduate program, different cohorts. Accomplished in their respective fields but lacking the social skills that so often accompany incredible intellect.

'I'm sorry for your loss,' Tristan murmurs, his voice barely carrying over the wind.

She gives a small nod, her throat too tight to respond.

The silence stretches between them before Quentin speaks, his voice cutting cleanly through the heavy air. 'We were wondering if you know everyone here? Tristan and Quentin look over the gathering as the question, loaded with suspicion, hangs in the air.

When she looks at him quizzically, he continues.

'What we mean is could there be anyone here that shouldn't be. Someone you don't know or recognise.'

Another shared look passes between them.

She lets out an exasperated sigh. 'Quentin, what are you getting at?' she asks as she holds up her hands, 'preferably before I go into labour.'

'Creepy guy, six O'clock,' Tristan says.

They all look in the direction he's indicating. There's a man standing high above the cemetery in a dark suit and sunglasses, despite the overcast weather.

She shakes her head. 'It's a cemetery guys, creepy goes with the territory. There's always someone with a morbid fascination on the periphery of a funeral. Think about all the people that slow down as they pass an accident at the side of the road. It's human nature.'

'Yeah, but...' Quentin starts.

'No,' she turns to them, aware of people watching and waiting for an opportunity to pass on their condolences while keeping a respectable distance. 'I don't need your paranoid conspiracy theories today.'

'It's only paranoia if you're wrong,' Quentin pouts.

She cocks her head to the side and her shoulders slump. 'What is it exactly you think he's doing then?'

Quentin looks at Tristan, and he steps closer. 'We've seen him before.'

Quentin nods to confirm Tristan's statement.

'He probably works for the company.' Over the last few days, she's had so many people she didn't know within the company offering her condolences. Popping by to check in on her. It's exhausting.

'That's not where we saw him,' Tristan continues.

Marcy smiles at the waiting mourners and shrugs an apology. 'Is now really the time?' she tries to hold back her frustration.

'He was there when we met up with Nathaniel.'

Marcy blinks, momentarily thrown. They had been meeting up

with Nathaniel without her; that wasn't part of their deal. They had agreed that whenever they met up with the other's work colleagues, they would always both be present if for no other reason than to make sure one was not exploiting the other's colleagues for information. This is all news, and she doesn't like it. Nathaniel never mentioned any of it. 'Why?'

'He asked to meet with us to talk about a project,' Tristan says.

'The one that was supposed to be theoretical, but he found out Tristan was working on a real-world application,' Quentin says, the tone demonstrating Quentin is put out by this revelation.

She shakes her head slightly, 'Why is that significant?'

'Because I didn't know Tristan was conducting human trials.'

She smiles tightly at the waiting onlookers and shrugs, as she can sense their ongoing frustration or quandary. Is it rude to leave without passing on condolences, even when the widow is obviously preoccupied with other things?

She looks from Quentin to Tristan. 'Is this true?'

Tristan nods, his eyes hooded and his cheeks flushed, 'but I didn't know I was doing anything wrong, until--'

Quentin shoves him.

They examine their shoes while she waits for him to continue. 'Until what?' Marcy prompts.

'Nathaniel.'

'What about Nathaniel?'

'He started asking questions and --'

'Then we worked it out.'

'Worked what out?'

'That they were trialling Quentin's technology on people.'

'Human trials are part of our work sometimes,' Marcy justifies.

A cough from one mourner draws her attention. She looks across and sees what could loosely be defined as a queue of people waiting to speak to her, but Quentin and Tristan have not finished. Torn between being the dutiful widow and understanding what's bothering them, she turns to the mourners. 'Please, don't wait for me. I'll see you back at the house.'

There's grumbling, but the mourners move off. The scuffle of feet and the murmurs of disapproval from the more mature among them.

Suspicious glances questioning why Quentin and Tristan have her undivided attention.

The baby moves inside her and takes position firmly on her bladder. Great. She's barely moved all day, and when she does, it's to the most uncomfortable position possible. She rubs her side to encourage the baby to move. It doesn't work, and the baby stays firmly glued to her bladder.

'Nathaniel said the trials weren't authorised,' Tristan says.

'And how would he know? It's proprietary knowledge.' Although Nathaniel had a way of finding out things people didn't want him to know. He was like a bloodhound. Once he had the slightest inkling of something, he would race down rabbit holes until he found out what was going on. His tenacity was one of the many things she loved about him. He was also charming and affable, which meant people talked to him, often revealing more than they intended.

'I told him.' Quentin's face flushes, and he looks at his shoes.

'Why?' She knows how persuasive and persistent Nathaniel can be, but he promised he would never compromise their relationship. It was the deal they made after a big argument the first time their work came between them.

Marcy slams the stack of reports onto the kitchen bench; papers fan out. 'I don't understand why you're taking their side,' she says.

Nathaniel exhales slowly, leaning against the counter opposite her, arms folded. 'I'm not taking their side Marce. I'm saying they have a point. What's the harm in someone independent taking another look?'

Her laugh comes out sharp. 'A point? They're accusing us of damage, and these drones are not capable of it. They are nothing more than glorified cameras taking pictures to identify mineral deposits, no agenda. It's a mapping exercise, nothing more. You really think I'd put my name on a project ...' She takes a deep breath.

'That's not what I said.'

'But it's what it sounds like,' she fires back. 'You're defending them.'

He pushes off the counter, his voice rising for the first time. 'I'm defending the principle, not the accusation, and besides, I'm allowed to have an opinion without you attacking me.'

Her breath catches, anger and hurt combined. 'Then why do I feel attacked?'

'I was drunk,' Quentin admits, bringing her back to the present.

Marcy cocks her head to one side, disappointed he should make such a rookie mistake, especially considering the non-disclosure agreements they sign not only when they take the job, but with every new project they get involved in. She's lost track of how many she's signed over the years.

Tristan pipes up. 'He pointed out that the people they are trialling the tech on are not exactly in a position to give their consent.' Eager to pile on from the embarrassment and guilt already weighing Quentin down.

'Who?' She's not even sure she wants to know, but the guys are not about to let this go.

'My patients at Greenwood.'

'Jesus,' Marcy breathes out. 'When was this?'

'Before the accident,' Quentin says.

'How long before?' Suspicion causes her eyes to narrow. She knows her employer is not always squeaky clean, but this is a whole different level. Tristan's patients are criminally insane. There's no way they would be able to legally provide consent. Even if they signed something, it wouldn't hold up in court if challenged.

'Not long,' Quentin looks at Tristan. 'A couple of days,' he says, but it's more of a question in search of Tristan's confirmation, which he nods.

'Creepy guy still there?' she asks after a moment. They both nod.

Chapter Seven

Aaron Dupree stands alone in his office. The morning light catches the dusty sheen of frames lining his 'brag wall'. His father's voice whispers up from memory, *Christ Aaron, no one cares who you shook hands with,* but the old man had always stopped in front of the photos anyway, pride hidden under his disdain.

Aaron's gaze drifts across twenty years of smiling politicians, ribbon cuttings and newspaper front pages. He lingers on one headline, DUPREE JUNIOR TO FOLLOW IN HIS FATHER'S MINISTERIAL FOOTSTEPS. It never happened.

A scandal broke out during the next election campaign, alleging that his father had taken kickbacks and bribes. Initially, he defended his father, but as they exposed more evidence, he tried to distance himself. Anna Levesque wouldn't let the story go. She constantly mentioned Aaron in every article uncovering his father's misdeeds, with carefully crafted words like, 'no allegations have been made against Aaron Dupree,' stopping short of slander.

He won his seat, but the damage was already done. The party had said it was too risky to give him a ministerial posting while his father's case was so prominent.

The day they arrested his father was the last time they spoke. When his father was sentenced to five years in prison, his mother stopped speaking to him. When his father died in prison, he did not attend the funeral. He's been fighting corruption publicly and privately ever since.

A soft knock breaks the stillness. Mira, a political science major, hired as a favour to a friend and because he didn't have the money to hire someone more seasoned. 'Here's those reports you asked for,' she says as she slips a thick stack of reports onto his desk.

'And the other thing?'

'The CCTV has been taken off the server and backed up. They couldn't get a good look at the person that delivered it,' she nods at the handwritten letter on his desk. The latest one, hand-delivered in the early hours. The handwriting is crooked and rushed. Scared. He can feel the panic baked into the ink.

I can't go to the police. You're the only one who can help.

'Anything I need to be across?' Jeremy asks too casually as he strolls in without so much as knocking and glares at Mira. She slips from the room with her head down. The party had foisted Jeremy on him and not having the kind of friends or connections to be choosy about his staff, he had agreed. Jeremy had more than his fair share of powerful friends and seemed willing to leverage those friendships to Aaron's cause. These days he's not so sure.

'I'm following up on something,' Aaron says. 'Grassroots.'

Jeremy snorts. 'Grassroots usually means potholes and school funding, not whatever that…' he nods at the letter, 'is supposed to be.'

Aaron doesn't blink. 'This could change everything.'

'For you maybe,' Jeremy says, and the mask slips for half a second, enough for Aaron to see irritation, or fear, or loyalty to someone else. 'I think you're chasing trouble, and you don't need that.'

'Have you called him yet?' Aaron snaps.

Jeremy's fingers twitch. A tell. 'There's history there.'

'Everyone has history. You're here because of that history, those connections, I expect you to use them and not just when it suits you.'

'He's dangerous and powerful, you need him on your side.'

'Power does not excuse corruption,' Aaron steps from behind his desk and closer to Jeremy. 'I need you to make that call.'

Jeremy holds the silence for a beat too long.

'And if it's a hoax?' Jeremy argues.

There's a brief silence before Jeremy finally sighs, a long, drawn-out exhale of frustration. 'Fine,' Jeremy mutters under his breath. 'I'll make the call, but don't say I didn't warn you.'

Chapter Eight

The sun has long since dipped below the horizon, leaving Anna's apartment bathed in the harsh, sickly glow of a single flickering bulb. The heat is stifling. She's changed into a pair of jean-shorts and a clean T-shirt; far more comfortable than the fleece tracksuit she was wearing when she came back from meeting Marcus. After showing her the photograph, he gave her a lead, a name.

She sits on the worn-out couch, her pulse still racing from the encounter with Marcus and the conversation she had with Carter. Her research on Carter paints a troubling picture. Officially, he's a security consultant at Redoubt Security Group, a private bodyguard company.

Anna had dug deeper, finding an article about Redoubt. Someone accused the company of pretending to be law enforcement to seize records about the business dealings of one of their major clients before a warrant could be issued. The CEO had denied it, calling the allegations baseless.

In the few images she could find, Carter's tall, standing head and shoulders above anyone else around him with the musculature of someone who spends his life at the gym.

She reached out to a contact with the Queensland Police Service after the shock of hearing from her after so long; he had confirmed her fears. 'Everyone's had dealings with Carter. That's why they suspected he was involved. He's nearly seven foot tall and has a scarab tattoo on his right bicep. A witness where Redoubt was accused of impersonating law enforcement originally said they saw the tattoo but then a few days later changed their statement. Said they were mistaken. Scuttlebutt was that someone got to them but with no proof there was nothing they could do. Thing is, they must have had someone with inside knowledge that the warrant was being sought. There's no other way they could have pulled it off.'

'Did the Ethical Standards Unit investigate?' she'd asked.

'If they did, nothing seems to have come of it, nothing public, and no one that was involved in the case was fired or moved on. Draw from that what you will.'

He tried to get Anna to talk about why she wanted to know about Carter. When she wouldn't tell him, he ended the call with one final warning, 'Watch yourself. He's a mean fucker.'

She looks down at her notes. On paper, Redoubt is a reputable security firm, not spotless, but they had avoided too many scandals. The CEO makes significant donations to food banks and sponsors local youth sports teams but still draws negative attention because of the men employed at Redoubt. To counter the negative press, a piece had been written by Veronica debunking the stereotypes of motorcycle culture, and the story had focused heavily on Carter.

There's precious little she can find online about him, even on the dark web. That he had so little online presence tells her one of two things. He is paranoid-level cautious about his identity, but that doesn't track with him taking part in Veronica's earlier interview. The other reason is something most likely dangerous and illegal. She suspects it's the latter.

Dropping in the reference to Carter's boss and Veronica's editorial was her hook, a follow-up piece she claimed, and it worked.

They arranged to meet later at a dive bar, away from Redoubt's headquarters. The location was smart, out of the way, discreet. It told her Carter was cautious, and he didn't want to be seen, which might work in her favour. She'd had leads in the past where someone's conscience finally got the better of them. A couple of deathbed confessions along the way. Cautious usually means they want to talk but with the safety net of plausible deniability and no witnesses.

For the last hour, she's paced her apartment, restless. The cramped space feels suffocating. A sense of unease sets in. She knows this story is dangerous, and she's not safe here. There's no security, and anyone can walk into the building and knock on her door. She tells herself that if she can get Carter's side of the story, then she can go to Jasper. Tell him she's resurrected the story, and given what happened last time she investigated this story, negotiate for him to put her find somewhere safer for the duration.

She had been careful, and even if he hadn't suggested somewhere public, she would have. Meeting in public comes with its own risks. Of course, the risks of an in-person meeting would have been mitigated if she'd had the sense to suggest a virtual meeting. Why hadn't she thought of that before? Not for the first time, she wonders if it's too late to change their arrangements.

She opens the door and checks the hallway, then closes it again, bolting it shut and sliding the chain in place. It doesn't make her feel any safer, but it's the best she can do.

The sounds of the city outside, distant traffic, muffled arguments, the occasional bark of a dog, filters in through the walls. Still, the air inside feels thick with tension. Her breaths are shallow, panic creeping in as she replays Marcus's warning. *They're always watching.* Who did he mean? Could he have finally let paranoia get the better of him?

The door splinters open. The sound is deafening. Two men rush inside, their movements swift and coordinated. One is Carter. The scarab tattoo on his right bicep is unmistakable. When he stoops to come through the doorway, she knows without a doubt who's stormed his way into her home.

Anna's blood runs cold. She has no time to think before her hands shoot out, grabbing the nearest object, a heavy ceramic mug. She hurls it at him, missing by inches as it shatters against the wall.

'Get out!' she screams, her voice raw with panic.

Carter doesn't flinch; his expression is cold. The first man lunges. Anna darts behind the couch, her feet slipping on the cluttered floor as she scrambles for the kitchen. The fear is overwhelming, but she fights to keep her head.

Her hands tremble as she rips open a kitchen drawer, grabs the first thing she can, a knife.

'Stay back!' she yells, turning on them, the blade shaking in her grip.

The men pause. One of them, smaller and wiry, lets out a cruel laugh.

'I told you this bitch would pick the hard way,' he sneers.

A tattoo on his arm catches Anna's eye, a chess piece, the rook, with Latin written beneath it.

'Try me,' Anna spits, tightening her grip on the knife. She focuses on every detail, hoping to get something she can use later, anything to give her a shot at escaping this nightmare.

Carter moves first, lunging toward her. Anna's aim is off, yet her blade still nicks his arm, resulting in a thin trickle of blood. He curses, retreating long enough for her to bolt.

As she nears the door, a third figure appears in the hallway. A woman. For a second, Anna thinks she's here to help her, but then she takes in what the woman is wearing, and she's in the same black fatigues as her pursuers. Before she has a chance to run, the woman grabs her arm, twisting it up her back and folds Anna in on herself so all Anna can see is her own feet.

'Enough,' the woman growls, her voice low and threatening.

Chapter Nine

The bar is a graveyard of faded neon lights and peeling wallpaper. Its air thick with the smell of stale beer and damp wood. The hum of a jukebox vibrates the air, filling the space with a haunting, distant melody mirroring the state of Victor's mind. He sits in a corner booth, nursing a half-empty glass, his fingers trembling around it.

The ice in his glass has melted into a lifeless pool, the whiskey diluted and forgotten. He doesn't have enough money left to order another. Three wet rings stain the tabletop, each one a quiet marker of how long he's been sitting here, watching the bottom of his glass, searching for answers he knows are not there.

The bar is half-empty now. The after-work crowd has thinned, laughter fades into inaudible murmurs, and the clinking of glasses. Above the bar, a muted television loops news headlines. He glimpses his own face in grainy footage flanked by reporters, eyes hollow, mouth tight, in the same clothes he's wearing. The chyron reads: *Appeal by disgraced former detective Victor Rourke fails.*

The volume is low but the subtitles march on. *Originating from the exposure of widespread misconduct uncovered by investigative journalist Anna Levesque.*

He turns away. Jaw tight.

A couple at the end of the bar catches his attention; they're looking at him. The woman leans in closer to her partner and says something and the man nods. He pretends not to notice.

Levesque's award-winning expose detailed years of backroom deals, cash payments, and confidential details of investigations disclosed to interested parties.

His shirt collar itches. The tailored suit, once crisp and a badge of authority, hangs loose. He hadn't noticed the frayed cuffs until he put the suit on for court this morning, too late to do anything about it.

He checks his phone. He's not expecting any messages, and he doesn't have any. Used to be his list of contacts was extensive and filled with powerful people. People he could call on to get things done and make problems disappear. Most stopped returning his calls as soon as the story broke; some waited until his suspension was announced. When he was fired, the remaining few all stopped.

The TV keeps going.

Multiple officers were implicated. Several took plea deals and turned on their co-conspirators. Others resigned quietly. Former Detective Victor Rourke has always maintained his innocence, and today was his last appeal against his dismissal.

The bartender flips the channel with an apologetic nod to him, acknowledging he hadn't realised the man subject to the story was sitting in his bar. She did her job well, Anna Levesque, too well. She gutted him. Exposed things well hidden. The only way she could have is with help, the kind of help he used to rely on.

She'd called it systemic rot. He called it survival. Justice doesn't always fit neatly into law books, not in his world. Not when the pressure comes from above. High above. He lifts the glass, hesitates, then sets it down again.

He had thought his circle was tight, impenetrable. Complacency was his downfall, and trust, trusting his secrets were worth keeping. He thought he was bulletproof.

He wasn't. Now he's forgotten except for the thirty-second news grab of his latest and failed attempt to save his career.

The door to the bar creaks open, cutting through the fog of his self-pity. Victor glances up in time to see a figure approach, tall and imposing, dressed in an immaculate suit. No fraying collar or cuffs for this guy. His eyes are dark and cold, a long scar down his face the only imperfection, an old ghost Victor thought he'd buried long ago. Without a word, the man slides into the booth, his presence filling the space. He smells of expensive cologne. Everything about him screams money, and lots of it.

'Victor,' the man says, his voice calm and measured. 'I thought you'd be easy to find. You've been making quite a mess for yourself these days.'

Victor swallows the bitterness in his throat, forcing himself to meet the man's eyes. His gaze never wavers.

'Why are you here?' Victor's voice comes out raspier than he intended, but he doesn't care. He's long since lost the taste for pleasantries.

The man doesn't answer right away. Instead, he slides a bundle across the table toward Victor. Cautiously, Victor unwraps the paper and rope. The contents: a security guard's uniform, pressed and pristine, and a swipe card gleaming bright white under the dim light. Victor's pulse spikes.

The man's fingers hover over the bundle before he speaks again, his tone low but firm. 'The Watcher wants to give you a second chance. A chance to prove you're still useful,' he nods to the clothes. 'This is it.'

Victor freezes. The Watcher. The same person who was behind Anna's story, the one who orchestrated his downfall, and now one of his minions is offering him a lifeline. His throat tightens with a mix of disbelief and resentment. He ruined him. He would be a fool to get into bed with him again, but he would be a dead fool to refuse.

'You're offering me a job?' The words taste like ash in his mouth.

'Not a job,' the man corrects, his eyes narrowing slightly. 'An opportunity to redeem yourself.'

Victor glances at the uniform, the familiar sheen of fear crawling under his skin. His hands shake as he picks it up, feeling the stiff fabric against his fingertips. The man's eyes bore into his, calculating, waiting. 'Sober up, wear this, and do exactly what you're told.' As he leaves, he places a mobile phone on top of the bundle of clothes.

Chapter Ten

The night is cool; a quiet Friday evening cloaks Brisbane in a sense of calm. The usual hum of the city has long passed, leaving the streets empty and silent. Marcus steps out of Greenwood, the doors closing behind him. The faint glow of the Story Bridge looms in the distance, its lights casting long shadows on the pavement.

He breathes in, trying to let the cool air wash away the constant ache in his chest. His brother's death, the years of guilt and grief, it's still there, lingering in the background. He can't shake the feeling that it was his fault. The thought always persists, no matter how far he walks or how hard he tries to outrun it.

He breathes in the city's quiet. There're still a few people milling around, coming and going from the bars and restaurants. A few cars glide past on their way to whatever life the drivers have. He wonders at the obliviousness of most people, unaware of the undercurrent pulsing around them. Lives untouched by the things he's seen. He envies them.

Without warning, three people leap out of an alley. Before Marcus can react, he's grabbed from behind. One hand clamps over his mouth, the other around his arms, pulling him back into the darkness. The force is too much. His body tenses in defiance, but it's useless. He can't break free.

A chill runs down his spine. His heart slams against his ribs as he struggles, trying to make sense of the sudden, violent turn his night has taken. He tries to scream, but the hand over his mouth muffles his voice. The man's grip is unyielding, their movements coordinated. No words; the sharp shuffle of boots on concrete, the quick tug of his arms, wrenching them behind him, rendering any resistance impossible.

He's being shoved forward, his body jerking as fights against the force moving him toward a waiting van. The door slams open with a harsh metallic clang. Before he can process what's inside, someone tapes his mouth, binds his wrists with zip ties, and throws a bag over his head. Relief fills him when he realises he can still breathe, but he can't see anything.

The van lurches forward and throws Marcus sideways, his shoulder grinding against cold metal. The hood muffles everything, his breath, the engine, the low hum of movement around him. Tape seals his mouth shut; plastic cinches his wrists tight behind him and bites into his skin.

He tries to breathe slowly, but his lungs won't obey. The air inside the hood is warm and stale. Too close. His pulse thunders in his ears, drowning out thoughts. He's suffocating, and not from a lack of air.

A sound beside him. A breath. Female. Not Lucy. He'd know her scent anywhere. Vanilla and jasmine. This woman smells of stale cigarettes.

His stomach drops.

He wants to call out, to ask who she is, what she knows, but the tape keeps him silent. The silence of the men is worse. They haven't spoken, not even to each other. He knows the quiet is deliberate, strategic, to put him on edge. It's working.

His thoughts spiral. Greenwood. His patient, Thomas. The story. His brother's face, pale and still. The funeral. The guilt. The years of trying to make it right. Agreeing to see Anna again when they both should have left it alone.

The van's interior presses in, claustrophobic. He can hear the people who grabbed him breathing. Who are they? What do they want? What did he miss? The van picks up speed. The road beneath them changes, becoming smoother and faster. They're leaving the city. Leaving everything familiar. His thoughts fractured. What if Lucy's in danger? What if the woman beside him is bait? What if this is punishment, not for what he did, but what he tried to do? For daring to challenge what he should have left alone.

He tries to focus. To stay rational. But the silence is corrosive. It eats at him. Every second without explanation is a new kind of violence. He's unravelling.

Marcus shifts, inching toward the woman beside him. The movement is awkward. His wrists scream against the cable ties, the hood brushing against her shoulder. She flinches. He freezes.

Then, slowly, deliberately, he leans again, enough to make contact. His shoulder against hers. A silent signal. *I'm here; you're not alone.* She doesn't pull away this time. Her breathing is shallow and rapid. He can feel it through the fabric. Fear, raw and unfiltered. He nudges her gently again. A question. A plea.

The van slows. His stomach knots. Gravel crunches beneath the tyres. The engine idles, then cuts. Silence. Marcus holds his breath. Doors open. One. Two. Three. The men climb out without a word. The van rocks slightly as their weight shifts away.

Then nothing.

Minutes stretch. The silence is unbearable. Marcus strains to hear anything. A voice. A footstep. The woman beside him trembles. He can feel it now. Her whole body is shaking. He wants to speak, to comfort her, but the tape holds him mute.

A scream. High. Piercing. Female. It rips through the silence. Marcus jerks upright, heart hammering. The woman beside him gasps. A muffled sob escapes her throat. Another scream. Closer this time. Wild. Panicked.

Chapter Eleven

The glow of the monitor is the only light in the lab, casting long shadows across the stark white walls. Quentin's fingers fly across the keyboard, his breath shallow, heart pounding. Every keystroke matters. Every second counts. Marcy may not have believed him and Tristan today, but he knew as soon as he left the funeral, he had to take precautions. He'd been working on something for weeks, but he hadn't felt a sense of urgency about it. Until now. Better to have it and not need it than to need it and not have it.

He copies the last segment of code and pastes it into the secure system, his pulse spiking as he watches the upload bar inch forward. Almost there. He glances over his shoulder. The lab is silent except for the rhythmic hum of the cooling fans.

Too quiet. He wishes he were not alone. The lab creeps him out at night as it is, but he can't do what he's doing now with potential witnesses.

Paranoia claws at his mind, a familiar sensation, but this time, it feels warranted. The facility is empty. Everyone else has gone home. Only a handful of people have clearance to enter his lab at this hour. The late-night benefits him, but he's also acutely aware of how quickly favours change.

The hair on the back of his neck rises as if he's being watched. He looks around for signs that he's not alone. Listening intently but when nothing triggers, he turns back to his task.

He forces himself to focus. With the last piece of the upload complete, the code locks into place within the encrypted system. He exhales and opens the Discord chat. Only two others have access to this private channel, two people he trusts.

Code uploaded. Line 40601.

He sends the message and then secures the chat. If something happens, they'll know what to do. They'll know where to look.

The door to his lab slides open.

Quentin turns to see who's there and freezes.

Three men step into the lab, dressed in black fatigues.

His mind screams this can't be happening, how the security controls meant he should have been safe. But everything he and Tristan have uncovered over the last few weeks tells a different story. Evidence of something much more sinister at work and he, Tristan and Marcy all pawns in a much wider agenda. An agenda he's sure Nathaniel was onto. He and Tristan argued over whether to tell Marcy, and once they agreed they should, it was a matter of doing it without raising red flags. They had thought the funeral would be the safest. They were expected to be there. Everyone was. A show of solidarity, but perhaps it wasn't. What if it were a trap, and they fell right into the middle of it?

They move around the lab in a pincer movement, no way for him to escape. He doesn't know why they bothered to send three; he's hardly in any condition to put up a fight. He can feel their eyes on him, watching, evaluating. It's a stalemate, and someone has to make the first move. Quentin's fingers twitch toward the laptop. With deft movements, he locks the screen. The leader smirks and shakes his head. They're not here for the laptop.

The second man reaches him in two strides, grabbing his wrist with crushing force. Quentin yelps, twisting to break free. The third man pulls a plastic tie from his belt, loops it around Quentin's other wrist and yanks it tight. Panic surges through him.

'No, wait,' his voice catches. His mind is still on the code, the message. Did he do enough? Did he hide it well enough? What will happen if they find the code or, worse, work out what the code does?

Chapter Twelve

The peace of her home envelops Marcy. Her pregnancy has grounded her. All she wants is to obliterate the day she never saw coming, the endless condolences and offers of help. She had been relieved when they had all finally gone home. Nathaniel's mother had offered to stay, as did her parents. She assured them she was fine and wants to be alone for a while. Now, she focuses on preparing the nursery for her baby's arrival. She arranges tiny baby clothes and adjusts the crib in the perfect corner of the room. The soft hum of the house, coupled with the light filtering through the windows, makes her feel safe.

Marcy glimpses her phone on the nearby table. It pings with a new message, but she ignores it. She tries to push the thoughts of the creepy man at the funeral and Quentin and Tristan's conspiracies to the back of her mind, but they persist to the point where she walks along the upstairs hall towards Nathaniel's office. Her hand pauses on the door. Even with him gone, this feels like an intrusion.

With a deep breath, Marcy steps inside. The space is foreign to her. A desk under the window with cables for his laptop, a lamp and an empty bookcase filling the wall where the built-in wardrobe used to be. She's confused. They had taken out the built-in and replaced it because he had so many books and file folders crammed with research. She had complained that his work took up every spare surface in the house until they dedicated this space to him. She looks around her. She had expected papers, folders, books or his laptop. Instead, there's nothing but dust outlines of where it all used to be. She opens one drawer after another, finding nothing but a few stray pens.

It's as if someone stripped the house clean, erasing every trace of his work.

Had Nathaniel cleared it all himself, trying to protect her, but she's sure she would have noticed? He couldn't have simply walked out with armloads of files and her not notice. A dark thought crowds her mind, what if someone else had come in and done it? What could he have been working on? What was so dangerous that every trace had to be eradicated?

The ringing of the doorbell interrupts her thoughts. She takes a deep breath. Someone else is coming to check on her, no doubt. To offer condolences and some kind of comfort food. She has enough lasagna crammed in the fridge and freezer that she will not need to cook for a month. She closes the door and takes one last look. 'I'm coming,' she calls out, knowing it will take a while for her heavily pregnant body to reach the door.

When she gets there and opens it, three figures stand before her, all in black fatigues, their eyes hidden behind dark glasses. Her heart skips a beat. The leader, a tall man, steps forward and looks down at her. He doesn't need to introduce himself. His cold, commanding presence is enough.

'Step back,' he orders in a low, gravelly voice.

Before she can process the situation, the woman beside him moves in, her grip strong as she grabs Marcy's arm. The third man, silent and efficient, closes the distance between them, securing her other arm.

'Let go of me!' Marcy manages, her voice trembling with shock.

She struggles, pulling against their grip with all her strength. But the woman's fingers tighten, and Marcy's breath comes in quick, panicked gasps. She screams.

'Please. What do you want?' Marcy's voice breaks as she struggles to keep her feet on the ground. Her thoughts race. Who are these people? Why her?

The woman calmly nods to the tall man, who gives a quick command. The next thing Marcy knows, they're dragging her away from the door.

The chill of the evening air hits her as they pull her out onto the front steps. Her mind is still reeling. She's pregnant, weak, and defenceless. These strangers don't care. The tall man's rough hand grips her arm, forcing her into an unmarked van parked across the street.

The third man, who hasn't said a word, opens the back of the van. Marcy struggles harder now, her heart hammering in her chest as the weight of the situation settles in.

'Stop! Let me go!' Marcy screams as she sees two other hooded people in the back of the van. She writhes against them, but she is no match for their coordinated strength. Tape slapped over her mouth, cable ties secure her hands, and a hood plunges her into darkness.

Chapter Thirteen

The hallway is dim; the flickering fluorescent lights cast long, jagged shadows on the concrete walls. The scent of damp cement lingers in the air, mixing with the faint metallic tang of old pipes. Sebastian stomps through the corridors with his fists flexing at his sides and his jaw clenched. He can hear Rook's footsteps behind him and Lauren's ahead. The collection of players is complete; he knows he needs to focus on what happens next. The adrenaline coursing through his veins refuses to abate.

He's spent years convincing himself morality is for people who can afford it, that jobs are jobs, but tonight, his conviction wavers. Something about this time doesn't sit right with him. He's taken people before. Hell, he's done worse, but this? A heavily pregnant woman yanked from her home as if she were nothing? He can still hear her muffled cries, the desperate way she fought, even knowing she couldn't win.

He exhales and turns to Lauren. 'He couldn't have waited?' His voice is low, controlled, but edged with frustration. 'She's eight months along. You don't think grabbing her now is a bit excessive?'

Lauren keeps walking, unbothered. She doesn't even glance at him as she responds. 'We didn't have the luxury of waiting.'

'That's it?' Sebastian stops in his tracks, forcing her to halt a few paces ahead. 'That's all you've got?'

She turns, arms crossed, her gaze cool and unwavering. 'What do you want me to say, Sebastian? I'm losing sleep over this. That I feel bad?' she tilts her head. 'We had a window. We took it. The mission comes first.'

'The mission,' he repeats, his voice lower.

Lauren sighs, her patience fraying. 'We weren't going to get another clean shot at her. Do you think they'd leave her unprotected after the baby comes? You think she'd be sitting in her nice little house with the door unlocked?'

She's not wrong, but he can't help but feel there's been a line crossed tonight he's not comfortable with. 'I've done a lot of things,' he mutters. 'But this, it feels wrong.'

Lauren steps closer, her voice dropping to something almost dangerous. 'What did you always tell me? Emotions are for the weak. The work is to do as you are told, execute the mission, keep your mouth shut and your opinions to yourself. You told me yourself when we first met, you have to have a certain kind of disposition for this work. Perhaps you don't have it anymore?'

Silence stretches between them, sharp and heavy. Lauren watches him, waiting. Daring him to argue. And then there's Rook. The man hasn't said a word, but his presence is impossible to ignore. Sebastian looks over his shoulder to check whether he's still even behind them. He is. He leans against the wall, arms crossed, head tilted as if he's pretending not to notice what's going on around him. Sebastian knows better.

Sebastian forces his muscles to loosen, his expression to smooth over. He can't afford to look weak, not in front of Rook. Not when he's already pushing the limits of acceptable defiance.

Lauren smirks, interpreting his silence as a concession.

'Thought so,' she murmurs as she walks away.

Chapter Fourteen

The pub is alive with the usual late-night chaos, laughter, clinking glasses, and music pounding through the speakers. Tristan leans back in his seat, a lazy grin on his face as his friend's crack jokes, the warmth of alcohol humming through his veins. For once, he allows himself to let go, to enjoy a rare moment. Today was hard. Burying Nathaniel, sharing their suspicions with Marcy and the strange, creepy man watching them.

His phone vibrates on the table.

He glances at it, then his brow furrows.

Code uploaded. Line 40601.

Tristan blinks, his buzz fading as he stares at the message. What does that mean? The numbers mean nothing to him.

Unease curls in his gut when the tension was ebbing away.

He taps out a quick reply, 'What?' but there's no response. He watches the screen for a few more seconds, waiting, but nothing comes.

'Earth to Tristan?' One of his friends nudges him. 'You look like someone texted you your own obituary.'

Tristan forces a chuckle and pockets his phone. 'Nah, work stuff,' he isn't sure why he lies. Maybe because he doesn't want to explain something he doesn't understand himself. He lifts his drink, deciding not to let Quentin's weird timing ruin his night. Whatever the problem is, it will still be there in the morning.

He excuses himself and heads toward the bathroom. Bodies press together in the pub's packed main room; beer and sweat thicken the air. As he steps into the hallway leading to the restrooms, the noise fades, swallowed by the dim corridor.

Something shifts.

The atmosphere is different here, quieter, heavier. The hallway light flickers, and Tristan feels unsettled.

Then he's overcome with the feeling even though there's no-one else in the hallway; he's not alone. He turns to head back to the bar, telling himself he can 'hold it.'

From the shadows, a figure moves fast, too fast. A hand clamps around his arm, yanking him backward before he can react. Another grips the back of his neck, forcing his head down with a powerful arm lock around his torso. Tristan snarls, twisting, instinct kicking in too late. A blow slams into his ribs, sharp and precise, knocking the air from his lungs. His vision blurs for half a second, long enough for them to drag him backward through the emergency exit.

The cold night air hits his face. His back slams against the side of a van, and before he can even think to yell, another fist drives into his stomach. White-hot pain explodes through him, his breath choking off as his knees buckle. A voice, calm and cold, mutters something behind him. He's bound, gagged, and with a hood slipped over his head.

Then the van door slides open, and they shove him inside. Tristan lands hard, his hands scrambling against the smooth metallic floor. He has little time to turn before the door slams shut, locking him in the darkness.

Chapter Fifteen

The hum of the engine is almost soothing; a steady rhythm lulls Aaron Dupree into a rare moment of calm amidst the whirlwind of his campaign. His chauffeur-driven car glides down the suburban streets; the blur of passing scenery offers a fleeting respite from the day's demands. The event in the next suburb is only minutes away, but for now, Aaron allows himself time to relax, if only for a few seconds.

He pulls his phone from his jacket pocket, fingers flying over the screen as he types a quick text to Jeremy. 'Any updates on the whistleblower's story?' the message sent. He sets his phone down on the seat next to him, focusing on his speech. Even though he has refined the words he planned, something feels wrong. He can't put his finger on it. The tension of the campaign creeps back into his mind.

As he leans back against the leather seat, his body jerks forward as another car hits them. Wham! The impact is sharp and sudden. Aaron's chest slams against the seatbelt, a violent pressure against his ribs and shoulder. His heart races, and before he can catch his breath, the car lurches forward again, skidding before coming to an abrupt stop. He blinks, trying to clear the fuzziness from his vision as his seatbelt digs into his chest.

The world outside is a blur, but through the passenger-side window, Aaron can make out the sight of a van screeching to a halt next to them. Panic rises in his throat.

'Jesus, what the hell?' his driver curses, his hands jerking against the steering wheel as he tries to regain control.

Before Aaron can react, the back door of the car flies open. Three men in black fatigues. The first man has the driver by his throat, pulling him out of the car with frightening ease. The second lunges at Aaron, rips the door open, while the third keeps watch, his eyes scanning the street. It's early evening, and while it's not a main road, it's not deserted. Cars pass by with shocked passengers and drivers, but no one stops to help. One man pulls over to video the whole thing on his phone, but one man in black grabs the phone, drops it to the floor, and crushes it with his boot.

Aaron doesn't have time to think. His body reacting, trying to fight, to push back against the steel grip of the man pulling him from the car. A gun pressed against Aaron's ribs causes his thoughts to shift. He's no longer thinking about the campaign, the whistleblower or his next speech. He's thinking about survival.

'Get out,' the man growls, voice clipped and commanding.

Aaron tries to resist and shouts, but the man yanks his legs out from under him. The man's grip tightens, pressing the barrel into his side as the first man steps forward to help force him out of the car. Having dispatched the driver with a shot to the head, he now lies on the street, blood oozing from his lifeless body. Aaron feels for the man's family before he exits the car completely. The man who was filming on his phone seconds earlier rushes back into his car and races away. He's not about to risk getting shot for social media likes.

The men don't speak to Aaron. Their movements are coordinated and practiced. As Aaron stumbles forward, he sees the van, its doors wide open, an empty, dark void waiting to swallow him. The men shove him toward it.

His mind races with questions. Is this about the campaign? The whistleblower? A political rival, perhaps, although this all feels too extreme. His thoughts scatter in a dozen directions as his body moves against its will. His feet drag across the pavement, and before he can even react, he's shoved into the back of the van with his hands bound, a hood over his face and a gag in his mouth. No matter what the reason, it all feels surreal.

Chapter Sixteen

The quiet of the alley is almost deceptive. The usual hum of the city seems distant, as though the world itself holds its breath. Sebastian's footsteps echo against the wet pavement as he approaches his car, mind racing through the calculations of his next move. He's always been careful, always aware of the risks his work brings, where the rules shift underfoot, and only the quick and clever survive. Tonight feels different, starting with him being told he was not needed any more for the mission. He's never been pulled off a mission before. The air feels charged, and he can't shake the feeling that something is about to go wrong. The kind of wrong he normally instigates.

Without warning, three figures step out of the shadows, moving with practiced grace, sending a chill down his spine. His fingers twitch at his sides, regretting now that he hadn't thought of bringing his gun. He doesn't move. Outnumbered, there's no escape. The leader of the trio steps forward, and Sebastian's heart skips a beat when he sees her face.

Lauren.

He's expecting anyone but her, or perhaps it was misplaced hope that they would not use her against him. He should have known better. His stomach lurches. This isn't another job; it's personal. She stands there, gun drawn, eyes cold but focused. Flanked by two other operatives, she looks every inch the soldier, the team leader, the enforcer of the Watchers will.

It's his own fault. When the Watcher had told him to recruit her, he didn't hesitate. He knew her skills in the forces made her valuable. He knew her family history made her vulnerable. He knew he was responsible for the latter, at least in part, and yet he still did it. He trained the humanity out of her. Now he's reaping the rewards of all his hard work. He always knew this day would come; the irony that they would send her to execute the task. Unless, of course, she volunteered.

'Watcher says it's time for you to retire,' Lauren says, her voice tight but clear.

Sebastian raises his hands, palms out, feigning surrender. His face remains unreadable. He's spent decades honing his craft to ensure all his opponents ever see is a mask of calmness. 'Here, now, or someplace else?' They both know what he means.

There's a flicker in her eyes, the briefest hint of hesitation, something she's fighting to suppress. The tension in the air thickens. His gaze shifts behind her, locking onto the imposing figure of Rook. The smirk on his face, the same satisfied grin he gets when he's screwed someone over.

'It was you, wasn't it?' Sebastian's voice is low, accusing. Of course, it was. Some fall into this job because they're disillusioned. Some, like Lauren, are trying to outrun something. Then there're men like Rook; they do it because they like it. It justifies their evil nature.

Rook doesn't respond, but Sebastian doesn't need him to. The betrayal is clear now. The air between Lauren and Rook crackles with it.

A bitter laugh escapes Sebastian, raw and jagged.

Lauren doesn't move.

'You don't even know,' Sebastian says, his voice quieter now, but still sharp with the weight of everything unspoken. 'Things I should have told you but didn't. I thought I was doing right by you by keeping quiet,' he can hear the desperation in his voice. He knows that if he doesn't say something now, he will not get another chance. But if he says too much, he might put her right here next to him.

Lauren's grip on her weapon tightens, the metal gleaming under the dim light of the alley. 'I know enough,' she shoots back, jaw clenched, trying to hold on to the control she still has. He knows her tells, the tick in her eyebrow. It twitches as if it has a life of its own. All Sebastian can think is, thank God Rook is behind her and can't see it. But she's aware of it and touches her finger to it to stem the reaction.

Sebastian shakes his head. A sad smile tugs at his lips. 'No. You don't. I know what really happened to your parents, Lauren. How the Watcher groomed you, how I helped him do it,' he pauses, his voice thick with regret. 'Guess this is karma, huh?'

For a heartbeat, the world freezes. He sees it then, doubt crossing Lauren's face before she suppresses it, forcing her expression back to something unreadable. She's aware of the consequences of expressing any kind of doubt or free will. She's looking at it. She's the tool they're using to execute it.

'Take him,' Lauren says, her voice hard, final, and the command leaves no room for argument, as he had taught her.

The operatives move in, their hands quick and sure, grab Sebastian by the arms. His heart hammers in his chest, but he doesn't resist. He's too tired. Too resigned to the truth of his situation. He made his choices, made them a long time ago, and now he's paying for them.

As they force him toward the waiting van, his mind spins. Lauren believes she knows everything about the Watcher, about the world they both inhabit. Sebastian knows better. Truth has a way of creeping up on you when you least expect it. When the truth catches up to Lauren, when the full extent of the Watcher's manipulation is revealed, will she question his orders, will she question everything?

Chapter Seventeen

Anna's head throbs. Her neck burns with a sharp, gnawing ache. She winces, trying to make sense of the dark, impersonal space around her. The gritty, unyielding concrete surface beneath her is hard and unforgiving. The flickering hum of industrial lights reveals a vast, cavernous warehouse. The high, rusted beams above cast jagged shadows across the floor, where graffiti and peeling paint vie for dominance on the walls.

The air is thick with the sour stench of mildew and the metallic tang of rust, creating a suffocating atmosphere. Disoriented, she attempts to sit up, her hands brushing against the gritty, dirty floor. Her neck protests; a searing pain shoots through her, and she reaches for the tender spot behind her ear. Her fingers graze at something hard and foreign beneath her skin.

'What the hell?' Her voice is a whisper, cracked and strained. She trembles, feeling the cool, metallic weight of a smart watch clasped to her wrist. It's more advanced than anything she's ever seen. She tries to yank it off, but the clasp is stuck, the watch refusing to budge. On its display, it reads 72:00:00. The reality of the situation settles in, but she doesn't know what it means yet.

A soft groan from the far side of the warehouse snaps her attention away from the watch. She's not alone. In the van, she was aware of a man next to her. Tape over her mouth stopped her from speaking but the man smelled like musk, like Marcus. There was someone else, but shortly after they picked up the last person, she remembers a cloth pressing against the hood covering her head.

Now, five others stir across the warehouse. Panic flickers in her chest as her eyes lock onto Marcus, hunched over, cradling his head in his hands. The person in the van didn't just smell like Marcus. It was Marcus. He feels his neck, then snaps upright, scanning the space. His eyes meet hers.

'Marcus,' Anna breathes, her voice weak. She scrambles to her feet, but dizziness overtakes her, and she staggers, bracing herself against a rusted steel beam. Marcus stumbles toward her, his steps as unsteady as hers. Between them, they take enough unsteady steps to come together.

'What the hell is going on?' Anna asks. Marcus looks around the room. She thinks she sees a flicker of recognition cross his face at one point, but it's gone as fast.

Marcus shakes his head, his expression grim, haunted. Before Anna can press him, a loud metallic clang echoes across the warehouse, making them all flinch. The others inch closer to each other, eyes darting to the shadows from where the sound came.

From the darkness, six men and one woman step forward. They're dressed in sleek black fatigues, their faces impassive, clinical. Behind them, a tall man emerges. His face marred by a long, jagged scar slicing through his left eyebrow. Carter might be the brawn, but this guy is both.

'Welcome,' he says smoothly, his voice devoid of warmth, almost rehearsed. He glances down at the paper in his hands, reading from a script. 'You've been selected for a unique game.' A sneer turns his lip up in one corner.

Anna's stomach tightens. Carter steps forward from behind the group. He flashes a thin, supercilious smile, his eyes narrowing when they land on Anna. She notices a bandage wrapped around his arm where she had cut him earlier. At least she knows he can be hurt.

'A game?' Anna echoes, her voice trembling despite her attempt at defiance. She can't hide the panic creeping in.

Carter's smile widens, but it's empty and cruel. 'Let me explain the rules.'

He steps forward, drawing closer to Anna and the others, who are huddling together, confusion and fear etched on their faces. 'For the next 72 hours, you are the prey. You have no phones, no money. Just whatever you're standing in.'

Anna checks her pockets. He's right. No phone, no wallet.

'These,' Carter gestures to the people standing behind him, 'are the hunters.' One of them, a woman, locks eyes with Anna. The hatred in her eyes is unmistakable, but Anna doesn't recognise her. The feeling that they've met before and the intensity of the woman's expression sends an icy shiver down Anna's spine.

Carter smirks, gesturing to the hunters, and they file out of the warehouse, disappearing into the shadows beyond.

'You will have a two-hour head start,' he continues, his voice dripping with malice. 'And seventy-two hours to survive.'

The weight of the words crushes Anna's chest. The countdown on her watch now makes sense. It's how long she has to live.

Another man, so small Anna hadn't noticed him until now, steps forward, holding up a tablet. 'Each of you has been fitted with a custom-programmed specifically to you. Inside each device is the means to kill you. Failure to comply with the rules will result in your death.'

Anna's fingers dart to her neck, tracing the hard, foreign shape embedded beneath her skin. The device pulses as if mocking her touch.

Carter steps closer, his expression cold and calculating. 'Don't bother going to the police, or family, or friends. The coordinates for those locations have already been programmed into your devices. Get too close, and the device will stop you. Permanently.'

Anna feels her heart skip a beat. She tries to control the panic rising in her throat, but it's no use. 'You can't do this,' she shouts, the mixture of fear and fury surging inside her. 'You can't.'

'We already have,' Carter interrupts smoothly, his voice colder than ice. 'Your lives are ours for the next three days. If you survive, you'll be free to return to whatever miserable existence you had before. If you don't...,' he lets the sentence hang in the air, its meaning clear.

'The watches on your wrists transmit your location,' Carter continues, his eyes scanning their faces for a reaction. 'We always know where you are, but the hunters don't have access to this information. They like to have their skills challenged,' he lets out a low chuckle.

Anna's eyes flit to the others, searching their faces for some sign of understanding. Marcus looks defeated, guilt written all over his expression. Does he feel responsible for Anna being here, and for bringing her straight to this nightmare, or does he blame her? Somehow, she can't help wondering when it's been less than 24 hours since she told him she was picking up the story again. Could it all be related or a massive coincidence? She swallows the bile rising in her throat, but Carter's voice breaks her focus.

'There's a map on your watch,' Carter explains. 'It highlights the no-go zones. If you get too close to these areas, you'll get a warning. Ignore that, and you'll get a second warning. If you ignore that, the device will administer a dose of something to remind you of what's at stake. Ignore that, and the device will execute its final protocol. Game over, can't say we're not being fair.'

The words hang in the air, heavy and final.

Anna's eyes dart to the other captives. She sees a woman standing nearby, tears streaking down her face, her hands trembling over her swollen belly. Her sobs are excruciating to listen to. A wiry man with tattoos and another who is a mirror image of him, only much heavier, stares at the ground. Another man in his forties, dressed impeccably, looks around, confusion clouding his face. Anna recognises him. He's Aaron Dupree. She exposed his father's corruption early in her career. Even though Aaron wasn't the focus, it still put the brakes on his political career, for a while, anyway. But as far as she knows, his name has never come up in connection with the Watcher's story. But what other explanation is there? Whatever it is, she knows it must have something to do with the people around her, and whatever it is, for the female hunter at least, it's personal.

'To keep it sporting,' Carter continues, his voice dripping with mock enthusiasm. 'There are equal numbers of hunters and prey, but as the prey...,' he pauses, looking for the right word. 'As the prey are eliminated,' he finishes, a sickly chuckle escaping his lips, 'the hunters can work together to track the rest of you down.'

The small man with the tablet steps forward again. 'We're still waiting for one more player before we begin.'

Anna's mind races; the magnitude of the situation crashes down on her. She feels the weight of the device in her neck. Her survival may no longer be hers to control.

Carter checks his watch. 'The last player will be with us shortly. Be sure to give him a warm welcome.'

As Carter walks away, the distant laughter of the hunters echoes through the warehouse, making Anna's skin crawl. The sound of a van approaching grabs her attention, and her heart skips a beat. The van screeches to a halt; its sliding door flies open, and someone shoves a person out before the door slams shut and the van speeds away. It's over in a blink.

Anna's smartwatch vibrates, the digital map flashing up on the screen. She looks around; everyone's watch is doing the same thing. Red dots mark the forbidden zones. A message flashes: Seven hunters active. Seven prey remaining.

Anna's breath catches. The game has begun.

Chapter Eighteen

The dim warehouse lights flicker, casting long, skeletal shadows stretching across the corrugated walls. Cold concrete presses through Tristan's clothes as he sits on the floor, back aching from tension. The air smells of rust, oil and dust kicked up by their captor's boots. Every breath feels thick, fighting its way out of his chest.

He tries to steady his racing thoughts. He doesn't know how long they have before the door creaks open again, before the hunters return, but he knows waiting here won't save them. If rescue is coming at all, it won't be fast enough. Not against men capable of orchestrating Nathaniel's accident.

Beside him, Quentin scours through the rubbish to find anything they can use as a weapon. His eyes gleam with something sharp and desperate. Quentin leans in, his eyes intense and determined. 'I coded a back door into the device,' he murmurs, his voice low but steady, a contradiction of the tremor in his hands. 'It's crude, but if I can get to a computer, I can deactivate it.'

Tristan blinks, his mind catching on to the words. A back door? His pulse quickens. 'How does it work?' he whispers, keeping his voice small, swallowed by the hum of a distant industrial fan.

Quentin's gaze remains unwavering, but there's a flicker of hesitation in his eyes. 'It's not perfect. I didn't exactly have a lot of time to work on it but if I can access a computer, I should be able to pull the plug on the devices.'

Tristan takes a slow breath. It's a glimmer of hope, but he's not convinced yet. 'I can disable them too,' he says after a pause, letting the words sink in. 'Because of my work at Greenwood, I know how these devices work. But...' He hesitates, his mind flashing to the critical pieces missing. 'I need my equipment.'

'What kind of equipment?'

Tristan hesitates. His fingers brush the skin beneath his collarbone, the spot where the implant pulses faintly with warmth. 'They have a special tool that can pull the device out without doing damage.'

Quentin's eyes widen. 'Damage?'

'Yes,' Tristan's voice cracks faintly. 'If you try to dig it out there's these claws that extend and grab onto the flesh around it. That's why they implant them so close to a major artery.'

Quentin mutters a shaky breath. 'Crap, that wasn't part of the original design.'

'Marcus's wife, she works with me at Greenwood,' Tristan says. 'She knows where the equipment is and how to use it. But I can't get close enough to the devices without triggering this thing,' he points to his neck, 'because they've programmed Greenwood as a no-go area.'

A heavy silence falls between them. Tristan can feel the weight of the moment pressing on his chest. He's always been a man of logic, of measured moves. But now, with the situation spiralling out of control, he's forced to decide without all the facts.

Quentin finally exhales, breaking the silence. 'Then we improvise,' he says, his voice calm but resolute.

'I've been thinking about something they said.'

Quentin's head lifts. 'When?'

'When they gave us the rules. They said they'd programmed them specifically to each of us.'

'What's your point?'

'My point is,' Tristan holds out his watch and shows Quentin, 'perhaps the no-go zones are custom too.'

Quentin taps the screen of his watch. The map with the red no-go zones fills the small screen.

Tristan smiles, 'Greenwood is a no-go for me, but not you.'

Quentin nods. 'Same for the lab, I can't go there but you can.'

Their euphoria is short-lived as Quentin realises, 'access cards, you can't get in without them.'

'OK, so I can't get into the lab, but you can wait in the car park at

Greenwood for Lucy.'

'I don't know what she looks like?'

Tristan thinks for a minute. 'I know what car she drives.'

Quentin squints. 'Do you know her work schedule too?'

'Ah shit!' Tristan sighs. 'No.'

'And if I hang around the car park too long,' Quentin lets the thought hang between them.

'The Hunters don't have access to GPS,' Tristan counters.

'True, but the program is designed to send a GPS signal every ten minutes. If you stay in the same place for more than 30 minutes, it sends up a flare. When they see where that flare is they'll probably work out why I'm there and then God knows what they'll do to stop us, and I suspect these guys don't exactly work to an honour code.'

Tristan presses both hands to his face. 'Fuck Quentin.'

'I know,' Quentin's voice cracks. 'When I coded it, I had no idea they were going to use it this way.'

Tristan thinks for a minute. Then he turns to Quentin. 'This flare, is it three consecutive pings in the same place or three pings regardless of when.'

'Consecutive.'

'Well, that's a small mercy.'

'How d'you figure that?' Quentin huffs.

'Shifts start at 8 am, and they're twelve-hour shifts.

'So?'

'So, if her car is there after 8 am then go back at 8 pm and you'll catch her.'

Quentin drags a hand through his hair. 'That's a long shot and leaves a lot of time in between.' Quentin says, 'and it assumes she doesn't finish late.'

'Nah, they're sticklers for that. But...' Tristan hesitates.

'But what?'

'She might not be at work, what with Marcus being ...'

Quentin stiffens. 'Being what?'

'Being in the same predicament as us.'

'What?'

'Yeah, he's one of the other people caught up in this with us.'

'Fuck.'

Tristan's voice softens, guilt pooling in his gut. 'I know. But I think he got dragged into this because of me.'

Quentin turns sharply. 'How'd you figure that?'

Tristan shifts uncomfortably, the cold concrete biting into his hip. 'You know the politician?'

Tristan nods.

'What about him?'

'I wrote to him about what's been going on.'

'And the journalist?'

'She was sniffing around this story a few years ago. She was off base but …'

Quentin exhales, long and defeated. 'They're not taking any chances. You know we're fucked right?'

'But what's the alternative? At the very least we should try and fuck up their plans,' Tristan smirks and shrugs.

'Challenge is going to be for me getting into your lab.'

Quentin smiles, 'there, I can help you.'

'Really?'

'Yeah, I know a guy. But he's on my no-go zone list.'

Tristan holds out his watch. 'Is he on mine?'

Quentin moves the map around until he finds what he's looking for. His shoulders slump. 'Fuck.'

Tristan exhales. The warehouse hums around them, a cold, indifferent witness. 'That back door of yours is no good if I can't get in your lab or get to a computer and that's assuming I can hack it in less time than it takes to send up a flare.'

'No shit,' Quentin mutters, voice tight with frustration.

Chapter Nineteen

The warehouse feels suffocating; the heavy air thick with fear and uncertainty. A growing sense of dread laces every breath she takes. Around her, the others react in varying ways. The two younger men rifle through the debris, scavenging for anything usable as a weapon. The politician stands frozen, eyes wide and vacant, while the pregnant woman sobs, clutching her belly. The last contestant, sitting on the ground, brushes dust off his pants as though waiting for a bus, detached from the surrounding chaos.

Marcus leans against a pillar. His eyes locked onto Anna with a burning intensity. 'This is your fault,' he spits, his words sharp and venomous.

Anna blinks, her mouth moving, but no sound comes out. She presses her back against the rusted beam behind her, trying to steady herself. 'It's not like I held a gun to your head. You could have said no.'

'You should have let it go,' he continues, his voice shaking now. 'The story you couldn't, wouldn't let go and now look at us. You think you're untouchable? You're not. None of us are. I tried to warn you, Anna.'

'I,' her voice trembles, but Marcus cuts her off before she can say anything.

'Seriously,' he snaps, his fists clenched so tightly that his knuckles turn white. 'Less than 24 hours after you show up, demanding help with your oh-so-noble ideal of exposing corruption. We both know that's bullshit. Your career's been on the skids, and now you think this story is the brake that'll stop you falling?'

Anna wants to deny it, to argue, but the side-eye he gives her silences her. She'd told him as much earlier in the café. He doesn't want her defence. He wants her silence.

'You think this is a coincidence?' Marcus's voice lowers, and he steps closer, his breath hot on her face. 'They obviously still see you as a threat. Probably never stopped. Now everyone you dragged into this mess is paying the price.'

'Now hang on,' she rebuffs. 'You didn't have to show up. You were the one that said the story was even bigger. You were the one that put me onto Carter. For that matter how do you even know it has anything to do with it?'

'Because ...,' he starts, then thinks better of it.

A new voice cuts in, sharp and mocking.

'Surprise, surprise. I almost didn't recognise you,' says a man standing a few feet away. The grime of the warehouse has dishevelled his suit, dulling his once-sharp appearance, but his manner remains refined, and his tone is laced with disdain. Anna freezes, a cold prickle running down her spine. Aaron Dupree.

His lip curls, and he points at her with an accusatory finger. 'Still finding ways to ruin people's lives, I see.'

Heat floods Anna's cheeks. 'I didn't.'

'Spare me,' Aaron interrupts, holding his hands up in mock surrender. 'Don't give me that integrity nonsense. You fell off that pedestal gloriously last year. This? This is another setup for your next big story isn't it. Probably some kind of reality show set up. Unless, of course, you're strung out like you usually are.'

'That's not fair,' Anna shoots back, her voice rising despite the lump in her throat.

Aaron lets out a bitter laugh. 'Fair? You think anything about this is fair? The only saving grace here is that you'll be the first to go, and good riddance. That's assuming any of this is actually real, which I doubt, but if it is, if they have any sense, they'll throw everything they've got at getting rid of you first, and maybe that'll leave the rest of us with a shot.'

A harsh cough breaks the tense standoff. The pregnant woman, her hand shielding her belly, glares at Aaron. 'Here's a thought,' she looks at him to make sure she has his full attention. 'I have no idea who this woman is, or what we're all doing here, but for now, instead of throwing each other under the bus and looking out for ourselves, how about we figure out a way to work together and try to keep us all alive?'

The two younger men, still gathering whatever they can use as weapons, stop and look at her, exchanging a glance before the larger one shrugs and turns back to the group. 'Strength in numbers,' he says simply.

'Good luck with that,' a gravelly voice interjects from the shadows near the entrance.

Everyone turns toward the source. The last player to arrive. A man in his late forties' steps into the dim light, his face half obscured by shadows. He moves toward them with a limp, his presence radiating a cold, unsettling calm. A scar runs down the side of his neck, half-hidden beneath his collar. His eyes sweep over the group, calculating.

'Who the hell are you?' Marcus demands, his voice low and threatening.

The man advances, his movements deliberate. 'Name's not important,' he says, his voice rough. 'What is important is that you all understand something. Teaming up is suicide. You stick together, you're dead. End of story.'

'How do you know that?' Anna asks, taking a step forward despite the rapid thudding of her heart. The man meets her gaze, his smirk devoid of any humour.

'Because I've seen what they do when you try to team up,' he replies.

'Meaning?' Anna presses, her mind racing. He seems to know more than anyone else.

'Meaning they'll pick you off one by one. Start with whoever they think is the strongest, then systematically break you. Turn you against each other. Offer you all kinds of deals but it's all worthless' His eyes flick across the group, assessing their worth with chilling indifference. 'That's the point, to break you. To break allegiances, you may already have or make along the way.'

'You could be wrong,' Marcus says, his voice sceptical.

'I'm not,' the man scoffs, 'I trained them.'

A collective gasp ripples through the group. Tension thickens the air, suffocating them.

'Wait,' Anna says, her pulse quickening. 'You trained them? You can tell us what they do, and we can protect ourselves that way.'

The man shrugs, as though the question is of little consequence. 'You have to understand, they're loyal without question. That's their strength. They don't ask why. They do. There's no point me telling you about strategies and tactics, each game is different with two exceptions. They hunt. You die.'

'Why?' Anna cries.

'I don't know, but that's where I made my mistake. I asked when I should have known better,' his gaze lingers on the pregnant woman, his eyes softening for a moment. 'That's why I'm here. And so, when I tell you this game isn't designed for teamwork, believe me. It's designed to break you.'

'How many times have you played this game?' Anna asks.

'Over the last two decades, enough to know what I'm talking about.' The grim certainty in his voice sends a chill through Anna, and she believes him. Why would he risk the group turning on him by lying?

Her breath catches as she takes another step forward. 'If you know so much, then tell us how we can survive. Even if as you say, there's no point. You could at least give us a fighting chance.'

The man looks at her. 'You're not listening to me. That's it. You don't.'

Before Anna can process his words, he turns and walks toward the far end of the warehouse without another word. A silent, unsettling finality hangs in the air.

'Wait,' Anna calls after him, but he doesn't stop.

The sudden vibration on her wrist makes her stomach drop. She looks down at her smartwatch as the countdown begins. The cold, metallic voice from the unseen speaker rings out, sharp and final.

'The Hunters are coming. Run.'

The words hang in the air, cold and unyielding. The scarred man vanishes into the shadows, his parting words echoing through the warehouse.

'The hunters never honour the head start they claim to give you.'

Anna's eyes snap back to the screen of her watch. The map pulses with ominous markings, forbidden zones flashing in red. Places tied to her past.

'Seven hunters active. Seven prey remaining.'

Chapter Twenty

The air in the warehouse is thick with the scent of rust and fear. Shadows stretch, casting long, eerie shapes across the debris-littered floor. Anna struggles to keep her breathing steady; the taste of panic lingers on her tongue. She grips the edge of a rusted workbench, the gritty surface scraping against her palms, grounding her in the moment.

Aaron Dupree paces near the door, his face flushed with anger and defiance. He sneers at the rest of the group, his voice rising above the creaks of rusted machinery.

'This is insane,' he spits, flinging a hand toward the others. His words echo in the cavernous space, the tension in the air palpable. 'Don't tell me you seriously believe this crap.'

His eyes scan the room, searching for any sign of agreement. The others, tense and wide-eyed, hesitate.

'They're bluffing,' Aaron asserts, a twisted grin on his face. His voice filled with arrogance, as if his position in the world could protect him from anything. 'They wouldn't dare kill us, especially not someone like me.' And like that his *I'm an ordinary man'* mask slips.

People exchange a few nervous glances, but no one dares to speak up. Anna knows why. The murder of a high-profile politician would attract unwanted attention, and the Watcher excels at remaining inconspicuous. She has to admit Aaron makes a strong yet conceited argument.

'What makes you so special?' Marcus growls from the back of the warehouse.

Aaron shrugs as if the answer were obvious. He huffs, dismissing the question with a flick of his hand.

'Listen up,' he continues, his tone growing more patronizing. 'This is obviously some sick prank. Empty threats. Do you really believe this nonsense? They're trying to scare us, and it's working, on you at least.' He meets Anna's eyes, then scans the rest of the group. 'But not on me.' His bravado is contagious, and she can see the rest of the group warming to his theme.

Anna's pulse quickens; a cold knot forms in her stomach. She watches as he strides toward the door, his back straight with pride. Despite Marcus's warnings, she feels a flicker of doubt. Could Aaron be right? Could it all be an elaborate ruse to frighten them into compliance, but compliance with what.

The door creaks open, and a few others trail him. Their faces are pale, but there's a hesitant curiosity in their movements. Anna's instincts scream at her to stay put, but something in her chest compels her forward.

'What if he's right?' Her voice trembles as she whispers the question. The hope in her words is fragile, but it's there.

Marcus appears at her side, his eyes narrow with disdain. 'He's an idiot, and he's going to get himself killed.'

Carefully, she steps through the door, exiting the warehouse, following Aaron. She can see now that they are in some kind of industrial complex with empty warehouses. The fence topped with barbed wire surrounds the buildings, but the gates to the complex are wide open. There's nothing stopping them from walking off. In the distance she can hear traffic, and there's the tang of exhaust fumes jockeying with the earthy smell of damp concrete. The rain still drizzles, but at least the downpour has abated.

Ahead of her, she can see Aaron striding confidently. Aaron stares off at something in the distance ahead, and when she follows his eyeline, she can see it. The blue sign of a police beat. Not a fully staffed police station, but there must be a presence there of some kind. He picks up the pace, more confident now. He strides up the steps toward the area bathed in blue light and spares them a look back. He touches his neck as he gets closer to the station and then, as he reaches for the handle, he stops. Both hands reach for his neck.

His hands claw at his neck. Anna blinks, trying to process what she's seeing. A metal collar, something none of the others wear, and from this distance appears to be constricting around his throat. Lights flash and glow. His face contorts in pain, his throat releasing a sickening gurgle as he struggles to breathe.

Anna's heart stutters in her chest. She can't look away as Aaron crumbles to the ground, his body twitching violently. His lips turn blue, and the horrible sound of his last gasps fills the air before he lies still, his life extinguished.

'No!' Anna screams, her voice cracking as she stumbles forward. But Marcus is faster, grabbing her arm and yanking her back. She struggles against him. 'Someone has to help him,' she cries.

'It's too late,' Marcus says and nods as a black Transit van arrives with a screech of tires. Two masked figures in black sprint out. They place an instrument around Aaron's neck, detaching the collar and his smartwatch. They drag his lifeless body into the van, which speeds off into the night, leaving nothing but the haunting silence behind.

Anna's legs give way beneath her, and she collapses to the ground, gasping for air. Her hands fly to her neck, fingers brushing the cold, hard lump beneath her skin. The faint red glow of the implant flickers in the dim light, its pulse matching the erratic beat of her heart.

A vibration on her wrist pulls her back to the present. Her smartwatch flickers to life with a notification:

Aaron Dupree: Deceased | COD: Unauthorised Zone Breach.

A photo she recognises from his campaign posters flashes across the screen, and Anna's stomach churns. Her vision blurs as she scans the digital map on her wrist. Green dots, each representing one of the remaining contestants, blink on the screen. Anna's own dot, 'A,' is almost next to Marcus's 'M,' while a 'T' and a 'Q' are further back down the road, still relatively close to the warehouse.

Behind her, she hears the footsteps of the two young men who had been trying to fashion weapons earlier. Another 'M' dot remains at the warehouse, but an 'S' dot is moving away, its pace increasing with every second.

It's moving faster than anyone else. It's the trainer. He had warned them about teaming up, and now they know what he meant. But what else does he know, and why wouldn't he tell them. Is he hoping to buy himself more time? Could he be a plant, his purpose to deliberately feed them misinformation? Is there anyone she can trust?

'Fuck this,' one of the young men yells, his voice full of terror. He bolts back toward the warehouse, the 'T' dot following him. The 'Q' dot moves in the opposite direction of the man he had been working with to fashion weapons.

That alliance didn't last long, Anna thinks bitterly, her mind racing.

Another vibration from her wrist.

Seven Hunters Active. Six Prey Remaining.

'Move, Anna,' Marcus yells, his grip on her arm tight. Urgency fills his voice, but she can barely focus. Every part of her screams to run, but her legs are unsteady, her body shaking with fear. Still, she clambers to her feet, forcing herself to move.

Aaron

I know it's all a game, a sick prank at best. Whoever is behind it wants us rattled, this strange group of strangers with apparently nothing in common. They are all jumping at shadows, not me. I refuse to sit here waiting for whatever they have in store, and I'm certainly not about to go hiding around the city for fear of these so-called Hunters finding me. Sure, the staging is good, meant to look dangerous and strike fear into them, but that's all it is. Some elaborate performance, and if they expect me to play along, they've misjudged me.

I can see the others scattered around the warehouse; panic fills their faces. Their footsteps clumping together as they seek safety in numbers. I refuse to be dragged into their hysteria. I push through the door and step into the industrial yard. My shoes click against the concrete, my pace steady and deliberate. The collar around my neck, which had felt so heavy a minute ago, shrinks to an afterthought. I see the police beat sign ahead. Now I have a plan.

Whatever this twisted setup is supposed to be, it's beneath me. When this is over, I'll hunt down the people responsible and turn their little spectacle inside out. And I know exactly where to start: the whistleblower. I'll drag him out of whatever hole he crawled into and remind him secrets don't protect cowards. Together, we'll expose the rot eating through this community, but he'll answer to me first.

'They're trying to scare us, and it's working, on you at least.' I shake my head, trying to shed the thin thread of unease tugging at me. The smartwatch flashes its warning again: You are in an unauthorised zone. Leave immediately.

Yeah, right. A hollow threat dressed up as authority. They wouldn't dare go further. They couldn't. Not to me. And even if they did ... how would they ever explain it?

The police station is close, a short walk, and I can already picture myself walking through the door, safe, sound, and laughing at how easily I escaped and then I'll save everyone else from this sick joke and turn the tables on whoever is behind it.

The smartwatch buzzes again, its warning flashing in bright red letters, but I don't care. It's a mind game, and they overplayed their hand by dragging me into the middle of it. I fight to keep my heart steady and my breathing normal. I pick up the pace as I walk down the road toward the distant light of the police beat. It's obviously a trick to manipulate me into keeping quiet and not rocking the boat. Perhaps the whistleblower lied when they said the only person they talked to was me; what if they told Levesque too? Could it be she's been digging into the same thing? If she has gotten too close, it explains why they want her silenced. When this is over, perhaps he will have to put his thoughts about her, and the role she played in destroying his father, and almost him, behind him. As much as he hates the thought, perhaps working with her is the way to go.

A little further, a few more steps, and I'll be free.

Then the collar.

At first, I don't notice it. It's subtle. A pressure, a tightness around my neck. I shrug it off, thinking it's nothing; the collar is adjusting to my movement. But as I near the police beat, the feeling becomes more pronounced. Tight. Almost unbearable. My fingers reach for the collar, brushing against it, but there's no relief. The pressure grows.

I keep walking.

It's nothing, I tell myself. *A glitch. A ruse to convince me they mean business. It'll stop.*

The door to the police station comes into view, the handle gleaming under the streetlights. I reach for it, pulling the door toward me, but as my fingers wrap around the cool metal. The collar snaps tight, constricting my airway completely.

I gasp. The sudden tightness seizing my throat. It's no longer a mere discomfort; it's a vice. My vision blurs. My hands claw at the collar, desperate to remove it, but it's as though it has fused with my skin.

No ... this is a mistake; it's a malfunction. They wouldn't...

I choke, staggering back from the door, but the pressure never relents. The world around me spins, my breathing shallow and frantic. I try to call out for help, but no sound comes out. Only the sound of frantic rasping, trying to take in air.

I drop to my knees, the cold concrete against my skin doing little to cool the panic swelling inside me. I need air. I need to breathe. My fingers are numb as I claw at the collar again, but it's hopeless.

Then I hear footsteps.

Distant, but real. Someone is coming. Help is coming.

As the footsteps grow louder, they seem to echo off the walls, mocking me. Every step makes my throat tighten more, the collar pressing into me, reminding me of how little control I have.

Chapter Twenty-Two

Veronica's phone buzzes, the screen lighting up with a message from an unknown number. Just because the number isn't in her contacts doesn't mean she doesn't recognise it. She knows exactly who it is. Watcher. The message is brief, urgent, and leaves no room for interpretation.

'Get the story online by the morning, after 6am. Aaron Dupree is dead. Apparent suicide. Spin it as follows: Aaron's anti-corruption stance was a smokescreen. Evidence of his own corruption was found at his home, same as his father. Rather than face the fallout, he took his own life. Jeremy, his Chief of Staff, found the body. A detective will be in touch with official quotes. Use them.'

She stares at the screen, her pulse quickening as the words sink in. She knows she needs to get these details before the message disappears like all the others. She needs the bones, and she can take license with the rest, as long as it's plausible. The problem is, she's been listening to the scanner all night and there's been nothing notable. She knows the code for suicide, and there have been none tonight. She looks back at her notes from the night. Scribbles of codes and suburbs. She scans her notes for Annerley, where Dupree lives and works when he's not in Parliament House or his constituency office. There are a couple of noise complaints, a break and enter, and wilful damage following the break and enter at the same address.

Her gut churns. Something feels off, and she considers sending a message back asking if he's sure of the information. But then, it's not her job to question. It's her job to report why she's here, what he pays her for. To report whatever he tells her.

She can't afford to hesitate. A moment of doubt could cost her more than her career. It could cost her everything.

Taking a steadying breath, Veronica sets the phone down and opens her laptop. The blinking cursor on the screen mocks her for a moment before she types, the story unfolding under her fingers even as unease twists in her stomach.

Aaron Dupree, the outspoken anti-corruption advocate, was found dead in an apparent suicide. Sources close to the family say that Dupree had been under intense scrutiny for the past few months. Allegedly, incriminating evidence of his own wrongdoing was discovered at his home, which led to overwhelming pressure to face the public's backlash.

Dupree's political allies expressed shock at the revelation, while his Chief of Staff, Jeremy Mitchell, discovered the body in the early hours of this morning. A close associate claims Dupree had been visibly distressed in recent weeks, though no official explanation has been offered for his decision to end his life. Aaron Dupree was the son of disgraced Senator Dupree who died last year while serving a five-year term for corruption and extortion. The old apple doesn't fall far from the tree adage, and there's plenty who will lap it up and run with it.

She wonders if it's got anything to do with something she heard on the police scanner earlier tonight about shots fired and Dupree's driver. When she called to get more information, she was told it was a random mugger, and they already had someone in custody. She wonders whether to tie the two together, then thinks better of it. If Watcher wanted the stories connected, he would have told her.

Chapter Twenty-Three

Anna presses her back against a rough brick wall, the jagged edges scraping through her thin T-shirt. The sensation is grounding, a harsh reminder of the world closing in around her. Her breath comes in shallow bursts, each exhale visible in the cool night air. The hum of distant engines and muffled voices echoes through the alley, mingling with the pounding of her heart.

'We don't have much time,' Marcus says, his voice low but laced with urgency. His eyes dart down the alley, scanning the shadows for any sign of pursuit. A streetlamp flickers nearby, its dull light casting harsh angles on his face, emphasizing the strain and tension etched into every feature.

'We have to split up. I think I have a place that I can get to that's safe, sort of, but I can't take you with me,' Marcus says.

'Why not?' she cries.

'First, you're not welcome there. Second, if they see that we're working together, that's going to make what we have to do that much harder. It also puts a bigger target on our backs that we don't need.'

'But what can we do?' She reaches out and grabs his arm.

'We survive,' Marcus says. His hands are steady, but Anna can feel the tremor in his voice. 'Whoever makes it,' he hesitates, his eyes locking with hers. 'Whoever makes it must stop them. Whatever it takes. Whoever these people are.'

Marcus lets her go, his hands falling away as he steps back. 'There's something you need to understand,' he says, his tone softer now, but no less intense. 'I have an idea of how to get help to you,' he continues, his voice lowering to a near whisper. 'But it's dangerous. For me, for you, and especially for the person I need help from.'

Her brow furrows, confusion clouding her mind. 'What do you mean?'

He glances over his shoulder, his eyes flickering with unease. The sound of footsteps in the distance grows louder. 'They have something important,' he says, urgency sharpening his words. 'Something I need to share with you, a way to bring them down once and for all. I thought it was my insurance policy against, well, this, I guess. Although this is not what I thought would happen. It's better you have it.'

Anna opens her mouth to protest, but he cuts her off with a sharp gesture. 'All I ask is that you do whatever it takes this time.' His voice trails off, leaving the unspoken words hanging in the air.

'Marcus...,' she starts, her voice barely a whisper, but he's already turning away. His silhouette melts into the shadows, and within moments, he's gone.

The alley stretches out before her, dark and oppressive. A single streetlamp flickers at the far end, its light failing to pierce the overwhelming darkness. Anna crouches lower, pressing herself deeper into the shadows. Her fingers graze the sticky, grime-caked walls. Every noise around her, the rustle of trash, the faint clink of bottles, the guttural growl of a dog rooting through garbage, puts her on edge.

Seventy-two hours. If she can stay hidden, find a dead zone for the watch, she might last until it's all over. But the thought settles before another dread creeps in. GPS doesn't need mobile service. And if they can't find her, neither can Marcus, and he's relying on her. She can't bail now.

Her watch buzzes again. She checks the map. Her heart sinks as she studies the screen. She identifies two M-dots, including Marcus. The other... the pregnant woman still at the warehouse. No surprise there. The poor woman is too far along to be chasing down the streets, so she must have hidden herself somewhere. If the hunters are looking for her, she has a two-hour head start. Assuming what the other guy, the trainer, said was a lie.

She grabs a nearby rock and smashes at the watch. The third strike cracks the screen. A warning flashes: *damaging this device will trigger its final protocol*. She stops, her fingers trembling as they hover over the screen. Her hand moves to scratch at her neck, digging at the recently damaged skin, but all it does is make her bleed. The device is embedded too deeply. The blood collects under her ragged nails.

Her boots stick to the grime-soaked ground as she shifts. The suction beneath her feet fills her ears, but she forces herself not to react. Water-damaged crates lean against the walls; stacks of trash and flattened cardboard boxes litter the alley in disarray. A rat scurries past, its eyes glinting in the dim light.

You can't stay here, her mind whispers, but she pushes the thought away. If she moves now, she risks being spotted. If she stays too long, the hunters will close in. There's no safe place, only the constant tension of trying to remain hidden while the seconds slip away.

A distant siren wails. Anna stiffens. The sound isn't close, but it sets her pulse racing. She presses herself tighter against the wall, her fingers digging into the splintered edge of a broken crate. The rough wood bites into her palm. She hears footsteps on the pavement.

Even if it's not the Hunters, it could be someone collaborating with them. She has no way of knowing who to trust, and if they can kill a politician and think they're going to get away with it, who else is working with them and what else are they capable of? She shudders.

Her eyes flicker to the chain-link fence at the end of the alley, its rusted metal glinting in the weak light. The edges are sharp and unforgiving. Beyond it, the street is quiet, save for the occasional passing car. She tries to focus on her breathing, inhaling, letting the air fill her lungs before exhaling in shaky bursts. Her heartbeat thunders in her ears, each beat a reminder that time is running out.

What if the hunters have already found her? What if they're watching from the shadows, waiting for her to make a move? The thought freezes her in place. She can't afford to make a mistake. If she sticks her head out to check, she risks giving herself away.

A faint clatter rings out at the far end of the alley. Anna's heart skips. A figure moves in the distance, its silhouette evaporating into the shadows. She freezes; her breath catches in her chest.

Do they see me? Is he one of the hunters?

Her body tenses, every muscle coiled, ready to flee. But to run now would be suicide. She has nowhere to go. The chain-link fence is too high to climb, too exposed. She's trapped.

The figure pauses, its head tilting as if listening. Anna holds her breath, her clenched fists digging into her palms. She forces herself to remain still. Every instinct tells her to run, but she knows it's too dangerous. The figure's presence only heightens her terror. Eventually, they move on, disappearing around the corner.

Anna slumps against the wall, her legs trembling beneath her. Her throat is dry. She swallows hard, trying to steady her nerves. *You're not safe here*, the thought echoes through her mind. The watch on her wrist catches her attention; the countdown blinking before her eyes.

71 hours, 32 minutes.

She feels paralysed by her own fear. With each second ticking away, she wastes precious time, but she can't decide what to do. To hide and wait it out, but there's no guarantee they won't kill her anyway. The more she thinks about it, the more she's convinced they will. Realistically, she's seen their faces. The faces of the hunters, at least. But it's so fantastical that even if she survives and goes to the police, would they even believe her? If someone came into the newsroom with this story, she wouldn't. What she knows is that the more she waits, the more vulnerable she becomes.

Chapter Twenty-Four

Anna pulls her jacket tighter around her, the fabric doing little to shield her from the biting wind. The rain soaks through her clothes as it runs in cold rivulets down her back. Every step she takes sends a sharp, burning ache through her spine, a cruel reminder. She grits her teeth, forcing her legs to move, but it's getting harder. The OxyContin is fading, leaving her raw and exposed. The pain is creeping in again, relentless, gnawing at the edges of her thoughts. The pattern is always the same. The pills wear off, and she's left with nothing but the agony and the realisation she needs more.

They don't understand. None of them do. The pain isn't in her head. It's real. As real as the rain soaking her through. More real than the slick pavement beneath her feet. She's tried everything. Nothing works. The pills help, barely. Alcohol helps too, smoothing over the jagged edges the medication leaves behind. But now, as her body stiffens with the withdrawal, she feels the cracks deepening. The need for more presses against her chest, suffocating. The anxiety builds, clawing at her insides, and she knows she has to find something. Anything. But how? Without money, without her phone.

Her family doesn't get it either. Her mother's voice rings in her head; every word laced with well-meaning but painful concern. 'You have to stop relying on the pills, Anna,' she says, the same words every time. 'The pain's not real anymore. It's the addiction talking,' her father's voice joins in with his endless stories of detoxes and yoga retreats that 'cured' someone he knew. They don't understand. They never will. How can they? They're not the ones lying awake at night, crippled by pain that won't stop, won't let go. They don't know how it feels when your own body is a prison.

Thunder cracks overhead, and Anna flinches; the sharpness stabbing at her already frayed nerves. The rain pours harder now, colder and more unforgiving, but she barely notices it. The overwhelming need to escape the pain and the gnawing fear consumes her thoughts. She won't last much longer without relief.

She stumbles down the alleyway, her steps slow. The shadows seem to shift, flickering with every movement, and she pauses, unsure if what she saw was a trick of the light or something more sinister. The hunters. She knows they're out there. The thought makes her skin crawl, but it also sharpens her focus. The pain in her back is becoming unbearable, but she pushes it down, shoving it aside for the moment. Although the effects of the pills and alcohol are fading, intensifying her anxiety, survival is her priority; she must find shelter. She needs to hide.

Her smartwatch buzzes as the screen flickers with a new notification.

Quentin Thomason: Deceased - COD: Capture.

A photo of his face flashes across the screen, and Anna's stomach drops. Quentin. The man who had fashioned weapons from scraps in the warehouse. Her eyes flicker to the next update.

Hunter's remaining: 5. Prey remaining: 5.

Quentin

I grip the rusted star picket tighter, the metal cold and rough in my hands. It feels heavier now. Not just from the hours of running with a heavy makeshift weapon. My only defence. My chest burns, each breath like fire as I back up step by step until my heel meets the wall of this dead-end alley. *Damn it, I should have known better than to let myself get boxed in.*

I scan the pack of hunters circling me, their shadows stretching long and jagged in the flickering light of a motion-activated security lamp. As soon as I triggered it, they knew where to find me. Seven of them all fit, disciplined, and I'm useless. I should have known they would send the whole pack after me first. I thought I was being clever. I wrote a backdoor into the device's code, which I hope is undetectable, but without access to a phone or a laptop, it's no use to anyone. I'm clever, but not invincible.

For a minute, I think about Tristan and whether he had set me up. Made a deal to save himself, but I'm nowhere near Greenwood, and they are all here. All seven of them. I should be flattered they consider me the greatest risk.

As they step closer, I swing wildly. I tighten my grip on the picket as the rusted tip slices ineffectually through the air. It's as if I'm swatting at flies, only these flies can, and will, kill me. There is no option but to face them head-on. I'm not stupid; I'm going to die in the next few minutes. The odds, even if I were fitter and in better shape, are against me. The only thing in my favour is that even though their guns sit on their hips, no-one reaches for them. Using them will draw too much attention. Even in the worst suburbs, a gunshot ringing out at night is going to draw attention. Attention, they don't want.

I lock eyes with the one I've heard be called Rook. His eyes are the coldest of them all, but there's something behind them. He's getting off on this. He steps forward a step only to move back again, playing with me. I'm a mouse cornered by a clowder of cats.

I already know the minute my heart stops, a clean-up crew will race to this location to sanitise the scene. Hell, they are probably already parked around the corner. I know because I created this. They said it was a war-games simulator. To let my creativity run wild and plan for every possible scenario. They said it was to train military personnel. I believed them. I'm responsible not only for the devices they are using to kill us, the implants in our necks, but for creating the simulator the men in front of me used to practice and hone their skills.

I thought I was being so clever, factoring in response times for emergency services. The clean-up crew was my idea to erase any trace of their activity. They said to use Brisbane as a backdrop to give it a sense of realism. They said the implants were for third-world countries. A way for regular medication to be administered from afar, particularly in remote communities. There was one feature of the smartwatch they hadn't mentioned back at the warehouse, but I told Marcy. Perhaps she can use it to save herself.

There's no escape. They have me cornered. But if I can take one or even two of them with me but then who am I kidding. Even so. I have to try. For Tristan to buy him the time he needs to come up with a way to help whoever survives.

They close the circle. My heart pounds an erratic drumbeat. I take a deep breath, my lungs screaming, and then I lunge. The picket's point drives forward with all the force I can muster, and I put my entire weight, the one time being on the heavier side is an advantage, behind it. It meets resistance, a body solid and unyielding. Then it sinks in. A horrible give sending a jolt through my arms. The Hunter's eyes go wide, his mouth open in a silent gasp as I yank the picket free. Blood gushes dark and hot as I swing wildly. The blood-slick tip whips through the air, flinging a fine mist of red in its wake. Another wild swing and I catch another one. I don't know where, but the sickening crack tells me I've done some damage.

Momentum carries me, adrenaline pumping through my veins. I

swing the picket crazily, ignoring the pain in my muscles, hoping to do as much damage as I can on my way out. Hands grab at me from behind. Another set of hands wrenches the picket from my grasp. I kick and scream, desperate. My fist connects with someone, but I don't know if it's done any damage. A blow connects with my ribs, the blunt end of the picket, my weapon used against me. It slams into me. Pain blossoms, white-hot and consuming. Another hit, then another. My knees buckle.

I try to hold on to the hope that my sacrifice might mean something, but it's slipping away. Darkness creeps at the edges of my sight as the beating continues. As I'm lying on the ground, I look into the face of the hunter I stabbed. His bloodied hand clutches his stomach. The only consolation I can take with me is that he's dying too.

Chapter Twenty-Six

The Q dot took out two of the hunters with him. Anna sends up a silent prayer of thanks that at least he's brought the ratio back to one for one. She checks the dot map. It covers a wider portion of the city now with one dot, an M-dot, far out to the west and the other M-dot appearing to be the closest to her still at the warehouse. Anna looks at where her dot is in comparison and wonders how the others have travelled so much farther away than her. Her dot is the closest to where she last saw the Q dot. If she's the one closest to the Hunters, will they come for her next? The watch reverts to the countdown timer.

69 hours and 18 minutes.

She needs to find shelter further out, and she needs to keep moving. She thinks about the other dots and figures if they are all in different directions, if they make the distance between them as far as possible, it might help them. The trainer was right about one thing, staying close to each other only gives the Hunters an advantage. The closer they are to each other, the less the hunters have to travel. She puts her head down and heads south, the one direction none of the other dots have taken.

After a few hours, she's a distance from the city, but as she pounded her way along the bike path hugging the motorway south, she realised the limitations on the Hunters don't include transportation. They have vehicles. Of course, she could always steal a car if she knew how. She doesn't. She had thought the bike path was a good idea until she saw a black SUV pull up on the side of the motorway near her. She had crouched down while she watched. She had breathed a sigh of relief when she watched a young mother take her toddler from the car and he pees off the side of the road.

She gets off the bike path, but she's on another main road. There's not a lot of traffic, but there's enough. She wonders if it's enough to keep her safe, too many witnesses, but she doubts it. She looks around her for options. She heads for what looks like bushland, but it's fenced in. She walks along the fence line, hoping to find a gap. A sign announces that the bushland is Karawatha Forest Park.

Yes, this could be a place to hide. Years ago, she wrote a story about the park and remembers its vastness. It has been part of a series of stories Jasper had given her to ease her back into work after the shooting. 'Nothing dangerous out there unless you count the snakes and spiders,' he laughed. He wasn't quite on the money. There were problems with vagrants and abandoned white goods and cars. The Council did a big clean up and installed security measures to limit access after-hours.

She follows the fence line and eventually finds a part of the fence broken and folded in on itself. She climbs over and trudges through the brush. The rain falls harder, and she picks up the pace. Bats fly above and screech, setting her teeth on edge. Then, in front of her, illuminated for a fraction of a second by a clap of lightning, is an old pickup truck. She holds her eyes on the spot where she saw it and speeds towards it, with the underbrush scratching at her and her boots sinking into the worsening mud. When she reaches it, she can see all the tires are flat, the paint is faded or peeling, and most of the shell rusts away. It's not going anywhere, but it's shelter and it's remote.

Cobwebs extend from the car to the bush, intent on swallowing it up whole. 'Please don't let there be spiders,' she sends up a prayer, but then, other than a redback spider or two, it's nothing compared to what's waiting for her. She approaches, her boots squelching. The driver's side door creaks as she tugs it open. She freezes, looking around to see if anyone heard the door. She waits a second. When she hears nothing, she holds her breath as she scans the interior. It's a mess.

The passenger side of the windscreen has cracks spider-webbing outward from what appears to be an impact. A layer of dust covers the dashboard. Sticky spots from old spills and discarded trash, wrappers, tissues, and a toppling coffee cup mar the floor as she climbs in. She grabs the coffee cup and rights it before she realises it's empty. Torn seats reveal foam padding poking out and jagged rusted springs. The smell of old cigarettes and stale beer makes her nose wrinkle.

Still, it's shelter.

Anna pulls the door shut with a firm tug. The handle sticks for a second before the latch clicks into place. The rain falls harder now, pelting against the roof and windows. She slumps against the seat. Her legs stick to the vinyl as she tries to manoeuvre herself into a position where the springs beneath the padding don't cut into her. Her hands tremble as she rubs them down her jeans. She tries to quell the unease creeping over her.

While the rain still pelts, she's grateful that the lightning has stopped. It's a flimsy barrier against the storm and whatever else is lurking outside. It's the safest she's felt since this started. Still, every sound feels ominous. The rustle of a bag caught on a tree branch being whipped around, the distant clang of metal.

She swallows hard. She closes her eyes and wills herself to calm down. *You need to wait it out;* she tells herself, *get through tonight and then work out a better plan in the cold light of day.*

The rain outside is growing heavier. The roar drowns out the occasional crack of thunder as the storm moves off. Time seems to stretch as Anna shifts restlessly in the seat. The musty smell of the truck mixed with the sour tang of old spills turns her stomach.

Exhaustion overtakes her. She curls up as best she can on the torn seat, her arms wrapped tightly around her. The sound of the rain becomes a distant hum as her body sags into the lumpy padding.

Chapter Twenty-Seven

Anna startles awake at the sound of a sharp rap against the window. Her heart leaps into her throat as she blinks, trying to focus on the figure silhouetted against the grey light of morning. A wiry man stands outside. His face weathered and creased. His beard is patchy and streaked with grey. He raps on the glass again, harder this time, his voice muffled but insistent. 'Hey, this is my car!'

Disoriented, Anna fumbles to sit upright, her body stiff and aching from the cramped back seat. The sharp pain in her back flares, and she bites back a groan as she turns toward the man. 'What?' she croaks, her voice rough from sleep.

'I said, this is my car!' the man snaps, tugging at the door handle. 'Get out of there. I live here.'

Anna's mind races; the events of the night before are a blur of rain, pain, and exhaustion. She presses her hands against her temples, willing herself to think. 'I'm sorry,' she mumbles, 'I didn't know...'

'You didn't know?' he cuts her off, glaring at her through the dirty glass. 'What, you think you can crawl in wherever you want? Get out!'

She scrambles to gather herself. 'I'm going, okay?' she mutters, pushing open the creaking door. As she scootches toward the damp, incredibly early morning, the man scowls and mutters something under his breath, but his focus is already on the car, checking to see what she might have disturbed or taken.

'I needed somewhere to.'

'Out,' he barks at her while grabbing at her, his long, dirty fingernails scraping into her skin.

Anna scrambles to comply as her face burns with embarrassment and fear. The man pulls at her. She stumbles out of the truck and almost slips in the mud.

'Don't care,' he snaps and pushes her out of the way, claiming the space she's vacated.

'Find your own spot,' he yells at her as he shuts the door. The rain soaks through Anna's clothes as she stands there, trembling. Her cheeks flush hot despite the night air. Her eyes sting with tears as it all comes flooding back. She tucks her head to avoid the man's glare as he locks the door.

Lightning flashes overhead. Anna turns away. Another storm threatens; her legs are unsteady. The storm intensifies into a torrential downpour. She runs, unaware of any direction, searching for shelter from the rain. She finds herself in a car park and sees the structure on the far side. Public toilets.

Headlights as a car turns into the main gate. Someone climbs out and tries the gate. Another person climbs out and flashes their torch into the park.

'Fuck this,' she hears one of them say.

'She's in there somewhere.'

'Yeah, and she's probably piss wet through with nowhere to go. Fucked if I'm trudging through that shit in the rain at night to find her. Bitch probably jonesing anyway. We'll catch her later. If she's still here in the morning, we'll come back. Right now, I'm more worried about the other geek. We need to find him first. She'll keep.'

The other one nods, and together they get back into the car and reverses out of the driveway.

Anna waits, shivering with the cold, wet, and in withdrawal. Only when she's sure they've gone does she race for the toilets.

The entrance is locked up with a solid steel gate and a giant padlock. An awning provides some relief from the rain, but not much else. She wraps her arms around herself to hold in what little warmth she has. Her skin is clammy and cold. She thinks if workers lock this block every night, they will unlock it in the morning. But how early and when will the Hunters be back? She can't risk being here when they do. But if the workers catch her there, can she risk they won't call the police on her for vagrancy? Getting carted off to the police station is the last thing she needs as Aaron's image crashes into her mind.

She needs to find another place to hide, but the thought of encountering another homeless person or worse, the hunters, makes her stomach churn. Her hands twitch by her side, and as soon as the rain lets up, she wanders away, aimless. Her mind foggy, and her body aching. Every street, every corner feels unfamiliar, her memory muddled with exhaustion and the creepy edge of withdrawal. Somewhere in the distance, a siren wails. Its sound swallowed by the night.

Chapter Twenty-Eight

Anna looks at the dots and can see the M-dot she thinks is the pregnant woman is still at the warehouse. She thinks about why her dot hasn't moved. Is it because she's simply too pregnant? But then why haven't the Hunters taken her out already? What if she has found a place to hide that the hunters can't find? She wonders if she can persuade the woman to let her hide there, too. She makes her way back to the warehouse. If there's a chance, it has to be better than wandering around in the rain and jumping at shadows.

When she arrives, the warehouse feels even colder, but the wind shearing through her wet clothes makes it worse. The faint echo of dripping water amplifies the emptiness in the distance. Shadows stretch long under the flickering fluorescent lights, sputtering and buzzing overhead.

Anna sits against a stack of wooden crates, her knees drawn to her chest. She's searched the place high and low and can't find the M-dot, but it shows on her map she's still here. If the M-dot were dead, the dot wouldn't be showing, as the dots for Aaron and the Q dot no longer are. Has M-dot got the tracker out of her neck and dumped it here? She scratches the device in her neck again. All she gets for her trouble is yet more blood under her nails.

She tries to calm her breathing. Her watch vibrates on her wrist, breaking the silence 66:00:00. She stares at the numbers. A sharp cry jolts her upright. It's coming from the far end of the warehouse. She had searched there and had seen no sign of anyone.

She makes her way back to the corner and searches again. Vehicle hoists stand stoic like sentinels. Soft sobs seemed to come from underneath her, but all she can see are metal panels.

'Tell me where you are, I can help,' she calls out.

The sobs stop. Wherever M-dot is, Anna can't see her. But if she can't see M-dot, M-dot can't see her either, so has no way of knowing if Anna is a hunter.

'It's me, Anna. I'm one of the...' She considers her next word carefully. 'Prey,' she says, using the Watcher's term for the collective group of victims subjected to their sick game.

'Oh God,' a voice calls out from somewhere beneath Anna. A great whirring noise erupts, and the metal plates under the hoist move. Anna steps back as the plates open to reveal a pit underneath them. Anna scrambles to the edge, her pulse racing.

Below her in the pit lies the pregnant woman. The pit wall supports her back; her knees raised and far apart. She clutches her belly. Her face is pale and slick with sweat. Her lips tremble as she pants through the pain. In her hand, she holds a mechanism with bright red and green buttons.

'It's too soon,' M-dot cries. 'I can't. Not here.'

Anna freezes. Her feet rooted to the spot, her mind screams at her to move, to do something, but she's paralysed.

'Anna, help me,' M-dot's voice cracks with desperation. The sound tears through Anna's chest. She stumbles forward toward the pit but stops again. Panic claws at her throat, and her breathing turns shallow.

'No,' Anna mutters as she shakes her head. She had hoped to find somewhere to hide and wait out the hunt. Not deliver a baby. Her hands tremble as she brings them to her forehead. She grips her hair and pulls, hoping the pain will help her focus.

'I can't do this. I can't,' she wants to run. To survive. *In these circumstances, abandoning a pregnant woman would be justified*, she tells herself.

'I'm Marcy' M-dot says, her eyes pleading with Anna.

Anna's legs turn to jelly. She backs away from Marcy with each step heavier than the last. Her breath comes in ragged bursts. She can't help Marcy. *How am I supposed to deliver a baby in these conditions, even if I knew how and we weren't being hunted*, a voice in her head screams.

You'll just make it worse. Run and save yourself.

'Please,' Marcy's voice cries out. Raw and hoarse. A sound so desperate it makes Anna flinch. She stumbles against a crate and falls to her knees. Tears in her eyes, blurring her vision, her fists clenched as she rocks back and forth, trying to drown out Marcy's pleas. But the sound cuts through everything.

Anna stares at the ground, unblinking. She can see the dusty floor beneath her hands. Her heart hammers in her chest so loud it drowns out every thought except one.

If you leave her, then you're no better than them. The Hunters. The ones who had stripped away their humanity and turned them into animals. Anna squeezes her eyes shut, but the image of Marcy's face burns into her mind. A woman brought to her knees, crying out for help, desperate and alone.

Anna slams her fist on the floor. The pain snaps her out of her spiral. She drags herself to her feet, her legs shaking beneath her. Her breath shallow but steadying, one step at a time, she climbs down into the pit with Marcy.

'I'm here, but we have to move in case the hunters come back.'

Marcy smiles. As soon as Anna is in the pit, she presses a button on the controller in her hands, and the large metal louvers close, leaving enough space for the electrical lead for the controller and only the barest crack of light.

'Hydraulics,' Marcy says. 'Even if they find us, without this...' she waves the controller, 'they can't get in, well not easily. They've already tried. They gave up. At some point they will be back, but they figure I'm not going anywhere and they're not wrong.'

Anna doesn't have the heart to say they are sitting ducks here. She should try to convince her to move, even though it will be hard, but it's also impractical. The woman is in labour and as if to reinforce the point, another contraction grips Marcy. Anna rushes to her.

'I'm here,' she kneels beside Marcy. She finds a rag and, despite its being filthy, uses it to wipe the sweat from Marcy's forehead.

'I don't know what to do,' Anna says.

Marcy's hand shoots out and grips Anna's wrist with surprising strength. 'Just don't leave me,' she whispers as tears stream down her face.

'I won't,' Anna says, trying to make her voice sound more convincing than she feels. 'I promise,' although she can't help but think it's only a matter of time before they come back and this time with something to pry open these louvers. But for now, the right thing to do is to stay, despite the risks.

Anna holds Marcy's hands throughout the last throes of her labour, her fingers curling around Marcy's trembling grip. Sweat beads on Marcy's forehead; her breaths come in short, ragged gasps as she fights against the overwhelming pain. Her free hand grabs Anna's shirt, shoving the fabric into her mouth to muffle the groans she can't suppress. The chill of the warehouse seeps into Anna's bones, but she forces herself to ignore it. She blocks out the distant noises by telling herself they are not footsteps and quelling the suffocating fear that staying in one place for too long will only increase the chances of the hunters closing in. All that matters is Marcy and the life she's bringing into the world.

'Marcy,' Anna says softly, her voice steady but insistent. 'You have to focus on something else. Look at me,' she squeezes Marcy's hand, willing her to stay present, to fight against the tide of pain threatening to consume her. 'Talk to me. Do you work?'

Marcy's body tenses again, a guttural sound escaping her despite her attempt to stifle it. After a few agonising seconds, she breathes through the contraction, her voice a whisper as she answers, 'I work for SkyForge Innovations. I develop drone technology. They said it was for environmental projects ... to map mineral-rich land for sustainable development.'

Anna nods, encouraging her to keep going. 'That sounds fascinating Marcy, what else?'

Marcy's eyes flutter open, clouded with pain and fear. 'You're a journalist, right?' she asks Anna.

'Yes.'

'Nathaniel, my husband, he started asking questions. He was an activist, and he cared about protecting the land. I thought what I was doing contributed to that. He was proud of the work I was doing, thought it could help. But then he noticed things didn't add up. The places we mapped ... the acquisitions.'

Anna frowns, her mind working even as she tries to keep Marcy calm. 'We don't have to talk about this now, tell me, do you and

Nathaniel have names picked out?' she asks as she clings to her hand.

'It was his funeral today,' Marcy whispers. 'Two of my colleagues pulled me aside. They said Nathaniel had been asking questions about their projects, things is, their projects have nothing to do with the environment. I had no idea they were talking, I didn't even know they met up when I wasn't around.'

Anna tries to keep her expression calm even though her mind is spinning. She doesn't know Nathaniel, doesn't know SkyForge. But she can see how scared she is and being scared will not help her get through this labour.

'SkyForge wasn't using the data for preservation,' she says. 'They were targeting land for takeover. Forcing people off their properties, telling them it was worthless when it wasn't. Cheating people who didn't know what questions to ask. And anyone who pushed back or started digging too deeply, well…'

The unfinished sentence hangs as a contraction hits her. She winces and breathes through it. Anna has no idea what to do, but she tries to mimic breathing patterns she's seen on TV, hoping she's at least a little helpful.

When the pain recedes, Marcy continues, voice thin and shaking.

'I started asking questions,' Marcy says. 'I thought Nathaniel was letting his hatred of big corporations affect his judgement. I wanted to prove he was wrong. But the more I asked, the worse things got. And then Nathaniel…'

She breaks, sobbing openly. 'They said it was a fatigue related accident. But it wasn't. He told me he was going to stay overnight in the motel and set off early in the morning. He knew he was too tired to drive, he told me so, and since I told him about the baby, he was careful. The only way he would have been driving that night was if something had happened, but then he would have called me.'

The next contraction slams into her, and she grips Anna's hand so tightly that Anna gasps. Marcy's apologetic glance flicks upward, but Anna shakes her head and squeezes her hand back—she's here; she's not letting go.

When the contraction finally eases, Marcy draws a shaking breath.

'And then … today at the funeral … when my colleagues told me Nathaniel had been asking about a project of theirs.' Her hand rises to her neck. 'This was the project he was asking questions about.'

Anna tries to find something hopeful to say, anything. 'Maybe your colleagues can get word out. Maybe someone will realise what's happened.'

Marcy cuts her off with a small, broken shake of her head. 'That won't work. They're both here. And one of them is already dead.'

Her words hang in the air, heavy and terrifying. Anna clenches her jaw. Her gaze darts toward the panels above them as distant sounds grow louder. She forces herself to push down her own fear.

Marcy cries out as another contraction overtakes her. Anna tightens her grip on Marcy's hand, grounding her. 'Breathe, Marcy. Focus. You're not alone. We'll get through this together.'

With one huge push, the baby's head crowns. Anna can feel the head between Marcy's thighs and, unless there's a complication they have no way of foreseeing or managing, she knows the rest should follow. The baby comes out. Marcy cries. The baby cries. The wail, unmistakable but Anna brings the baby to Marcy's chest, and it suckles on Marcy. Anna wraps the baby in the folds of Marcy's clothes in the absence of any other option to wrap the child. Marcy sobs as she watches her baby.

They have nothing to cut the umbilical cord with, which makes it almost impossible for Marcy to move, to protect or defend either herself or her child. Anna sits back. A wave of exhaustion crashes over her. She wants to run, to hide. But how can she? She can't leave Marcy like this, not now.

Marcy senses Anna's dilemma and reaches out her hand. 'Have you checked out the watch?' she asks and nods to it.

Anna shakes her head. She has to admit she had been afraid to touch it after she cracked the screen with a rock for fear of triggering the final protocol, as it had warned.

'One thing Quentin did tell me is there is a phone icon with only one number programmed in it.'

'We can call for help,' Anna cries, hopeful.

But Marcy shakes her head. 'No keypad to dial numbers, but the caller ID says, *let's make a deal*. He told me to call it, to do a deal and save myself and my baby. He says that the person on the other end is the only one who can pull me out of this game if the price is right.'

'And what if the price is your life?' Anna sits back on her heels. 'Who will take care of the baby?'

'My parents.'

'You can't do a deal with these people Marcy, you know that,' Anna says.

'What choice do I have?' Marcy nods at the baby suckling at her breast and the umbilical cord still attached to her body. 'But you need to be long gone by the time they get here. I'll hold off as long as I can,' Marcy says with a wan smile, clearly resigned to her fate. Her only option now is to make a deal to spare her child.

Anna cries. 'But.'

'But nothing. You did what I asked. I get to hold my baby. And I know my parents will do a good job if they let them. It's not like my baby knows anything that can hurt them.'

Anna clenches her fists. Her nails dig into her palms. She wants to scream, to rage at the injustice of it all, but the words die in her throat. Instead, she shuffles forward, her footsteps echoing in the confined space.

'Marcy, don't do this,' she murmurs. 'There must be another way.'

Marcy turns her face to her. Tears glistening in her eyes. 'Another way, like what Anna? Run and hope they don't find me? They'll hunt me down and my daughter with me. This way I might get to keep her safe.'

'No,' Anna says, shaking her head weakly. 'You're giving up. You don't have to surrender. We can fight.'

'Fight,' Marcy laughs bitterly. 'I can't even stand,' her expression twists with pain. 'This is not a fight any of us can win. Haven't you worked that out yet? These people. They don't lose.'

Anna stares at her, searching for the right words, but all she feels is the weight of resignation weighing down on her. She's tired to the bone. Her shoulders droop as she bows her head and says. 'I'm sorry.'

'Don't be,' Marcy smiles kindly. 'If anyone can win this, it's you. And if you do, promise me you'll do everything you can, everything you have to, to survive and then bring these bastards down.'

Marcy pushes the button to open the louvers. For a moment all Anna can do is sit there. They're exposed, and she wants to grab the controller and close them in again. Marcy gives her a shove. 'You have to go,' Anna stands and then sits again, shaking her head. 'Go!' Marcy demands. 'I won't make this call until you do. I won't risk you being here when they come for me. You stayed. You...' she looks at her daughter then back to Anna. Her eyes filled with tears. 'You have to stop them. I can't, we both know I can't. The best I can hope for now is to save my child. I need you to give me that chance.'

Anna nods and cautiously climbs out of the pit, scanning the dark warehouse as she does. She takes one last look before she steps away, walking through the tears obscuring her vision. The baby's cries echo throughout the warehouse. Anna hopes, for the baby's sake, Marcy gets her deal before the hunters come back.

Chapter Twenty-Nine

The streets feel like a maze. Each turn tightens the grip on her chest, suffocating her further. Anna's boots scrape against the damp pavement; the sound is hollow in the heavy air. Her trembling hand brushes against a grimy handrail, but the touch does little to steady her. The dampness clings to her, and the stifling heat makes every breath an effort. She flinches at every noise, the rumble of a passing car, distant arguments, the eerie squeak of a shopping trolley being pushed by a shadowy figure.

The aftermath of Marcy's encounter has drained her, and the hunger for a fix pulses within her. The ache in her back is relentless, and her throat is dry, desperate for relief. She checks her watch. 65:12:00. It beeps, but no notification appears about Marcy. She holds her breath, waiting for something, anything. Her chest tightens as her mind spirals into a mess of fragmented thoughts. What could she even say if she found someone to talk to? Who would believe her now? She swallows hard.

Her stomach growls, reminding her of the hunger gnawing at her insides. The nausea hits, waves crashing over her. She wipes the sweat from her brow, eyes darting down the shadowed street, the darkness pressing in.

She needs a fix. Enough to ease the ache. The words claw at her thoughts. *The drug will clear your mind. It will make you sharp. Strong.* Without it, she's nothing but a shell, weak and fading. The darkness intensifies.

You're useless. You can't survive like this. You'll die like this, a pathetic husk.

She turns a corner and spots Ray, leaning against a graffiti-covered wall. He has his hands buried in his pockets; a sight she's witnessed countless times. The early morning light cuts through the shadows, casting long stretches of darkness across the pavement. Ray's always there early, catching the city's elite on their way to work, supplying whatever they need to get through the day.

She watches him from the shadows, waiting for the right time to approach. Wondering what she can say to him to persuade him to let her have what she needs, even though she has no way to pay him. But what choice does she have? She can't think straight right now, and she needs her wits about her. She steps out towards the road, towards Ray, when her watch vibrates against her wrist.

Warning: Unauthorised zone. Turn back immediately.

Her heart sinks. It hadn't occurred to her to check to see if Ray's place fell within the 'no-go' zones. But for them to know about Ray, they must have been tracking her for months. Panic twists in her gut. Can she risk whatever penalty her presence here will cause? She glances at the watch. If she can get Ray to come to her, she might avoid triggering the alarm. But first, she has to get him close enough that she can talk to him. Shouting about a drug deal over a busy street goes against the premise of the clandestine nature of the transaction she's trying to complete.

Ray sees hesitation in her step and nods in greeting. He doesn't seem to notice the fear in her expression. She waits for him to come to her, but he looks confused. He shrugs, stepping closer.

'Anna,' he calls out, his voice slicing through her fog. 'You look like shit, babe.'

His words make her cringe. He checks the traffic and crosses the road, but the moment he moves, the proximity field tied to him shifts.

'Need something?' he calls out, reaching into his pocket, but with each step he takes toward her, she instinctively steps back.

'What the fuck, Anna?'

Her feet falter. She's torn between retreat and surrender, each step heavier than the last. The proximity alarm blares louder, and the device in her neck pulses, sending shockwaves through her. She remembers Aaron. She doesn't have a collar, but whatever they have planned for her, she's not in a rush to find out.

'Stay back!' she screams, raising her hands in a desperate plea.

'Don't come any closer!'

Ray stops in his tracks, frowning. There's only a narrow street separating them now.

'What's going on, Anna?' he calls, tilting his head slightly, his voice dripping with concern. 'Babe, you're shaking.'

He steps closer, but she retreats, her back scraping against the damp brick wall.

'I can fix you up,' he says, his voice softer now, almost coaxing, as he reaches for his pocket. The watch vibrates harder, sending a high-pitched hum through her skull. She looks down.

Unauthorised zone violation imminent.

'No!' Anna cries, backing away faster.

Her head throbs as panic overtakes her. She clutches at her scalp, trying to steady her breath. She can't think, can't breathe, can't keep her footing.

Ray steps closer.

The watch emits a shrill beep, the sound sharp enough to make her jump. Her eyes widen, and she spins around, breaking into a panicked run. Her foot catches on the slick pavement, and she stumbles, losing her balance. She grabs a grimy wall to steady herself and then sprints away, her heart pounding in her chest.

'Anna, wait!' Ray calls after her, but his voice fades into the distance. She keeps running, not daring to look back. Her legs ache, her chest burns, but she doesn't stop, pushing herself through alleyways and darkened streets, putting as much distance between herself and the danger as possible.

When she finally stops, her muscles scream in protest. She collapses against a boarded-up storefront, gasping for air. Tears stream down her face, the pressure in her stomach rising again. She doubles over, dry-heaving. Cold shakes wrack her body, tremors coursing through her.

'You're pathetic.'

The voice in her head. No, not in her head. She looks up, startled, only to find herself face to face with the woman. The only female hunter. The one who had stared at her with such loathing back at the warehouse. But Anna doesn't remember why.

The hunter steps forward with cold precision, cutting off Anna's escape.

'This is a mistake,' Anna gasps, her voice trembling. 'What do you want?'

The hunter's lips curl into a bitter smile.

'You don't even remember me, do you?' she hisses, her voice seething with venom. 'After everything you did?'

Anna's mind races, struggling to place the woman, but nothing clicks.

'I don't know you,' Anna insists. 'You must have me confused with someone else.'

The hunter lets out a hollow laugh.

'Confused? No, I know exactly who you are. Anna Levesque. The "Voice of the People," The hero with a newsprint cape, exposing corruption.'

A flash of memory surfaces. Newsprint cape. A cartoon from years ago, after she'd exposed a corruption scandal involving a defence company's CEO.

The hunter's eyes blaze as she spits out the next words. 'Heroes don't ruin lives, do they?'

Anna flinches but stands her ground. 'I don't ruin lives. I expose the truth,' she says, her voice shaking with conviction.

The hunter sneers. 'My father,' she seethes. 'You exposed my father. The architect of greed, you called him.'

'Thomas Greer,' Anna breathes. The words barely leave her lips before the hunter cuts her off, voice tight with fury.

'You destroyed him. You destroyed my family.'

Anna's mind spins, the pieces falling into place. Greer faced accusations of embezzlement, and following his mental breakdown, he shot his wife and tried to kill himself. Anna remembers the daughter confronting her. The woman standing in front of her now only younger.

'You didn't think about the consequences. You painted him as a monster.'

Anna opens her mouth, but nothing comes out. Whether he was guilty of the embezzlement, they still don't know, but she knew he murdered his wife. Not that it mattered, they decided he was incompetent to stand trial. He is one of Marcus's patients at

Greenwood. She knows there's nothing she can say even if she could; nothing about this woman gives the impression she'd be willing to listen.

Before she can react, the hunter swings, landing a punch that sends Anna reeling.

Instinct takes over. Anna kicks out, her heel catching the hunter's shin. The blow doesn't stop her, but it gives Anna a moment to scramble away. The fight is ugly and desperate, each move pushing her closer to her breaking point.

Finally, with a surge of adrenaline, Anna slams her shoulder into the hunter, knocking her into the brick wall. The impact stops the hunter cold, and Anna sees blood staining her hand as the woman touches the back of her head.

This is her chance. She bolts. Ignoring the pain in her side, ignoring the exhaustion, she runs, weaving through the labyrinth of alleys. The rain is falling harder. She doesn't look back. She won't. When she finally stops again, she collapses against a boarded-up storefront, gasping for air, shaking with fear and exhaustion. Her heart pounds in her chest, and tears streak her face.

You're an idiot. The voice in her head mocks her, relentless. *Of course, they watched Ray.* They knew she wouldn't be able to stay away. All they had to do was wait for her to come to them.

Anna leans against the door, the smell of garbage and petrol in her nostrils, but she doesn't care. The weight of the world presses down on her. She checks the watch. 64:08:34. It's not even been one full day. But if she's going to survive, she needs a plan. But the pain is unbearable as her body betrays her.

Chapter Thirty

As the city's cold, grey dawn breaks, faint light casts long shadows on the pavement as Tristan leans against a streetlamp, eyes fixed on Greenwood's staff entrance. The night drags on, but the urgency in his chest keeps him alert, every tick of the clock pulling him closer to some unknown, looming deadline.

His phone buzzes, pulling him out of his thoughts. He checks the screen. The no-go zone warning: he's too close. He had hoped the periphery of the car park would be far enough away to keep him safe. He'd also kept moving to avoid the 30-minute flag from triggering. With Quentin dead, he has no choice but to reach Lucy himself.

The sound of footsteps breaks the silence. Tristan looks up to see Lucy emerge from the institute, exhaustion written all over her face. Dark circles ring her eyes, and her shoulders slump. She glances around before spotting him. Her expression mixes concern with fatigue, but there's something else in her eyes, something he can't quite place.

'Tristan,' she says, voice barely a whisper. 'What's going on? You look like you haven't slept in days.'

Tristan rubs a hand over his face, the roughness of his stubble reminding him how long it's been since he's felt normal. 'I haven't. But this can't wait. It's about Marcus but I can't stay here. I need you to get in your car and start driving and not ask too many questions, but I promise I'll explain.'

She lets out a sigh and gives him a wary look, pulling her jacket tighter around her body as she leans against the brick wall of the building. 'You're not going to ask me to do something crazy, are you?' Together they climb into the car, and he's relieved when the proximity alerts finally stop.

He shakes his head, trying to mask the desperation in his voice. 'I need your help. I need to get my hands on my equipment, stuff from inside Greenwood. Without it, none of us stand a chance. Have you heard from Marcus?'

'What have you done and what does this have to do with Marcus?'

He pulls down his collar and shows her the device in his neck. He knows she'll recognise it and what it does straight away.

'Oh my god,' she almost drives up the back of a car stopped at the lights, slamming on the brakes just in time as the safety features blare out. *A collision is imminent.*

'Short version. I have to get this thing out of my neck and you, and I are the only people I know that can use the equipment to do that.'

'Then let's go back.'

'Can't, if I get too close to Greenwood, they'll set it off.'

The light turns green and slowly she moves off, her hands trembling on the wheel.

'And Marcus?'

'He has one too.'

'Where is he?' she cries desperately.

'I can show you on this map,' he holds out his hand, 'but I suspect if he gets too close to you, they'll trigger it.'

Lucy chews her lip, brow tightening as she processes the impossible mess he's dropping in her lap. 'And you think I can waltz in there and grab it? The security's been tightened. Now I know why.'

'I don't have anyone else,' Tristan says, urgency creeping into his tone. 'I wouldn't ask if I had any other option. Please, Lucy.'

She bites her lip, torn. 'And if I get it out how does that help Marcus?'

'If I can get it out then all I have to do is get to a computer and I think I have a way to disable it.'

'You think.'

He sighs heavily. 'it's the only chance I've got; we've got.'

'You and Marcus?'

'There's others too.'

'This is ridiculous.'

'Lucy, they've already killed two people. One of them wrote the code.'

'But if he's dead?'

'He wrote in a back door.'

'That's why you need a computer.'

He nods.

She thinks for a moment as she slowly makes her way through traffic. 'Is this something to do with Greer?'

Tristan nods. 'Yes, but more than that. It's about Anna, too. We don't have time to waste. We need this equipment, or we're dead.'

Lucy's eyes narrow, a flash of concern crossing her face. 'Marcus has been in touch. He wanted me to get something to Anna.' She pauses, looking around before lowering her voice. 'He's hiding out with some of his brother's biker friends. He's been using their phones to contact me, but it's always a different number...'

'So, you already knew?'

'Some, not much, but Marcus said that I had to act like everything was normal. That I was probably being watched. He's probably right so you coming up on me like this has probably put me right in it with you.'

'I know, but unless you have any better ideas, we'll all be dead come Monday night.'

'Marcus said that things might get weird and I have to trust him.'

'And do you?'

'Of course I do.'

'And the people he's with?'

She hesitates. 'I don't know them, but he promises me that where he is, he's safe, for now. Something to do with his brother but he didn't have time to explain.'

'I can't help him without getting the equipment. You know this,' Tristan says, voice low but firm.

Lucy exhales, struggling with the weight of the decision. 'I know. But I can't risk it. Not today. I can't afford to raise any more red flags,' she rubs her forehead, exhaustion clear in every line of her face. 'I'm on shift again tonight, I can try then.'

Tristan's heart sinks. He knows the risks she's facing. He knows that asking her could put them both in jeopardy. But the more he thinks about it, the more he thinks what he's asking is too much.

'You can't,' he says, his voice suddenly sharp with the realisation. 'It's too dangerous, Lucy. If they catch you ... We'll both be done. I shouldn't have asked. I'll find another way.'

Her gaze softens, but her weariness doesn't fade. 'I can't leave Marcus hanging, Tristan. I can't.'

Tristan steps forward, lowering his voice as the tension between them thickens. 'I don't care about Marcus. I care about Anna. And right now, that's the priority.'

Angrily, she asks, 'why is she the priority?'

'Because she's got the best chance of all of us to stop them. She can bring the whole mess into the light.'

'Like she did last time when Marcus' brother was killed. Where was she then?'

'It's different now.'

'That's what Marcus said.'

'I know you're tired, Lucy. But I'm asking you, if you can't help me get that equipment, everything will fall apart. We're running out of time.'

There's silence for a moment, the only sound being the distant hum of the surrounding city. Tristan feels the weight of the moment, the tension thick between them.

Finally, Lucy speaks again, voice quiet but resolute. 'If they catch me--'

Tristan interrupts, his voice urgent. 'Get me the equipment. I know we can stop them; we just have to stay alive long enough.'

Chapter Thirty-One

The clubhouse looks different from what Marcus remembered, older, harder around the edges. Outside, a wall of chrome bikes gleams under strip lights, and the air smells of oil, leather, and scorched rubber.

Dingo stands in front of him; arms folded over his broad chest. The last time they saw each other was at Jonas's funeral. Marcus still doesn't know his real name; he suspects it's something like George, but the man's stare is sharp enough to carve truth from ice. He's lean, weathered and confident. He has the steady, magnetic pull of a man who's survived more than he ever talks about and knows exactly when to smile and when to bare his teeth.

'So, you're saying,' Dingo says slowly, 'that some kind of black-ops outfit is hunting you because of that story that you fed to the reporter. The one that got Jonas killed.'

Marcus nods, his throat feels tight.

'Hunted,' Dingo echoes. 'By mercs.'

A few of the club members snort. Marcus knows how ridiculous he sounds, but he also knows there's a lot this club has seen over the years with Jonas at the centre. Jonas had always kept Marcus from the real underbelly of their world, but he was observant; he saw more than he let on and said less. It was a world he wanted to be part of, to follow in the footsteps of his big brother before he was killed.

'I'm not asking you to believe me,' Marcus says. 'I'm just asking for a place where they can't get to me.'

Dingo leans in. His eyes are dark and searching for any sign of a lie.

'You can stay,' Dingo says. 'For now.'

Marcus exhales. Relief, or something like it, loosens his spine. Then it snaps tight again as one of the other club members rushes from inside and shouts. 'We got company.'

Everyone follows him inside. It's dim and smoky, lit mostly by the neon glow over a battered snooker table and the warm spill from a well-used bar. Mismatched leather couches line the walls, their surfaces cracked from years of use, and the air carries the low hum of conversation and clinking bottles. In one shadowed corner sits a bank of monitors, their shifting grey-scale images revealing live CCTV feeds from the perimeter outside.

On the monitors, three figures emerge from a dark van. They're clad in black. They are looking around the fence and through cracks.

'Say hello boys.' Dingo says.

Almost everyone races outside, and seconds later, the entire building vibrates with the sound of motorcycles revving. On the monitor, one figure looks toward the locked gates, then turns to their colleague. The one with the phone tries to step away from the noise, but it's no use.

Inside, Dingo looks at Marcus. 'This the trouble that got Jonas killed?'

'I think so.'

'You think?'

'I can't be sure. All I know is that I was grabbed off the street last night, thrown into the back of a van and woke up in a warehouse with this thing,' he points to his neck. 'I wasn't alone. I recognised one of the other people as someone I work with. He knows about these things, how to get it out, and he works with my wife. She knows too.'

Dingo's jaw flexes for a moment. They watch as the men outside pile back into the van and disappear. Dingo nods and one of the few remaining men inside races outside. Seconds later the motorcycles fall silent and the riders return to the clubhouse.

'Alright, say I believe you. What do you need?' Dingo says.

'Boss,' his sergeant at arms, Havoc, says. Havoc has broad shoulders, thick arms and the kind of solid weight that makes people think twice about crossing him. His face is a roadmap of old fights, a broken nose set crooked, and a thin scar beneath his chin. Marcus remembers how Havoc got that scar. Remembers him racing into the clubhouse years ago with blood pouring from his chin. Jonas had been livid.

Havoc had been working security at a club in the Valley, and some guy had come up with two razor blades taped together with a matchstick in between them. Designed to make two sharp incisions guaranteed to leave a scar because it is almost impossible to stitch together. Rumours had been circulating for weeks of a gang of youths going around the clubs and pubs referring to the scaring of security personnel this way as collecting trophies.

They patched Havoc up and then went out to find the culprit. Marcus was all set to go with them, but Jonas had refused. When they came back hours later, they were laughing and joking about how they had found the culprit and what they'd done to him. 'He won't do that again,' Jonas had said and then shut down any more talk of it in front of Marcus. Marcus had been desperate to be part of the life; Jonas had insisted otherwise. He could hang out with them, but nothing more. He was a clean skin and Jonas intended to do everything possible to keep it that way.

Havoc steps forward now with controlled precision. A quiet heaviness belies an undercurrent of violence. His sleeveless leather *kutte* is worn at the seams, patches faded from sun and years on the road. He radiates a steady, dangerous calm, reminding everyone why he's the one who keeps the club's chaos in line.

'You sure about this boss?' Havoc asks.

'It's what Jonas would want.'

Havoc nods. Loyalty is the blood running through all these men's veins, especially Havoc.

'I need to call my wife, Lucy, but I think they'll be monitoring her phone. They've already taken mine,' Marcus says.

Dingo and Havoc smile and nod at each other. 'We can work around that,' Dingo says, and immediately the young man monitoring the CCTV feeds jumps up. From under the desk, he pulls out a tool bag with the logo of a telecommunications company on it.

'There's something else,' Marcus says.

Dingo raises his eyebrow as if to say he expected nothing less.

Marcus ploughs on. 'This thing in my neck, they can send a signal to it, and it can kill me.'

Havoc sighs, exasperated. 'You didn't think to lead with that?' He turns to the young man monitoring the feeds, 'Buzz?'

Buzz jumps up from digging around in his tool bag. The furious clicking on the keyboard fills the room, then Buzz turns around and nods. 'We good if he stays inside, nothing will get through. But you might want t' let the boys know their phones won't work.'

Chapter Thirty-Two

The city feels alive. Its pulse throbs through the streets, a cacophony of distant sirens, barking dogs, and muffled arguments. Anna trudges through a shopping centre food court. Hyperaware, she's too exposed. She makes her way to the toilet and puts her head under the tap to get some water. The sign says it's not drinking water, but at this point she doesn't care.

Acting as casually as she can, she finds an empty cubicle as far away from the entrance as possible. She steps inside and locks the door behind her. Taking a deep breath, she puts down the toilet seat lid and sits down. It dawns on her she's put herself in another box, the one thing she swore after the encounter with the Hunter she wouldn't do. But what choice does she have? They can hardly come here and get her; there will be people coming and going all day. Even if they find her here, dragging her out in front of witnesses, surrounded by CCTV, gives her a sense of calm and pseudo safety, but she can't stay here all day.

She looks at the watch and all the places she can't go. The places on the map she recognises as work, friends' homes, although there's not many of those. The paper, her parents' place, and one zone that moves around, she realises now to be Ray. She uses her fingers to zoom in and out of the map, looking for places she recognises, street names, anything to inspire her. A street name appears on the screen and she's sure she recognises it. Then she remembers. Her storage locker. The one her mother rented when Anna was evicted from her apartment while she was in rehab. It is possible they didn't know about it because she hadn't organised it and never been there.

Her mother explained that there was no rhyme or reason to how things had been boxed up from the apartment. They had emptied drawers into boxes and taped them up. Her whole life stored away, save for the few sticks of furniture her mother had retrieved from the locker to furnish her new place when she checked out of rehab.

I've used one of those combination locks and used your birthday; I figure you can't forget it and this way you don't have to worry about losing the key. She had barely acknowledged her mother's words the other day.

She had been using her laptop to pull the threads of the story about the Watcher; she had found out the name he was hiding behind not long before the shooting. When she came out of the hospital, she had abandoned the story to follow something safer. They will have it by now, she's sure; it had been lying on the coffee table when they grabbed her. Even if they haven't, her apartment is a no-go zone, so she can't retrieve it. But her original notes, all scrawled in notebooks, will be in the storage locker. She recalls how she used her hospital time to compile everything into a single notebook, which then made her wonder, was this the story she had been shot for? She had collated all the threads, even the things she discounted as potentially not relevant, into one place.

Thankfully, she had always used shorthand for her stories and not the standard Pitman's, but a mash-up of Pitman's, Tee line and her own made-up squiggles and codes making it efficient when taking notes and almost impossible for anyone but her to decipher.

She thinks about how when she first started out, her job was everything she had. Relationships had been superficial at best, and she was always on the lookout for stories. Even with what appeared to be insignificant facts and events, she would note them down. She learned early that she had an instinct for stories, and crime was where she excelled. But the more success she had, the more pressure she felt to find bigger and better stories.

Exposing corruption became her niche, and Jasper became increasingly lenient with her deadlines because he knew when she had a story for him, it would be gold. But the more she immersed herself in the city's underbelly, the more dangerous the stories were to write, and the more enemies, some of them powerful, she made.

The faint hum of fluorescent lights fills the restroom, broken only by the distant murmur of voices and the occasional echoing footsteps outside. Anna sits on the closed lid of the toilet in the cramped cubicle, her legs drawn up to her chest. Her heart pounds against her ribs, and her breath comes in shallow gasps as she strains to hear anything beyond the flimsy partition.

With each second that she stays here, the more on edge she gets. A few times people have tried the door, and one even asking if she was okay. 'Dodgy curry' had been her reply and sufficient for a few murmurs of understanding. But with each passing moment, the anxiety increases. She imagines the Hunters coming up with ways to grab her without too much attention. Pulling the fire alarm and posing as security or as ambulance officers attending to a medical emergency. Her imagination runs wild with possibilities.

There's a knock on the cubicle door. 'Anna?' a woman's voice calls softly, barely more than a whisper. Anna freezes. Her first instinct is to ignore it. Stay quiet. Whoever is on the other side might move on. But then the voice comes again.

'Please, Anna, I need to talk to you. Marcus sent me.'

Anna's blood runs cold. She doesn't recognise the voice, but the mention of his name sends her mind racing.

'Who are you?' Anna hisses through the door.

'I'm Lucy,' the voice replies. 'Marcus is my husband. He told me how to find you.'

Anna's mind reels. She clutches the edges of the toilet seat; her knuckles turning white.

'How?' Anna asks suspiciously.

There's a pause, and when the woman speaks again, her voice trembles. 'Marcus sent me your GPS coordinates.'

'How?' Anna demands, her voice low but sharp.

'He said you'd ask that, and he told you to check the map on your wrist.' Anna looks at the smartwatch. 'He said you can see where he is, and he can see where you are, but meeting up was dangerous and that's why he asked me to help him.'

Anna opens the door a crack. The woman in front of her looks wrecked. If she's playing her, she's doing a good job. Anna opens the door wider and gestures for Lucy to step in. The two of them squeeze into the tiny space. Lucy looks pale, her blonde hair pulled back into a messy bun, and dark circles underline her eyes.

'But he doesn't have a phone?' Anna questions, still unconvinced.

'He found a way around that. For now, anyway, but how long it will be secure is anyone's guess. He told me where to find a video on his cloud and download it to my phone and then he told me you were here.' Lucy chokes back tears. 'I was waiting until there was no-one else around before I called out your name. Marcus said not to let anyone know where you were or what I was doing.'

Anna's stomach churns. It could be a trap. She hesitates, her instincts screaming at her not to trust anyone. But then she remembers the way Marcus looked at her the last time they spoke, worn but resolute. He had told her he would help, or send someone if he could. Is this the someone he was referring to?

'Talk,' Anna says, her tone clipped.

'This is the video he wants you to watch.' Lucy opens her phone and taps the screen a few times before holding it out to Anna.

Anna's throat tightens. She takes the phone, her fingers trembling as she takes the earbuds Lucy offers and then presses play.

Marcus's face appears on the screen.

'Anna,' Marcus begins, his voice hoarse. 'If you're watching this, then something has happened to me. I couldn't tell you before because I never know if anyone is watching, listening. I'm sorry I was so cryptic, but I was too afraid to say too much. But if you're watching this, then it probably doesn't matter anymore.'

Anna's grip on the phone tightens.

'The woman showing you this video is my wife, Lucy. She's the only person I trust to get this to you. We met when Jonas died and we both work at Greenwood now. I work as an orderly there.'

Marcus's voice cracks, and he pauses, running a hand over his face.

'There's a patient there. His name is Thomas Greer, but then you know that already. Officially, he's in for killing his wife, but... something doesn't add up. The facility uses experimental tech--chips implanted in patients' brains to deliver medication automatically. The chip in Greer's head malfunctioned and for the first time in years, he was lucid.'

The video perspective widens and shifts to reveal a patient's room at Greenwood. The patient, sitting upright and completely lucid, is

Thomas Greer.

'I didn't kill my wife,' he says, his voice strong and confident. 'But I made a mistake, I told them I had enough evidence on them to take them down. That I'd suspected what they had been doing for some time and that I had documented everything that I found,' He takes a deep breath and sags his head before he looks back at the camera.

'I told them that I had set everything up so that if anything happened to me the information would automatically be released to the police and the press. I should have just gone along with their plan and then betrayed them when I had my wife and daughter safely out of harm's way. But I was proud and I was angry. They have done this to me to keep me quiet. Besides, even if by some miracle I get out of here, who's going to believe me now.'

There's a noise in the background and instantly Greer looks afraid and the footage stops. When it restarts, Marcus leans closer to the camera, his face filling the frame, but it looks like he's somewhere dark. 'Anna, he swore to me he didn't kill his wife. He was adamant that he was innocent, and he made sense. When I first came to you the story was about how the patients were being mis-treated, but after this, I know there's more to it.'

Anna's chest tightens as Marcus's voice grows more urgent. 'I started digging. The more I looked, the clearer it became someone wants him there. Someone powerful. I think they're using that place to bury him--to keep him from talking. I don't know what he knows but keeping him there and quiet is big enough to make people jittery.'

He exhales shakily. 'Anna, if you want to find the truth, start with who benefits from Thomas Greer being locked away, and I don't think it's about the money.'

The video ends, leaving the restroom silent except for Anna's ragged breathing. She stares at the screen, her mind spinning.

Anna looks at Lucy, searching her face for any sign of deception. She finds none. Her instincts tell her Lucy is genuine, but the knot in her stomach persists.

Lucy shifts in the confined space and holds out her hand for her phone. 'I'm never going to see him again, am I?' Lucy asks.

'I don't know what to tell you,' Anna says as honestly as she can. Lucy cries and slips out of the cubicle, but Anna locks it again behind her. She needs to think.

Marcus came to her not long after the Greer story broke. She had noticed a powerful undercurrent with high-profile accidents and suicides. The man who seemed to benefit the most was a guy called Mark Thorncroft, but his reputation for philanthropy and charitable projects was renowned. A plausible cover and one used many times over, but it's also possible he doesn't know and he's being set up as a patsy for someone else's agenda, but whose?

For her stories, though, she worked on the reverse of Occam's Razor principle. She assumed everything was more complicated than it appears. Just because something looks one way doesn't mean it's the truth. She started asking questions. Drawing connections between powerful players who didn't want those connections exposed. The closer she got to the truth, the more anxious she became. The more anxious she became, the more she turned to drink to take the edge off. But the more she drank, the more careless she became. The first time she heard the reference to the Watcher; she had laughed it off. The more she learned, the more serious things became, including death threats. Burglars ransacked her apartment and her office at the newspaper.

Then, driving down Mount Tamborine one night, her brakes failed. Later, when the mechanic told her someone appeared to have tampered with them, she knew she was in real trouble. The last straw was when Marcus's brother was gunned down while he was standing right next to her. The irony being he was telling her to stay the fuck away from Marcus.

Chapter Thirty-Three

The engines of many motorbikes thunder to life all at once, the ground shaking beneath his feet. Rook stands close by, his hands shoved into his pockets, kicking the tyre of the van, itching for a fight he's not allowed to start. Briggs raises the phone tight against his ear. He needs distance and quiet but gets neither. He nods for everyone to get back in the van, and they move away far enough that Watcher can be heard through the speaker.

'Sir,' he shouts. The roar swallowing his words. 'Marcus is with his brother's motorcycle club. We don't have eyes on him anymore.'

'You don't have eyes because your intelligence was flawed,' Watcher snaps back, although Briggs can hardly hear him over the din.

Briggs swallows hard. 'I'm sorry sir. There were no indicators in the intel that he had kept in touch since his brother's funeral.'

'Yeah, well, it looks like he's feeling sentimental,' Rook mutters, and he pulls over to the side of the road.

Briggs shoots him a *not now* look.

Watcher's voice sharpens. 'Do you think this is amusing Rook?'

Rook straightens. 'No sir, just unexpected.'

'What is unexpected,' Watcher says, 'is your team's failure to verify basic patterns of behaviour. Marcus is unreachable, which means everything you were certain of is now worthless.'

Briggs winces.

'We could always take out the entire building, gas leak or something like that. Clean. Quick.'

Briggs closes his eyes. *Idiot*.

'Rook,' Watcher sighs.

'Sir.'

'Don't think. You're not good at it.'

Briggs smirks and looks at Rook as if to say, *you asked for that*.

'Marcus stays alive,' Watcher continues, 'for now.'

'He's a sitting duck,' Rook continues.

'And that is the point,' The anger in Watcher's voice booms through the speakers. 'We know where he is, where Anna is. They are contained. You still have others that need to be removed, and Rook, clean means no spectacle. Blowing up a building hardly meets that definition, wouldn't you agree?'

'Yes sir,' Rook pouts.

'An organisation is only as good as the people that belong to it. Clearly mine has some weak links,' He lets his reproof sit in the air. 'Find theirs.'

Chapter Thirty-Four

The metallic door of the storage locker groans as Anna rolls it up. Mum hadn't been exaggerating; everything really had been dumped inside and forgotten. Most of the box's list to one side, teetering against a dusty wall.

A second door sits at the back of the locker. She tests it carefully. It opens into an internal hallway and a fire escape. Another way out if they find her. Ground floor, two exits. It steadies her more than she wants to admit.

Dust motes drift in the weak glow of the overhead bulb. Shadows stretch over the clutter. The air is stale with cardboard and old paper. She steps inside, her boots scraping the gritty concrete, and pulls the door down behind her. With the light sealed off, she can breathe again.

The labels on the boxes aren't much help. A few say kitchen, but most read office, unsurprising given her old apartment, shelves stacked with notebooks, papers in unsteady piles, no proper system. It will take hours to sift through it all in search of the sky-blue A5 dot-journal she used while investigating the Watcher. She went through so many, even if she finds the right size and colour, it still might not be the one.

A familiar ache flares in her back. Only one box says bathroom. She lunges for it, dragging it from the far wall with a grunt. Inside: makeup, empty pill bottles, nothing she can use. She checks three times before the truth sinks in. Sitting back on her heels, she closes her eyes and forces her breath to slow down using the mindfulness from rehab. She gives herself only a moment before pushing on.

She cracks open a dust-caked office box. A chaotic mix of notebooks, files and printouts spills out. Memories flood with them, newspaper clippings, unsolved murders, police corruption, backroom deals.

Briggs had steered her toward Victor Rourke back then. Briggs always had a lead ready, vague enough to hook her, detailed enough to reel her in: *Rourke makes problems disappear. Evidence, witnesses. When they try to move him, the transfer gets blocked.*

She'd trusted him. Worse, she believed her best stories were earned. Now she sees how carefully he fed them to her, how conveniently he arrived with something 'better' whenever she got traction on the Watcher.

Her hand freezes on a faded notebook, the cover stamped with old coffee rings. Inside, her own notes on Victor Rourke stare back. Regret twists in her chest. She'd abandoned the Watcher story for this one, exactly as they'd wanted. Victor hadn't been the threat; he'd been the pawn. A distraction.

You knew they were dangerous. The thought flashes and she forces it away. Regret won't help her now.

Something cold brushes her fingertips beneath the papers. She lifts a gun from the bottom of the box. Its weight turns her stomach.

She remembers Jasper's low, urgent voice forcing her to take the cold weight, unfamiliar in her hand. 'You need to learn how to use this,' he said. The urgency in his voice left no room for refusal.

Now, the coldness of the gun in her hand is a reminder of how much things have changed. A tool, not a burden. She checks the chamber, then the clip. Three bullets. Not enough to wage a fight, but enough for an emergency. Her stomach churns at the thought of needing it, but she pushes the fear aside and forces herself to focus. *If it comes down to it, will I remember what to do?*

She doubts herself. She'd made mistakes before, letting ego drive her, letting fear stop her. She forces the doubt away and scans the room again.

In a flash, her eyes lock onto a stack of three blue notebooks. She grabs the closest one, flipping through its pages. She tosses it aside and picks up the next one. As she flips through, names, dates and places stand out, pieces of a puzzle she couldn't see before. Her breath catches when she sees the name.

The CEO of a multinational conglomerate. Famous philanthropist.

She remembers interviewing him years ago for a fluff piece about Vita Core Biopharma, a subsidiary of his company that delivers a program to provide life-saving medications to developing nations.

Her heart races as she reads the details she had overlooked. The Greenwood Mental Health Institute had a connection to his company, and Thomas Greer was being held there. She'd been trying to get an interview with Greer after his incarceration but had come up against brick walls every time.

You'll get yourself killed, she thinks, but then another thought creeps in, quieter but insistent. If you don't try, you've already lost. *You let them bully you off this story before.* Her resolve hardens. *You can't afford to make that mistake again.*

Anna forces herself to exhale, refocusing. *I can either hide and wait for them to pick me off, or I can fight back and expose them. They've made a mistake in thinking I'll stay quiet.*

She grabs the gun, feeling its weight settle into her hand.

She stuffs the notebooks and files into a canvas backpack. As she picks it up, her hand brushes against something hard. Coins. She finds a small inside pocket with a zipper and opens it. Two twenty-dollar bills and a handful of gold coins.

With this small victory, her plan forms. She has two goals now. First, find painkillers for her back. Something to take the edge off so she can focus. Second: Keep digging, keep looking for something to expose the Watcher. If they don't shut her up now, they'll always risk exposure. She needs to make sure the world knows who he is.

She slings the bag over her shoulder; her resolve sharpening. The clock is ticking, and there's no more time to waste.

Chapter Thirty-Five

Anna trudges along the uneven pavement, the soles of her boots scuffing against loose gravel and patches of trash. Her eyes dart between the shadowy figures lingering at the edges of the street. Their eyes follow her, suspicious and calculating, and she's all too aware that her own suspicion mirrors theirs. She keeps her movements steady, but her senses are on high alert, tuned to the slightest flicker of danger.

The man leans against a wall painted with layers of graffiti, each tag shouting over the other in an urban symphony of defiance and decay. He pulls his hood low, masking most of his face, but Anna recognises his stance and the casual way he flips a coin in his hand. She can't remember his name, but she knows he's been on the periphery of a story she's covered, a minor player in a larger scandal. She's confident he'll be holding.

The man's eyes flick to hers, sharp and wary. Neither of them offered pleasantries. Moments later, she's sitting on the pavement of a narrow alley with two precious pills in her hand. She tears the packaging open and pops the pills into her mouth and dry swallows. She waits for the desired numbness and for the dull ache in her back to subside, but when nothing happens after a few minutes, she knows she's been cheated.

She goes back to the dealer. 'What the fuck did you give me, 'cause that wasn't what I asked for?' Rage surges through Anna, hot and blinding.

'What' ya gonna do, go the cops?

Chapter Thirty-Six

The metallic creak of the roller door echoes through the storage locker. Its sound cuts through the stale air. Anna resumes her place, slumped on the cold concrete floor with piles of discarded files around her. Her back pressed against the metal wall with enough pressure to dull the ache radiating from her spine through the rest of her body. The dim light from the overhead bulb flickers and casts uneven shadows across the stacks of crudely labelled boxes surrounding her.

Dust motes float in the narrow beam, giving the space an almost dreamlike quality. Her chest hitches as she lets out a hard sigh. Hands wrapped around her knees, she tries to stretch out her back for some relief. She stopped crying long ago, or maybe it had only been minutes. The pain makes it hard for her to decipher the symbols and codes she'd scribbled throughout the notebooks.

Her hair hangs in her face. Staring at the floor, she is damp with sweat. The temperature inside the unit becomes unbearable, but she dares not open a door to let out the heat. Then, at the bottom of yet another box of memories she'd rather forget, was a bottle of pills. A stash she'd forgotten about, and her mother hadn't noticed, stuck inside a file wallet.

The sight of them brings relief, and when she opens the bottle, she can see there's enough not only to manage the pain she's in now, but enough to slip into blissful oblivion. The label, faded and peeled away, makes her wonder if the contents expire as she turns it over in her hands. But even if they do. What does that matter now? She's no closer to finding answers. She swallows two and considers taking a third, but she needs to ration them. She doesn't know when she'll be able to get her hands on more.

Anna's head snaps up as the sound of footsteps in the hallway outside breaks through her haze. She holds her breath, listening as each step comes closer. Sure-footed, they stop at the door leading to the fire escape. The door opens. Her heart beats in her chest as she scrambles to shove the pills into her pocket and out of sight, but her movements are clumsy and sluggish.

'Hey. You're not supposed to be here,' a man yells at her.

As she shields her eyes from the doorway, Anna's breath catches when she sees Victor Rourke standing in front of her.

Is her mind playing tricks on her because she was looking at his photo and the story of his imploded his career earlier? But she's confident it's him. The problem is, will he recognise her? But as she takes him in, she notices he's wearing a security guard's uniform, with the logo emblazoned on his chest.

'I... I rented this unit. It's mine.'

Victor's tall frame obscures much of the light coming through the doorway. But with a no-nonsense demeanour matching the gruffness of his voice, he steps closer.

'What's your name?'

'Diana,' she says, remembering her mother organised and paid for the unit. She swallows hard and tries to keep her voice steady.

He watches her closely. His expression suggests he's weighing up whether to believe her. 'I'm going through some stuff,' she spies a photo of herself with her parents and grabs it, holding it in front of her. 'See,' she points to herself in the photograph. 'That's me.'

Victor looks from the photograph to Anna and back a few times, his brow furrowed, before he says. 'You look like hell.'

After Anna received her first death threat, Jasper insisted on not publishing her picture as part of her byline anymore. She sends up a silent prayer of thanks and lets out a bitter laugh as she leans forward with her elbows on her knees.

'Thanks,' she mutters.

He hesitates, then steps further into the locker. He takes in the houseful of furniture. She has moved the sofa to one side of the unit, with cushions and a blanket tucked at the far end.

'This place isn't a shelter.'

'I promise I'm trying to find something, and I can't remember which box I packed it in so I'm having to go through each one.'

'You sure you're alright?' he asks as he leans in closer.

Anna shrugs. 'I'm fine,' she says as she fingers the pill bottle in her pocket, and the pills fall against the plastic and make a noise.

He eyes her with suspicion. 'What's that?'

'Nothing.' she says and steps away, but his strides are twice as long as hers, and he covers the distance between them in a couple of steps. He pulls her hand out of her pocket and reaches in and grabs the pill bottle. He looks at the label, then back at Anna. 'You not thinking of doing something stupid, are you?'

She grabs for the bottle, but Victor pulls it away.

'No,' but her voice cracks, betraying her.

Victor takes in the state of her and checks out the bottle of pills. She's thankful the label had peeled away so most of the identifying information is no longer there.

'Look, I don't know what kind of trouble you're in, but I've seen enough people hit rock bottom to know the signs. Whatever you're thinking, this,' he holds up the bottle of pills, 'is not the answer.'

Anna's jaw tightens and tears well up in her eyes. 'You don't know anything about me,' she snaps, as her voice trembles.

'Maybe not,' Victor says calmly, 'but I know that giving up doesn't fix anything. Think about your parents,' He nods at the photo she'd shown him moments ago. 'Is this what they would want?'

She looks away. Her shoulders sag. 'I've managed to piss off some very dangerous people.'

'Criminals?'

'You could say that.'

'Go to the police.'

She shrugs and looks at him with a deep sigh.

'You recognise me, don't you?' he waits for an answer and when she doesn't give him one, he continues, 'from all the stories that bitch wrote about me in the papers.'

He shakes his head, but Anna wants to sigh with relief when he doesn't appear to recognise her. 'It's not true, you know,' he growls. 'You're not the only one who's made enemies and when you have someone like her on your payroll to help spread misinformation, the truth doesn't stand a chance.'

The nagging doubt she's harboured for the last few hours that the story about Victor was a fabrication, something to discredit him and toss her a convenient distraction, now confirmed.

The Watcher has already stripped her of everything, her career, her safety. The thought of confessing everything to Victor and begging for his help crosses her mind, but she's already done enough to him without putting him in danger now and getting him killed as well.

'You don't have to tell me,' Victor says after a moment. 'But whatever is going on this,' he says, shaking the bottle, 'is not the answer,' He pockets the pills and steps forward towards the hallway side door. 'I'll leave you to it. But I'm going to check on you again before I go home.'

Chapter Thirty-Seven

Briggs takes the team back to the depot, the familiar rattle of the roller door echoing as they slip inside. He heads straight for the office, ignores the paperwork scattered across the desk, and says, 'I need a clean car.' The man digs into a drawer and tosses Briggs a set of keys.

Briggs catches them without slowing, walks past the others, and takes the car out alone. He circles back to the back of the compound. His patience pays off when a young kid trudges from inside towards a small, beaten-up hatchback.

'Hey Colby, don't forget my egg rolls,' a voice calls from an upstairs window. Colby nods as the engine coughs to life and the car rolls out. Colby is twenty if he's a day with a mess of uneven curls. His clothes hang off him, and they need a wash.

Briggs follows, keeping a safe distance.

Colby pulls up outside a takeaway shop. The kind with sticky counters, loud fans and a tired teenager behind the counter. Briggs parks at the far end of the lot and steps out only once Colby has disappeared inside. Briggs enters the shop and orders a burger he has no intention of eating, then stands near Colby to wait. Colby preoccupies himself with his phone.

'Hey Colby, how's it going?' Briggs asks casually.

Colby tenses, his eyes squinting at Briggs. 'Do I know you?' he says, mustering bravado Briggs knows he can't back up.

'No,' Briggs says. 'But I know you,' Briggs studies Colby for a moment, then lets out a low, almost sympathetic breath. 'You know,' he says, tapping a finger lightly against the counter, 'I get it. Being bottom of the totem pole. Fetching food. Cleaning up after blokes who can't even be bothered to remember your name,' he tilts his head, voice dropping. 'That was me once.'

Colby blinks, thrown off. 'You?'

Briggs gives a small, humourless smile. 'Look at me now.'

He gestures to the tailored suit hanging perfectly, sharp and expensive. He knows everything about him screams power and money; it's meant to. He pulls his wallet from his pocket; flips it open just long enough for Colby to see the fat stack of crisp notes inside. Then he jerks his chin toward the sleek black car outside, paint gleaming in the sun.

'I earned all that,' Briggs says quietly. 'Not by being loyal to people who kept me small ... but by recognising opportunity when it walked up and sat beside me.'

Colby goes still. Briggs lowers his voice, making the space between them feel sealed off from the world. 'If you want what I have, you have to work for the right people.'

Colby swallows. 'What ... what people?'

'Powerful people, genuine power not the bullshit they sold you,' Briggs murmurs. 'Someone who rewards initiative. Someone who recognises loyalty. Someone who can offer you more than fetching burgers for bunch of arseholes on bikes.'

Briggs leans in closer.

'Thing is, I don't think your boss realises what he's doing. Hiding that bloke there. Do you even know who he is?'

Colby puffs out his chest. 'I know enough.'

Briggs laughs. 'No, you don't. You don't have a fucking clue. Neither does Dingo. Were you even around when Jonas was murdered?'

Colby swallows.

'All I'm saying is that if we can get to Jonas, we can get to anyone,' Briggs continues softly, calmly. 'Question is, when we make a move, and we will make a move soon, what side of the equation do you want to be sitting on?'

'You want me to rat,' Colby says a little too loud. The girl behind the counter looks up, but Briggs gives her a charming smile, and she returns to her task.

'No,' Briggs corrects, eyes steady. 'I want you to survive the future that's coming ... and be standing on the winning side when it does.'

Briggs holds Colby's gaze a moment longer, then turns back to the counter.

With a movement so subtle it could be mistaken for adjusting his sleeve, he slides a small, black mobile along the Formica surface toward the kid. It comes to a stop in front of Colby.

Colby stares at it. His throat bobs once.

Behind the counter, the girl calls out, 'Order for Colby!'

Colby jolts, grabs the paper bags, and backs toward the door ... leaving the phone exactly where it is.

A beat later: 'Hamburger with the lot,' the girl shouts.

Briggs stands, collects the burger, and walks out without a backward glance. The bell chimes softly as he leaves. In the car park, Colby's hatchback idles. Colby stares at the takeaway shop.

Briggs settles into his own car, one hand resting lightly on the steering wheel. He waits. Thirty seconds. Forty.

Then the hatchback's door opens. Colby climbs out, shoulders tight, resolve and fear ricocheting through every line of his body. He strides back toward the takeaway, re-enters looking around, patting his pockets before seeming to notice something on the counter. He walks over and scoops up the mobile from where it still rests. He gives the girl behind the register a sheepish grin and a little wave; the universal *forgot my phone* gesture, then turns and walks back out.

Marcy

I don't have time to think. My daughter is in my arms, warm and fragile, the umbilical cord still pulsing between us. Anna is long gone. It wasn't safe for her to stay, and I've waited as long as I dare to give her time to put as much distance between us as she can. Now it's me and my daughter, and the clock is running. Any second the Hunters are going to find us.

I stare at the smartwatch on my wrist. One number. The only way I can even try to save her. My hands shake as I tap it, the device slick under my fingers. One press. Two. I have to call before they find us.

I don't even know why this is happening. I don't understand how Nathaniel's death tied me into this, or why someone decided I was expendable. I only know what matters right now: her. My daughter.

I cradle her closer, feeling the weight of her tiny body, and tap the screen again. The line connects. 'Yes' is the only reply.

'Will you let me take my daughter to my parents?'

I have no idea whether I can trust the man on the phone, but within a few brief minutes people surround me. They appear to be a team of medics. They cut the umbilical cord and wrap my baby in a clean blanket. They clean me up and give me IV fluids. Then the one in charge makes a call, and soon after, the man in the tailored suit shows up.

He watches me with cold detachment, and for a moment I wonder if I've made a mistake.

'Your devotion is touching,' he says.

His voice is smooth but laced with condescension. 'You have until the end of the day to say your goodbyes. You cannot tell anyone what has transpired here. You will return here no later than 6:00 PM. If you fail to return, we will come and find you.'

He looks at me with a direct and pointed look. I nod.

'If we have to come and find you, we will also punish your parents, your siblings, your siblings' families. And' He nods to my baby, 'Your daughter.'

'Punish. Punish how?'

The man in the suit raises one eyebrow as if the question answers itself, and I wish now I hadn't asked.

'We have provided transport and a driver. He will take you wherever you instruct, within reason of course,' he chuckles at what he clearly thinks is an amusing joke.

'The proximity thing?' I ask.

He nods at my wrist. 'The proximity feature has been disabled.'

When I look at the map, I can see that the red areas no longer display.

'You must stay with your driver for the duration. Wherever you go, he goes. Until your return no later than 6:00 PM.'

I nod and allow myself to be guided into the car.

Chapter Thirty-Nine

The storage locker is dim and musty. The yellow glow of a flickering overhead bulb casts long shadows on the piles of forgotten boxes. Dust hovers in the stagnant air, particles suspended in time. Anna sits on the cold concrete floor, her fingers trembling as they sift through files, papers scattered around her. The mountain of clutter feels overwhelming. Her mind spins, the chaos of the files matching the chaos in her head.

A light tap on the door breaks her concentration. Victor steps inside, his face framed by the doorway.

'Still at it, I see,' his voice is soft but laced with concern.

Anna doesn't look up. 'Yeah.'

He pauses, then adds, 'Will a second pair of hands help?'

She shakes her head. 'No, but thank you.'

Victor doesn't press. Instead, he hands her a bottle of water. 'You need to keep hydrated.'

'Thank you,' she pops the cap and takes a long drink, the cool liquid soothing her parched throat. She hadn't realised how thirsty she was until it hit her, and she keeps drinking until the bottle is empty.

Her watch vibrates, the screen lighting up with a notification. She pauses, staring at the message.

Marcy Lynch: Deceased: COD proximity violation.

A soft, choked sound escapes her throat. Her hand flies to her mouth, her vision blurring.

'News?' Victor asks, watching her closely.

'A friend died,' she says, her voice barely above a whisper.

'I'm sorry,' he replies, his gaze gentle but probing.

Anna's chest tightens as she fights to hold it together. She can feel Victor's eyes on her, waiting, but she doesn't know how to keep the words inside anymore. Finally, she says, 'She was in trouble with the same people who are after me.'

Victor's brow furrows. 'You think they did something to her?'

'I know they did,' her voice breaks. She wipes her eyes with the back of her hand, trying to regain control.

Victor shifts his weight, the scuff of his shoes the only sound in the cramped space. His voice softens. 'And something in here will help you?'

'I hope so,' she gestures to the scattered files around her, the pages, the notebooks, everything she's gone through, hoping for some piece of clarity she hasn't found yet.

Victor leans against the doorframe. 'If you tell me what you're looking for, I can help you look.'

Anna gives a short laugh, though it doesn't feel like one. 'It's not that simple.'

He shrugs. 'Okay,' he turns toward the door but pauses when she speaks again.

'Company would be nice,' she says, the words slipping out before she can stop them. She regrets it, but it's too late. Being near her is dangerous, yet the idea of being alone again feels unbearable.

Victor doesn't hesitate. He sits down on the floor next to her, glancing at the notebook in her lap.

'You some kind of secretary?' He chuckles and holds up a page. 'How can you read this?'

'Some days better than others,' Anna forces a small smile. She doesn't tell him how today's been harder than usual. Her hands tremble more with each passing minute.

Victor nods, his gaze shifting to the mountain of files in front of her. 'They really got you spooked.'

She nods, her breath shallow, her jaw tight. But her chest is tightening for another reason now; despair is giving way to something else, something colder. Determination.

She leans forward and digs through more papers. She has to do this. For Marcy. For herself.

Victor's voice breaks the silence again, but this time, it's sharp with disbelief. 'Well, I never.'

Anna looks up, processing the words, until she sees him holding out his phone. The headline grabs her.

Senator Dupree found dead in apparent suicide.

Her pulse spikes as she steps closer, her eyes narrowing. Beneath the bold headline is a photo of Aaron Dupree, composed, stern, the man who always appeared in control.

She snatches the phone from his hand and starts scrolling through the article.

'That's not what happened,' she mutters, feeling her grip tighten around the phone, her stomach lurching.

Victor's voice is calm but edged with suspicion. 'What do you mean?'

Anna's voice cracks as she stares at the screen, her heart hammering. 'I was there. He didn't die at home. He didn't hang himself. They killed him.'

Victor stares at her, scepticism creeping across his face. 'Who?'

'The people after me. They were after him too. But he didn't believe them.'

'So, they killed him?' He sounds incredulous, as if the idea doesn't quite land.

She nods, her throat tight, eyes locked on his.

'Who are these people?' Victor presses, his tone more serious now.

'He calls himself the Watcher. Surrounded by powerful people. Aaron pissed him off somehow, and so did I.'

Victor looks at her for a long moment, trying to process her words. 'And you saw them kill him?'

'Yes,' her voice is small, but the certainty in it is undeniable.

Victor rubs his jaw. 'Then you definitely need to go to the police,' he's standing now, urgency in his posture.

'Are you kidding?' Anna snaps. 'That's how Aaron got killed.'

'By going to the police?' Victor asks.

Anna wipes away a stray tear, shaking her head. 'He tried.'

Victor's gaze doesn't waver. 'Who are these people?'

Anna swallows hard. 'I think I have something in here that can expose him. I just don't know what it is.' Her frustration spills over.

'Nothing makes sense.'

Victor leans against the wall, arms crossed, considering her words. 'Right,' he nods. 'I think you should tell me everything.'

Anna opens her mouth to protest, but the weight of his words hits her. She's already shared too much, and she knows she can't do this alone anymore. 'Being near me puts you at risk. You should go.'

Victor meets her eyes, unflinching. 'If I told you that I think the Watcher framed me because I was asking too many questions, would you believe me?'

Her breath catches. It sounds as impossible coming from his mouth as it did from hers. Still, she can't deny the truth of his words. Slowly, she nods.

Victor exhales. 'Then maybe we can help each other.'

Anna's watch beeps again, the sound cutting through the tension.

Prey remaining four. Hunters remaining five.

The odds have shifted again.

Chapter Forty

It's been a long day and Victor's tired. He's been at the storage unit since last night, and now he's on another errand. Dealing with Anna and her 'woe is me' bullshit has tried his last nerve, and now he has to deal with Jay.

The apartment sits on the second floor of a brick block in one of Brisbane's older housing estates. Long overdue for a face-lift, but no-one's in a hurry to gentrify this neighbourhood. Built in the seventies with little thought for beauty, only for function. Its narrow balcony overlooks a patchwork of cracked concrete and stubborn weeds.

Victor doesn't knock; he bangs his fist against the door twice, hard and deliberate. It's a message. One Jay will understand. A moment later, the door creaks open, and there's Jay, leaning against the frame with a cigarette dangling from his lips. His eyes narrow when they land on Victor, but he doesn't seem surprised.

'What do you want?' Jay's voice is rough, wary.

Victor doesn't wait for an invitation as he pushes past Jay. Inside, the air is thick with the stale bite of cigarette smoke, layered over years of dust and the faint metallic smell of old electronics. The walls, once cream, are now the colour of nicotine. Cables snake across the floor.

A multitude of desks bear the weight of a mismatched array of monitors. Their glow casts a bluish tint across the clutter. Empty energy drink cans, overflowing ashtrays, a half-eaten packet of dry two-minute noodles. The balcony door cracked enough to let the smoke escape rather than for the view, which offers nothing but the peeling façade of the next building over.

Victor's gaze sweeps across the room, his eyes lingering on the computer monitors stacked on every available surface, the half-finished projects scattered around. Jay bristles at the intrusion.

'I need a favour,' Victor says, his voice steady but carrying a weight behind it.

Jay snorts, flicking ash from his cigarette. 'I'm not doing anything for you. You're not a cop anymore. What makes you think I'd help you?'

Victor's lips curl into a faint, knowing smile. 'Because I can make you disappear, Jay. like that.' He snaps his fingers for emphasis, letting the silence hang heavy in the air. 'I don't need a badge to make people vanish.'

Jay scoffs, rolling his eyes, but there's something in his expression that gives Victor pause; something flickers, for a second, behind his defiance. It's fear masked by bravado. Jay knows what Victor is capable of, and they both know it.

'I'm not scared of you, Victor,' Jay mutters. 'You're a washed-up security guard now. You don't have the muscle to make anyone disappear.'

Victor steps closer, his presence closing in on Jay. 'You're right. I'm not a cop anymore,' he says, his voice low and cold. 'But I still have connections. People who can make sure you're erased from the world. You really want to take that risk?'

Jay hesitates, his gaze flickering toward the exit as though contemplating an escape. But he knows better. There's nowhere to run. Not from Victor.

Victor doesn't give him a chance to respond. He continues, his words deliberate and forceful. 'I'm going to bring someone to you, someone who needs your help. And you're going to help them, whether you like it or not. Or I'll make sure your past catches up with you.'

Jay's face tightens, his lips pressing into a thin line. He exhales, smoke curling into the air.

'Who?' Jay asks finally, his voice barely above a whisper, but Victor can hear the curiosity buried beneath the defiance.

Victor smiles, with a small, knowing twist of his lips. 'You don't need to know.' He takes a step back, eyes locking onto Jay's. 'What matters right now is this: when I call on you, you'll answer. You'll help.'

Jay's jaw tightens, but he doesn't argue. He doesn't need to.

Victor turns toward the door, his hand already on the handle. 'I'll be in touch.'

Chapter Forty-One

The lunchtime rush is already a memory clinging to the smell of fried onions and over-worked oil. It's the kind of place you'd miss if you blinked and you weren't already looking for it. A low tin roof, a concrete forecourt, a few tired pot plants baking in the sun.

Inside, the warm, still air is broken only by the dull clatter of cutlery being cleared and the occasional hiss from the flat-top grill as someone coaxes the last of the day's burgers into shape. A tired server wipes down tables with disinterest, leaving behind swathes of an unclean table. A radio mutters through the static behind the counter.

Through the wide front windows, the Brisbane River catches the afternoon glare. A cruise ship moves sluggishly toward the port; the decks filled with passengers watching the city float by.

Victor sits across from Anna in a sun-faded booth, the vinyl cracked beneath him. He'd ran an errand, and when he got back, had insisted she come with him and get some food. While driving there, she shared the little information she had with him. He'd bought her a burger and chips and now pushes the plate toward her with a small, quiet gesture.

She's figured out which notebooks she was using around the time Jonas was murdered and while she was investigating the story Marcus had told her about Greenwood. Safely tucked in her backpack, she doesn't want to let them out of her sight. Anna's backpack sits at her feet, the zippers pulled tight, and she has one foot on the strap so someone can't walk past and grab it. Victor has been eyeing it off since they sat down.

'You know,' he says in a faint voice, 'I don't mind holding onto them for a while. No-one's looking at me.'

Anna doesn't look up. 'That's exactly why they should stay with me.'

He laughs softly, part humour, part frustration. 'You haven't stopped watching the door since we got here.'

'I can't afford to let them out of my sight, not for a second.'

Victor leans back; arms crossed loosely over his chest. 'You don't trust me?'

'It's not about trust. Whoever has them is in danger,' then she pauses. 'Besides, half the stuff in there won't make any sense to anyone but me. I have my shorthand and I'm the only one that can decipher it,' a flash of Jonas's body pooled in blood assails her senses. 'Try to anyway.'

He watches her carefully and then nods once, slowly. 'Smart.'

'Paranoid,' she corrects, 'but useful,' she finishes the last of her coffee.

They sit in silence, the background noise of the café settling into a kind of urban symphony. Chairs scraping, someone coughing, the clink of cutlery against plastic tubs.

Victor checks his phone and then slides it back into his pocket. 'We should get you back. There's a lot you need to get through in that locker and not much time.'

Anna nods, takes one last chip, and pops it into her mouth.

Chapter Forty-Two

Victor's car rattles along as it climbs the slope toward the edge of the industrial estate, suspension groaning with every pothole. Receipts, takeaway coffee lids, and an empty pack of gum clutter the dashboard, and all of it skitters with every turn. Anna sits in the passenger seat, her backpack wedged tightly between her knees, her eyes fixed on the road ahead but unfocused, her mind ticking over faster than the speed limit signs blurring past. She's confident most of what she needs is in the notebooks in her bag, but she has to be sure.

Victor opens his mouth to speak when he sees something up ahead before the turn into the storage facility. 'Shit,' he mutters, tightening his grip on the wheel.

Black transit vans, three of them, parked along the main row of units, all unmarked, all with their doors open. Victor keeps driving, eyes forward. 'I think they've found you.'

Anna doesn't need to ask who they are. She turns in her seat, tracking the units as they drive past.

He takes a sharp left at the end of the road and turns onto a narrow access road curving around the back of the storage facility. Tyres crunch on the gravel road. The car lurches over a rise.

Behind the facility, the land slopes up, a scrappy, forgotten hill covered in waist-tall grass and rusting fence posts. At the top, they pull in behind an old maintenance shed, out of sight of the buildings below.

Victor kills the engine.

The silence is heavier than before. In the distance, Anna can make out the curve of the chain-link fence ringing the back of the storage facility, sagging in places, half-swallowed by grass that hasn't seen a mower in years.

Anna squints against the harsh afternoon sunlight as she crouches behind a row of waist-high bushes at the edge of the storage yard. The sharp tang of dry earth and faint chemical odours fill the air. Her smartwatch alerts her that she's approaching a proximity violation. She searches for the map on her watch. They have added the locker to the list of places she can't go.

Together, Victor and Anna watch as the hunters search the storage locker. A male voice booms from within, echoing off the walls, making it sound even louder and travels far enough for Anna and Victor to catch his words, 'check that', or 'move that', every now and again.

There's a loud crash, and Anna can only imagine the destruction they're causing, but better they destroy her furniture than capture her. She's now grateful Victor had persuaded her to take a break. At least now her stomach wasn't grumbling so loud, and she hadn't been there when they arrived.

After the hunters leave, she makes to move when Victor pulls her back to the ground and nods. Another group of people drive up and step into the locker. Carter exits the lead car and directs others with whatever he wants them to do. Among them, the Weasley Rook. Only this crew opens every box, slicing open cushions. This is not a search for her, she realises. This is a search for something else.

At one point she thinks Rook looks right where they're hiding, and while she can't see clearly from this distance, she could almost swear he smirks. Her breath catches as a figure emerges from her locker, dragging a box with him. Others follow with more boxes; they put them in a van.

She can also feel Victor tense up next to her.

'Should have known that fucker would be mixed up in this,' Victor growls.

Anna freezes, her breath catching in her throat as she catches sight of the man across the car park. Broad shoulders, a distinctive limp. It's Briggs. A chill runs through her mind, and her grip tightens on the very edge of the crate she's crouched behind. He's dressed more casually now, directing the others as they load the van, but there's no mistaking him.

The last time she saw him, he had been in a crisp suit, clean-shaven, his appearance polished and professional. Back then, he had been her contact for the story about Victor. A supposed whistleblower. There's no way she can explain who he is to Victor without unravelling everything, but as she watches Briggs move with practiced authority, her stomach churns.

She remembers him spoon-feeding her the story. Checked in with her daily, always eager to know how she was progressing. His attention had flattered her. She had allowed herself to be impressed by his dedication. He had seemed earnest, maybe even a little idealistic. Now, with hindsight, she recognises it as manipulation. He wasn't feeding her the story out of altruism; he was keeping her on track, making sure she stayed on Victor, keeping her too focused to ask questions.

Her mind drifts further back to their first meeting. It had been a fluff piece; she wasn't even supposed to write. Veronica was supposed to cover the Pathway to Purpose article, a non-profit supporting veterans, and Briggs, its public face. Anna had thought little of it. A last-minute reassignment, Veronica's frustration, the routine of it all. But she remembers now how strange it had felt sitting across from him in the small coffee shop where they met.

'You're young for someone with your reputation,' Briggs had said, his voice warm, his smile easy. 'I hear you've broken some big stories over the last couple of years.'

Anna shrugged, brushing off the compliment, uncomfortable with the attention. 'Lucky, I guess. What can you tell me about Pathway to Purpose?'

Briggs leaned back in his chair, his casual air almost too casual. 'It's about giving back, helping veterans find their footing after life in the services. Jobs, housing, mental health support. You know, the works.'

But he hadn't lingered on the project. Instead, he pivoted back to her. 'So, what's next for you? I can't imagine they'll have you doing nickel and dime stuff like this for long. You working on something big?'

She'd dodged his questions, redirecting him to the topic at hand, but his interest in her career had struck her as odd. Why was he so curious? She remembers jotting it down in her notebook with a brief note, 'Briggs,' before letting it slide.

A few days later, Marcus's brother died. Anna had been grappling with the aftermath, her emotions raw, when Briggs made his next move. He approached her about the Victor story, claiming she had made such an impression on him that he felt he could trust her with it. 'I know you're the right person for this,' he had said, leaning in as though sharing a deep secret.

But now, as she sits behind the fence with her heart pounding, she sees it differently. Her potential did not move Briggs. He was orchestrating her involvement, planting seeds, steering her toward Victor and away from the actual story. The one everyone was so desperate to hide.

Anna shifts slightly, the dry grass whispering against her legs as she adjusts her position behind the fence. Her eyes stay locked on Briggs. Without looking away, she slides her backpack onto her lap and unzips it slowly. Her fingers move deftly as she grabs one of her notebooks. She flips through the pages. She knows the page she wants because he'd given her a promo sticker for Pathways to Purpose. She'd stuck it in the notebook. Nothing in the first notebook, but then halfway through the second, there's the sticker.

There's nothing else, no detailed notes or revelations, the barest thread of a connection she'd dismissed back then. But now, as she watches Briggs, it all clicks into place. The reassignment, his probing questions, the timing of his approach, it had all been deliberate. Briggs played her from the start.

'Something?' Victor asks as she closes the notebook slowly and puts it back in her bag.

'Thought it was, but no.' She's not about to tell him the guy who used her to destroy his career is only a few feet away. Selfishly, she needs Victor's help. She can always tell him later, she justifies. Of course, if they catch up with her, later may never come. Maybe it would be better for Victor if he doesn't know.

Anna shrinks lower, her fingers digging into the dry, uneven ground. She wants to run. All her files. All her research. Everything she had pieced together over months carted away. She puts her hand on the backpack, glad she'd merged her notes into a handful of notebooks, now secreted with her. She's glad she took it with her, and it will take them a while to get through the materials she left behind and longer still to decipher her notes.

Victor crouches beside her. He's doing something with his phone, and she's grateful he's too distracted to press her further. His presence comforts her. But would he still help her and risk his life for her if he knew she was responsible, at least in part, for his downfall?

She already knows he hates her and what she's done to him. Not the person sitting in front of him, but the woman she truly is.

'What are you doing?' she asks. He smirks as he points his phone toward the locker.

'Binocular app.'

'Seriously.'

He smiles and shows her the phone, then focuses back on the locker.

'They're thorough,' he notes, as they watch the searchers go through every box and take out only what they think they need. 'On the plus side,' Victor notes, 'you can probably work out what they've taken by what they leave behind.'

What they leave behind will tell its own story. She has to stay alive to tell it. 'I can't go back there,' she says.

'Why not? We can wait for them to leave.'

She shows him the smartwatch and points out the locker's location.

'The places shaded red are programmed into this thing and if I get too close; I have no idea what it will do to me. But I saw what it did to Aaron Dupree, so I'm in no hurry to find out.'

'I can bring the contents to you,' he suggests.

'First off it would take hours, time I don't have and second, I wouldn't be surprised if they leave someone behind to watch over the place to see if I come back.'

'But if they made it a no-go zone, why would they wait around to see if you come back?' His eyes squint with confusion.

'Because it's what I would do to see if someone's helping me.' A wry smile passes over her lips. 'If you go anywhere near that locker now, you'll be putting an even bigger target on your back.' She doesn't add how she suspects there may already be one, but what's done is done and she can't undo it. But she is not about to expose him to any more risk than she already has.

'They've already destroyed me, what more can they do?' he says.

'Kill you.'

Briggs barks orders at the other men, his voice carrying across the yard. The crew loads the last of their haul into the van. As they slam the van doors shut, Anna's chest tightens as she watches them secure the unit with one of their men still inside. Victor places a steadying hand on her shoulder.

'We'll figure something out,' he says. 'But not here. We should move in case they decide to search the surroundings.'

Anna nods, and together they retreat deeper into the overgrown wasteland, back to where Victor had hidden the car.

'Where now?' she asks, hopeful Victor has a plan, because she sure doesn't.

'I work from multiple locations,' he smiles. 'We can go to another nearby. I have the keys and it's a site where they don't staff it on the weekends.'

'And do what?'

'Decipher those notebooks of yours,' he says as he nods to her backpack. 'Maybe Google some shit. Speaking of which, here,' he hands her a laptop, 'this should make research easier. 'It's my personal one, so don't lose it, and you'll have to find your own Wi-Fi.'

Anna gives Victor a nod, and they crawl away from the fence, only standing when they are far enough away not to be seen. Victor and Anna climb into the car, careful to open and close the doors as noiselessly as they can. He rolls the car down the hill, and only when he's satisfied they are far enough away, does he engage the engine. They take the long way out, winding through industrial back streets until the storage unit disappears behind them.

Chapter Forty-Three

It's after three when they arrive at the second facility hidden behind a defunct panel-beating shop; its sign is half blown off, and weeds crack the gravel lot. The facility is smaller than the other one, with sun-faded units behind a rusting sliding gate. Victor keys in the code on a weathered pad. He glances over his shoulder once, twice. The gate groans open reluctantly. He guides her towards the office tucked away in the corner. She feels the familiar anxiety of boxing herself into a corner again, but there's nothing she can do about it now, and besides, whether or not she likes it, she needs help, and Victor is the only one around.

Fluorescent lights hum overhead, casting a harsh glow on the cramped, unremarkable office. A desk cluttered with loose papers, an outdated computer and a mug emblazoned with the logo of the storage company occupies the room. Security monitors mounted on the wall display grainy footage of the surrounding facility. The rows of lockers stretch into the distance. The branding of the original company is still present in places. The new company had focused only on replacing the front-facing signage.

Anna perches on the edge of a plastic chair, her arms crossed over her chest. Her gaze flits toward the monitor.

'How is this setup?' she asks, now more aware than ever that everything she touches, everywhere she goes, could put both of them in even more danger.

'It's a cloud thing. All the sites security feeds are in a cloud. Don't ask me how it works, I just know it does.'

She smiles and nods. She's not great with technology either. 'If it's on the cloud, does that mean it can be hacked?'

'I guess so, but the security company in charge of all this claims they have the best cyber security money can buy.'

She points at the screen. 'But let's say the hunters can, do you think this is how they found me?'

'I guess, but this shit is beyond me.'

She shakes her head. These days, she's lucky she even knows how to access her email on her phone with all the hoops she has to go through to get to it. Victor stands by the desk, his posture casual but his expression sharp. He leans one hand against the desk; the other grips a disposable coffee cup he'd grabbed from the break room.

'We need help,' he says, his voice firm. 'You can't do this, but I know a guy that...' He waves around at the technology.

'No,' cutting him off before he can elaborate.

She shakes her head and looks away, avoiding his gaze. 'The more people who know, the greater the risk they could talk or be followed. Or worse.'

Victor raises an eyebrow and takes a deliberate sip of his coffee. 'You think you can take down the Watcher all on your own or survive the next...' He reaches out and checks the countdown on Anna's watch, 'fifty-four hours without help and I don't mean me.'

Anna's lips press into a thin line. She looks down at her hands clasped in her lap. 'I don't trust anyone. Not with this.'

'What about me?' he challenges with a sharp tone. 'I have as much reason as you do.' He waves at the uniform representing what he's been reduced to.

'Do you?' she points to the device implanted in her neck. 'Do you really? You don't have this thing in your neck or this,' she points to the smartwatch. 'Every move I make. And who's to say they won't give the hunters my GPS coordinates if I get too close again, and they work it out before I can do anything with it?'

'That's exactly why we need help because they can't track me. They don't know I'm helping you.'

'Yet,' she says. 'They don't know yet but look how quickly they got on to the storage locker.'

'Yes, because they're tracking you,' he says. 'They probably tracked you through the GPS in your watch, which I suspect is more likely. They probably have facial recognition trawling CCTV for you too. I know people who can help. One guy in particular owes me a favour. I kept him out of jail and his help might give you the edge you need.'

Anna's stomach churns with unease. She feels the weight of his words pressing against her already frazzled nerves. Her mind races, imagining all the ways involving other people could go wrong. Someone leaking her plans, someone leading the Watcher straight to them, or someone deciding to turn her in is a safer bet or more lucrative. She's learned most people have a price, even the ones who have no need for money, because they already have more than enough. Greed, in her experience, is a persuasive motivator.

'I can't,' she murmurs. She swallows hard and shakes her head as she stares at the floor. 'I can't take that risk.'

Victor lets out a frustrated sigh and sets his coffee cup down. 'What if you can't get that thing deciphered?' He nods at the notebook with her scribbles. 'Or worse, you do, and you still can't work out what it is they are looking for. What if you don't even have this magic bullet.'

'If I don't have it, why are they looking so hard?'

He runs his hand through his hair. The muscles in his jaw flex as he tries to maintain his composure. 'You're going to get yourself killed if you keep thinking like that. You need help, whether you like it or not.'

Anna's shoulders sag. She doesn't want to let on that she's having more trouble with the notebook than she had expected. She rubs her temples as if trying to will the doubts away. 'I need time to think. OK, let me, let me figure this out.'

Victor's eyes narrow, his frustration clear, but he gives a terse nod. 'Fine, but don't take too long because time is the one thing you don't have.'

She looks up at him then, his expression a mix of weariness and quiet resolve. 'I'll think about it,' she says.

Victor grabs his coffee and heads for the door. Before he steps out, he looks back at her. 'Don't think too hard. Sometimes you have to trust people, even if it scares the shit out of you.'

Chapter Forty-Four

The ballroom is a study in excess. Crystal chandeliers blazing overhead, velvet-draped tables, champagne that fizzles. The air hums with polite laughter and the soft clink of glasses, every guest dressed to be noticed. These galas exist solely for wealthy people to congratulate themselves.

Mark Thorncroft thrives in it.

He enters with the practiced grace of a man used to doors opening before he even reaches them. His shoes click on marble; his trophy wife glides beside him, her smile bright enough to qualify as stage lighting. She squeezes his arm as a cluster of donors approach, all eager to bask in Thorncroft's glow.

He gives them his usual smile, warm, benevolent, expertly hollow.

It's a dance they all take part in. The organisers taking pains not to know where their benefactors get their money, or how they make it. In return, the benefactors are generous for the air of respectability these types of events afford them. Everyone wins. Although how much of what is raised reaches the people it's intended for is another question entirely?

The auction begins. Thorncroft sits front and centre, his wife perched elegantly beside him. He raises his paddle with casual confidence, outbidding everyone without hesitation. The applause is warm and admiring. His wife tilts her head proudly, as if she's the one bankrolling half the room.

But something is off. Thorncroft's phone vibrates in his pocket, again and again and again. Urgent. Insistent. He checks the screen under the tablecloth, smoothing the tension from his face as quickly as it forms.

Across the room, Veronica weaves through the crowd with the grace of a woman who's attended a thousand functions she never wanted to be at. She sips her champagne but doesn't taste it. Her father insisted she make an appearance. And when he sponsors the event, refusal isn't an option.

She finally reaches Thorncroft's table, offering a polite nod to his wife.

'Veronica,' Mrs. Thorncroft gushes, leaning in for a cheek-kiss. 'You look stunning tonight. Doesn't she, Mark?'

Thorncroft glances up from his phone, the mask sliding neatly back into place.

'Yes. Veronica always makes an impression,' a veiled compliment. Or a warning. Depending on the day.

Veronica's gaze flicks briefly to the phone before returning to Thorncroft. 'These events are always … enlightening,' she says dryly. 'Though honestly, they're such a drag.'

Mrs. Thorncroft laughs, the airy, chiming kind perfected for public spaces. 'Oh, I know. Mark adores them, but I always feel like I'm melting under these lights.'

Thorncroft's smile stays fixed. 'It's important work, dear.'

Veronica glances toward the stage, then back to him. 'Speaking of important work, what do you make of the news about Aaron Dupree?'

Thorncroft stills for the smallest beat before placing his phone facedown.

'I'm not surprised,' he says smoothly. 'People are very rarely what they seem.'

'Does that include you?' Veronica asks.

His wife gives a too-bright laugh. 'Oh, Veronica, always digging for a story.'

'I can't help my job,' Veronica replies lightly. 'Actually, I'd love to do one on your rise to success someday, Mark.'

'There's not much to tell,' he says. 'Hard work and luck.'

'You do seem very lucky,' she lets it linger.

Thorncroft's jaw flexes. 'Luck favours the prepared.'

'And the well-connected,' she murmurs.

Mrs. Thorncroft jumps in with a cheerful deflection. 'Speaking of prepared. Did Mark tell you Mia made the select squad? Her coach says she's got real talent.'

Veronica smiles, but her eyes stay on Thorncroft. 'She really does. Exceptional control for her age. Should we expect Thorncroft United next? A soccer club to add to the empire?'

Thorncroft gives a tight smile. 'I invest where it makes sense.'

'And where it shines well on you,' Veronica says pleasantly.

Before he can reply, the auctioneer unveils a rare collector's piece. Bidding erupts. Thorncroft lifts his paddle instantly, drowning the room in confidence. Another bid. Another victory. Another round of applause.

He shoots Veronica a pointed look. 'In my experience,' he says, 'actions speak louder than words.'

The crowd claps louder.

Under the table, his phone vibrates again.

Chapter Forty-Five

Anna sits at the desk, her back hunched over the notebooks and longhand scribbles on a notepad next to it. She highlights the symbols she still can't decipher. The faint aroma of stale coffee mingles with the dusty undertones of old papers. She highlights another symbol.

'Damn it.' Her voice is a whisper, filled with frustration and despair.

Victor leans against the door frame, his arms crossed over his chest, the sharp angles of his face set in a grim line.

'What now?' He steps forward and, noting all the highlighted symbols on the page, realises she's struggling. 'You'll work it out.'

'And what if I can't?' Anna's voice rises. She yanks the chair back. The legs scrape against the tiled floor.

'What if it's like you said and...,' she falters, glancing toward the security monitors on the wall. Victor frowns, following her gaze to the grainy live feed.

A black SUV pulls up at the front gate of the facility. The SUV's tinted windows reflect the late afternoon sun.

'Did you lock the gates?' she asks as she scoops everything into her backpack.

'Of course,' Victor growls as he helps her. They watch as the driver rolls down his window and reaches for the intercom. It buzzes in the office, and even though she watched Briggs press it, the sound still makes her jump.

'Don't answer that,' she screams as Victor reaches for the button.

'If I don't, it will go through to head office.'

'And then what?' she stares at him.

'It will go through to head office,' he says, restating slower and with a clipped tone.

'And?'

'And they can remotely open the gates.' Victor reaches for the button and answers with the company name.

'Hi,' the voice on the other end says disarmingly. 'I need to grab something real quick from my unit but I've left my pass at home. Any chance you can buzz me in?'

'You really need your pass, I'm afraid,' Victor says, keeping his voice calm and neutral, sticking to the company script.

'Come on mate, just this once. I promise I won't be long.'

Victor thinks for a moment, checks he's not transmitting, then looks at Anna. 'You got everything?' he asks her. She nods. He presses the button.

'I'll have to come down to swipe you in,' he says, as if a little put out. 'And if you haven't got your key or combination to your lock, you're on your own.'

'Really appreciate that.' The voice is crackly through the speakers, but she would know Brigg's voice anywhere, even if she hadn't seen him on the monitor.

'I'm on my way,' Victor says, and disconnects the buzzer.

'What the fuck?' Anna exclaims.

'There's a way out around the back. If we leave now, we can buy you a few minutes, but when they figure out I'm not coming, they will buzz again and this time they'll get in because I bet you dollars to donuts, they have come prepared with enough information to talk their way in. They need the name of an account holder and a unit number. All of which is stored on computers which they probably have someone with the skills to hack.'

He pushes her towards the door. 'So, we have to go now.'

Anna hesitates. Her gaze flickers between the screen and Victor.

'No, if I go with you, they'll follow and that puts you in more danger.'

Victor grabs her arm and pulls her toward the back door of the office. 'When they start asking questions it's not going to take long for them to work out I was here and even if I wanted to, I can't stay behind and try to bluff it out because I'm not supposed to be here either. I'm supposed to be on my mandatory ten-hour break. And because I used my key card to get in...'

Anna gasps.

'Whether you like it or not, I'm in this now.'

She should have sent him away the minute she saw him.

'If they catch us, they'll kill us both.'

He steps into the car. She hesitates. His dark eyes lock onto hers intensely. 'And you think that scares me, that I will walk away because it's dangerous? I'm not that guy. I don't run from a fight, and I don't leave people behind to fend for themselves,' he says as he drags her out towards the car.

He turns on the ignition and reaches across and pushes open the passenger door. 'I do, however, get the hell out of dodge so I can live to fight another day when I can see the odds are stacked against me. Sometimes retreat is the smartest move.'

Anna's still not sure.

'Look,' he says, 'we get out of here, then we work out a way you can do what you need to do, and we can regroup. But we can't do any of that if they catch us.'

Chapter Forty-Six

Lucy hasn't heard a word from Marcus since she left Anna in the toilets hours ago now. Anna and Tristan have no safe way of reaching her, and Marcus told her he needs to stay off the grid. Silence stretched throughout the day, now sharp, brittle and unbearable. Her thoughts loop through worst-case scenarios. Were they safe? Were they even still alive? Every time her phone buzzes with nothing but spam, the dread settles deeper. They need this equipment, and she's the only one who can get it.

Lucy's heart pounds in her chest. She checks the clock. The late afternoon light filters through the blinds, casting long, jagged shadows across Greenwood's floor. The sounds of the building hum around her, footsteps, the muffled chatter of her colleagues, the distant clang of metal tools.

Her hand trembles as she slips her ID lanyard around her neck. She keeps her eyes on the floor as she walks past her colleagues, blending into the background, hoping no one notices the nervous energy radiating off her.

The equipment room is a small, shadowy space tucked away behind a nondescript door at the end of a corridor. It's usually locked, but Lucy knows the code. Her hands sweat as she approaches the door. The cool metal of the handle slips under her fingers. She looks both ways down the hallway. No one. She slides inside.

The fluorescent lights cast an eerie glow over the room filled with racks of machines and sterile shelves stacked with equipment. She spots what Tristan needs. A small, portable kit, one of only two in existence, tucked near the back. Her pulse spikes, but she forces herself to steady her breath as she reaches for it.

She stuffs the kit into her bag with quick, deliberate movements. The weight of the bag is noticeable now. She hears a sound outside the room, footsteps, too close for comfort. Lucy freezes, her breath hitching in her throat.

The door creaks. She feels her heart leap into her throat as she takes a step back. She watches the door handle turns, but it stays firm; the person on the other side moves away. The footsteps fade into the distance. She lets out a breath she didn't realise she was holding. Her pulse still hammering in her chest. Her fingers tremble as she adjusts the bag, making sure its zipped shut.

She steps toward the door, her body tense. She slinks out of the equipment room, her movements smooth but hurried. She wants to race for the exit, but she forces herself to slow down. She takes a deep breath as she steps back into the staff area.

Lucy's nerves are so frayed as she approaches the head nurse.

'I'm feeling a little off,' Lucy says quickly, her voice sounding more strained than she intended. 'Think I might be coming down with something. I'm going to head home. Can you cover for me?'

The woman furrows her brow. After a beat, she nods. 'Alright, go home and get some rest.'

Lucy nods. She gathers her things, keeping her movements slow and deliberate. She heads toward the exit, trying to look casual.

The night air hits her the moment she steps outside. She strides towards her car, her mind racing. She glances over her shoulder, half-expecting someone to be following her. A motorcycle roars up beside her. The rider wears all black. A helmet obscures their face. The engine rumbles menacingly. The rider's voice cuts through the noise as he lifts his visor.

'You get it?'

She nods.

He reaches behind him and hands her a helmet. 'Get on.'

Chapter Forty-Seven

Victor's suggestion of hiding out at the library turns out to be a good idea. It's cool, has access to the internet, and no one would dare do anything here. Too many witnesses. Rows of bookshelves stretch into the distance. Sturdy and unyielding. Their spines bear titles hinting at worlds far removed from her own. Students hunch over desks. The soft scratching of pens on paper blends with the tapping of keyboards. Anna moves through the aisles with purpose. She needs a desk where no one can sneak up on her.

She carries Victor's laptop under her arm. Her fingers tighten around it. She finds a secluded workstation on an upper level near the back of the library. Through the window she can see the library's main entrance. She wonders if she would notice the hunters coming in, but then the black fatigues might raise some alarm bells with the building security.

She slides into the uncomfortable plastic chair, sets down the laptop and boots it up. Her fingers tap on the polished desk. The low hum of the library's air conditioning and the murmur of voices provide a strange sort of comfort, a steady backdrop to her racing thoughts. Anna connects to the library's free Wi-Fi. She needs to pull together the threads she has.

Briggs.
Carter.
The Redoubt Security Group.
Aaron Dupree.
Quentin Thomasson

Thomas Greer

Marcy Lynch.

She opens the browser and takes it into in-private mode. She starts with Marcy and an old-fashioned Google search. It pulls up several stories with photographs of many Marcy Lynches, but a quick scan discounts most as either too old, too young, or already dead. But then one headline catches her attention. It's only a couple of weeks old. She follows the link, 'Tragedy strikes SkyForge Engineer's family.'

There's a picture of Marcy. It's one of those corporate headshots. She reads the story. *The SkyForge Innovation team is rallying around one of its brightest minds, Marcy Lynch, after the sudden and tragic death of her husband, Nathaniel Hawthorne, weeks before the couple are to welcome their first child.*

Nathaniel, 42, passed away suddenly. While the police have not released the cause of death, they have confirmed they are not treating it as suspicious. Marcy Lynch, the engineer behind SkyForge's revolutionary drone navigation and communication systems, has been a key figure in the company's success.

Her husband's passing has left colleagues and friends shocked. Nathaniel, a respected environmental consultant, was working on an independent project examining the potential use of drone technology for environmental conservation in the Australian Outback.

That tracks with what Marcy had told her.

Friends close to the family described him as perpetually curious. In a brief statement, Marcy expressed her gratitude for the support she's received from the SkyForge family and the conservation community during this challenging time.

'Nathaniel was my anchor, my best friend, and my biggest supporter. While my heart is shattered, I look forward to welcoming our child and will keep his memory alive through her.'

SkyForge Innovations has launched a scholarship fund in Nathaniel's name to further environmental research.

Anna sits back and looks at the page. Veronica's smug face accompanies her by-line. Anna scans more results for Marcy and opens them in separate tabs. She starts a new page in her notebook for Marcy. This time her notes are in longhand. If she doesn't survive, she wants her notes to be readable.

At the top of the page, she writes Marcy's name, then the name of Marcy's husband, Nathaniel Hawthorne and the name of Marcy's employers, SkyForge Innovations. Anna's heard of them, but they didn't factor in her stories. She checks Marcy's LinkedIn profile and shared connections; there are two that stand out. Both are trapped in this game. One of them is already dead. There are also several academic papers, but they seem to have dropped off over the last few years, as did her public speaking engagements.

Then Anna searches up Nathaniel Hawthorne. Minutes tick by, marked by the quiet movement of the hands on the clock on the wall. Anna leans back for a moment, stretches her arms above her head and then pinches the bridge of her nose. The tightness in her ribs hasn't eased since the hunters' near miss at the storage facility. She can still picture the SUV. The men who climbed out.

A noise to her left snaps her attention back to the present. A tall man in a dark hoodie browses the shelves nearby. Her muscles tighten as she watches him out of the corner of her eye. Is he one of them?

She packs up the laptop, sliding it into her backpack. She moves past the children's section, weaving through beanbag chairs and low shelves filled with colourful picture books. She finds another workstation on the opposite side of the library and quickly sets herself back up. Her fingers dance over the keyboard as she resumes her research on Marcy.

While Marcy had been pulling away from the limelight over the last few years, her husband had not followed suit. He had grown more vocal within the conservation community, and many articles reported his arrests at protests. One article catches Anna's attention.

Reforestation projects spark land rights controversies.

It's dated three weeks before Nathaniel's death.

Project Renewal, a reforestation initiative backed by Mark Thorncroft's Charitable Foundation...

Wait, Anna stops reading. Thorncroft. Could it be his entry in her notebook wasn't a red herring, but this article is only a few weeks old, six at the most. Her notes were from years ago. She scribbles Thorncroft on the page with Nathaniel's name on the top in her journal and keeps reading.

Mark Thorncroft's Charitable Foundation is facing allegations of displacing Indigenous communities in northern Australia. Environmental activists allege the project is a ploy to seize control of resource-rich land while...

A paywall hides the rest of the article, and despite many other searches, she cannot find any other information on the story.

A group of students rush past, chattering and giggling and

swinging their bags around, which knocks Anna's notebook onto the floor. It lands splayed open on a different page. There's an IP address. She can't remember where she got it from, but it must mean that at some point she considered it important.

She types in the address, and it appears to be a chat room on the dark web. At first, what she reads makes little sense, but then she figures it's some kind of code. She retrieves her notebook, flips to a new page, and records the words occurring most frequently out of context, along with their frequencies and any accompanying sequences of numbers. Each entry has a user tag. Two catch her attention: Rook, which is the chest piece on the arm of one hunter, and further down Scarab. She figures this is not a coincidence.

At 7:50, an announcement comes over the intercom. *The library will close in 10 minutes. Please prepare to leave.* Anna's pulse quickens. The hunters could be waiting outside. She shoves the laptop into her bag and stands, her jaw tight as she scans the room.

As she passes the exit, the librarian at the desk offers her a polite smile. Anna nods in return, focusing on the glass doors ahead. The cool evening air greets her as she steps outside. She looks out at the shadows stretching across the car park. No SUVs. No hunters.

Chapter Forty-Eight

The clubhouse is an urban fortress. High fences topped with barbed wire. As soon as they get close, a door in the fence opens and they ride through. The air smells of oil, sweat and cigarette smoke. She climbs off the bike and a man approaches. His leather vest proclaims him to be Havoc and his title as Sergeant at Arms.

'This way,' he says and nods for her to follow him into what appears to be the primary structure. At one point, she could have been mistaken for considering it a house, but the makeshift additions disguise it. She steps into a large room with a bar and a snooker table, and couches and coffee tables filled with overflowing ashtrays and empty beer bottles.

Over in one corner, Marcus sits on a bar stool, shirt off, blood dried along his collar where the device sits embedded beneath the skin of his neck.

Lucy doesn't hesitate. She crosses the room in three strides and throws her arms around Marcus. He catches her instantly, pulling her tight, burying his face in her hair.

'I'm okay,' he murmurs, though his voice is rough. 'You got here.'

Tristan steps up behind them and puts his helmet on the nearest table.

'Yes,' she breathes, as she grabs hold of Marcus's hand.

Tristan inspects the small device embedded in Marcus's neck. Lucy had removed Tristan's the moment they got far enough away from Greenwood.

Tristan clears his throat. 'Let's get this done because my hands are starting to shake,' as he reaches for the equipment from inside Lucy's bag, the floor shakes.

A deep boom rolls through the compound. The concrete floor trembles beneath their feet. Glasses rattle off shelves and clatter across the floor. For a beat, no one breathes.

Dingo appears in the doorway a heartbeat later, Havoc a looming shadow at his shoulder. Both men scan the room in an instant, Marcus half-dressed, Lucy bracing him, Tristan frozen mid-reach toward the kit.

Dingo lifts a hand, sharp and commanding. 'Stay put.'

Havoc nods to the men who, until moments ago, had been relaxing, now on their feet. 'I want to know what the hell that was.' Dingo strides down the hall. Havoc calls out for bodies to fall in behind him. Their voices fade into clipped commands, boots pounding towards the noise.

The sudden quiet they leave behind is somehow worse than the explosion.

Seconds later, Colby stumbles into the room, wild-eyed and panting. 'Dingo says you gotta get out. Now. Compound's been compromised.'

'What?' Tristan blurts. 'How?'

Colby shakes his head. 'Don't know. Don't care. There's a way out, but it's narrow. Can only take one of you at a time. Dingo said I have to start with him.' He jerks his chin at Marcus.

Lucy is already grabbing her bag. 'Then I'm coming too.'

'I can't get everyone out, Dingo said him first.' He nods to Marcus.

'And I'm not letting him out of my sight,' Lucy snaps.

Marcus grips her wrist to reinforce that they are staying together. His jaw clenches. He kisses her forehead. 'Stay close.'

Colby hesitates, but only for a heartbeat. Marcus takes her bag from her.

Colby leads them through a service corridor, down a narrow ladder, into the tunnels beneath the compound. The air is damp and sour. Their footsteps echo in the tight, claustrophobic space.

'We're nearly there,' Colby says. 'Exits around this bend.'

Three silhouettes stand at the far end of the tunnel, rifles shouldered as they round the bend. Hunters.

Marcus reacts first. He shoves Lucy back behind a jut of concrete, disappearing her from the line of sight as Briggs steps forward.

'Well done,' Briggs says to Colby, voice dripping satisfaction. 'You actually pulled it off.'

Colby flinches. 'Yeah. Now we just, now we get out, right? Together?'

Briggs's smile fades. 'Oh, Colby. Not you.' He places a heavy hand on the young man's shoulder. 'You stay here. Sell the story. Tell the bikers you were ambushed.'

'Wait, no. The other guy...' Colby blurts. 'He's still...'

Briggs's fist snaps forward, striking Colby across the jaw. The young man collapses like a puppet with cut strings.

Lucy clamps her hand over her mouth to stifle a gasp as Briggs gestures for his men to take Marcus. Panic claws at her, but she forces herself to stay silent.

Marcus catches her eye from the corner. *Quiet.*

She nods. Only when the sounds of the footsteps echoing off the walls have gone does she dare move.

She races back through the tunnels, lungs burning, heart hammering. When she bursts back into the compound, she finds Dingo and Havoc storming toward Tristan, fists clenched.

'No!' Lucy gasps. 'Marcus ... they took him. It was your man that helped them.' The accusation in her eyes as she stares Dingo down.

Dingo and Havoc exchange a look. Minutes later, Havoc's men drag Colby inside, bruised, groggy, barely conscious.

The moment his eyes land on Lucy, he knows he's done for.

Tristan steps to Lucy's side, steadying her shaking hands. 'There's still a way to find him, and disable the device ... I think,' he murmurs.

'You think!' Lucy turns on him.

'Yes, but I need a computer. And a hacker. A good one.'

Dingo nods to Buzz. 'Will he do?'

Tristan looks at Buzz. 'Can you crack military grade encryption?'

Buzz shrugs and shakes his head. 'Sorry. But I can try.'

Dingo steps closer. 'Unless you know someone who can do that, Buzz is the only option we got.'

Tristan winces. 'I do, but there's a problem.'

'What?'

'These guys don't exactly advertise in the yellow pages and he's not really my guy.'

'Meaning?' Dingo's voice is menacingly close.

'He was someone my mate used in the past.'

'Then call your mate,' Havoc growls, holding out a phone.

'I can't,' Havoc steps closer still, and Tristan leans back. 'They already killed him.'

'So how do we find him?'

'There're ways but we can't just broadcast that we're looking for him. I'll have to reach out to … people. Carefully. It might take time.'

Buzz appears at Tristan's elbow, slapping a laptop into his hands. 'Use mine. It's secure. And tell me what you need from me.'

Tristan flips it open and gets to work, fingers flying. 'I can give you a list of places on the dark web, what his handle is, what to say. At the end of the day though, we have to hope he sees the messages and that he gets in touch.'

Dingo turns to Buzz. 'Work with him, find out everything you can about this guy,' he nods to Tristan. 'Then work your magic to get me an address. Fuck this waiting for him to come to us shit.'

Lucy sways, knees threatening to buckle. Dingo steps beside her, his presence unexpectedly gentle. 'We'll get him back,' he says, voice steady as steel. 'You have my word, Lucy. Whatever it takes.'

Chapter Forty-Nine

Anna's boots scuff against the uneven pavement, the gritty crunch of loose gravel and shattered glass underfoot, a constant reminder of where she is, nowhere safe. The streets stretch before her, and she needs to stay within the radius the free city Wi-Fi provides if she's going to use the laptop. Victor had offered to let her hide out at his place, but she refused. While the security of a roof over her head for the night was tempting, if the Hunters have already worked out Victor is helping her, given what went down at the storage sheds, it won't be any safer than where she is now.

Flickering streetlights casting jagged shadows dance in her peripheral vision. Her heart races as her eyes dart to each corner and scans for danger. She moves through the streets, doubling back twice to make sure she's not being followed. The muscles in her legs ache, and her body screams for rest, but her mind refuses to relent. Every car idling too long, every shadow shifting in the dim light, feels threatening.

She thinks about the words from the dark web chat room. The words themselves make little sense to her; she wonders what they mean for the people who are using the chat. Packages, deliveries, drivers, all of it could be about drugs, but she doesn't think these people are drug dealers. She's investigated enough drug-related stories to know there's more to this story.

She had already worked out that the people who died mysteriously, accidents, suicides, were all powerful men or experts in their fields. Then there are words which don't belong together. Planting seeds in the same sentence or message as broken wheels and fog.

A distant siren wails, and she flinches. Her eyes dart to the source. The sound fades, swallowed by the city's constant hum. Somewhere down the street, two men argue, their voices echoing against the brick facades of shuttered shops. Anna picks up the pace and averts her eyes. Her pulse hammers in her ears.

'Just keep moving,' she mutters under her breath. Her hands fidget, pulling at the fraying ends of her sleeves. She ducks into an alley and finds a spot behind a dumpster, but with a streetlight close enough so that when she pulls out her notebook and reads the pages, she can still make out the words.

Each chat has four numbers beside it, and as she scans the pages, focusing on the numbers, she realises they are timestamps in the 24-hour clock. It's so obvious now she's pissed she didn't see it sooner. There's a flurry of messages between 6:00 and 7:30 last night.

She hadn't noted the messages word for word. She didn't have time but tried to capture what she thought was relevant. She can see multiple packages scheduled for delivery between 7:00 and 7:24 PM. The last timestamp is moments before 7:30, when the game began. She counts them up, seven, although originally there had only been six. The message accompanying the last timestamp talked about a package delivery, so nothing was out of context except that the delivery was a late addition to the schedule.

She recalls the way the trainer had looked at Marcy when he talked about getting caught up in the game. Could he have been one of the men in fatigues collecting everyone and perhaps balked at taking a pregnant woman? It's a plausible explanation for his late addition to the schedule.

Each package displays a series of numbers upon collection, followed by a letter. She recalls the dots on her map and brings it up to be sure. On her watch, each dot has a corresponding letter, and they match up with the prey being hunted based on what she knows about the names of the people she's worked out so far.

Package means prey. She writes it in her notes. The numbers following each package's delivery match, but the collection numbers differ. Could those numbers represent coordinates?

'Hey you,' a shout from the back door of a restaurant startles her. 'You can't stay there. Fuck off.'

She holds her hands up, and she stuffs the notebook back into her backpack as she scrambles to her feet. She passes a rundown shop with bars over the windows. A neon sign buzzes 'open.' A group of teenagers loiter on the corner, their laughter sharp, jarring.

One of them glances at her, and she averts her eyes. She needs somewhere to fire up the laptop to check her theory about the numbers. She can feel the fatigue heavy on her eyes.

She spots a narrow alley ahead. She veers into it. Her shoes splash through a shallow puddle smelling of damp concrete. The alley is littered with discarded cans, broken bottles, and papers. She finds a spot sheltered from the wind and the rain, and she's hidden from view.

She crouches down and finds a dry spot for the backpack. She arranges the debris at both ends of the alley, cans at one end, broken glass at the other. This way, no one can creep up on her, and depending on the sound, she'll know which direction they're coming from. Her hands tremble as she works.

Satisfied, she leans against the brick wall of her semi-safe space. Exhaustion threatens to drag her under, but she forces herself to stay awake. She pulls out the laptop, connects to the free citywide Wi-Fi, and pulls up maps. She holds her breath while plugging in the numbers of where all the deliveries were made. The pin displayed is for the location she thinks is the warehouse where the game started.

'Yes,' she says, then checks herself for making a noise and peeks out of her hiding place. She looks along both sides of the alley, then sits back and checks the screen. She presses the button for street view and confirms what she had thought. She uses the mouse pad to get the 360 views of the location and uses the cursor to follow the route she, Marcus, and Aaron took when Aaron was looking for help.

The screen fills with the police station as the memory of Aaron's murder consumes her. She shakes it away. She looks at the numbers for the pickup points for the deliveries, and a letter follows each set of coordinates. There're noises all around her. The squeak of a shopping cart's wheels. A dog barking in the distance and the sharp crack of a bottle kicked against the curb.

Anna presses her back against the icy wall, her knees pulled to her chest, and she closes the laptop so the light from the screen doesn't give her location away.

Her thoughts spiral. The paranoia sets in. What if someone had seen her set up her makeshift alarm and is waiting out of sight? She shakes her head and tries to dislodge the thoughts.

'You're fine,' she whispers. Her voice trembles. 'No one knows you're here.' But that's not true. The watch has GPS, and while the Watcher said the rules were that the hunters don't have access to the GPS data, what if they realise she's digging and poking around the story again and decide to change the rules?

Her mind refuses to let her rest, so after a few minutes and with no one in sight, she reopens the laptop. She enters the coordinates for the first 'A' package. It's Parliament House. She enters the numbers for the second A package and gasps as the screen displays her apartment block. They must have grabbed Aaron from Parliament House, but there's a second set of coordinates for the first A package, and it's a house in Annerley.

She clenches her jaw, and her muscles are taut. But now she knows these numbers are coordinates. She needs to work out what the other codes and the other coordinates represent.

She shuts down the laptop. She's too tired to focus and too alert and on edge to sleep, but for the first time since this all began, she feels hope. She had planned to meet Victor and his hacker friend in the morning. After what happened at the lockers, she had agreed to accept help, but Victor's guy is not available until the morning. She has to keep out of sight until then.

Then her watch vibrates, and she looks down at the notification.

Sebastian Garcia. Deceased. COD captured.

Pray remaining three. Hunters remaining five.

Sebastian

The shadows stretch long and lean under the fluorescent glare of the streetlights. My breath fogs the air as I press my back against the cold brick wall of the alley. I taught them this: how to corner prey, how to hunt.

I hear the faint crunch of boots on gravel, a sound so subtle it would've gone unnoticed by anyone else. But not me. Never me. I've drilled them a thousand times, taught them to be silent predators.

'Sebastian,' a voice calls, low and measured, floating on the still air. Lauren.

My chest tightens. Of all the mercenaries I've trained, Lauren was the one I had the most hope for. She was sharp, determined, and relentless in her pursuit of justice, or perhaps vengeance.

When I recruited her, I asked her why she chose this path. Her answer was raw, the truth that cuts through all pretence. Emotion choked her voice as she spoke of her mother's murder. The anguish in her eyes burned, a pain so vivid it made me look away. This was what they used to recruit her. Her loss of family, her loneliness, her desperate need for meaning in the chaos of her life. They had seen the gaping hole her mother's death left behind and promised to fill it with purpose, with belonging, and she believed them with a little help from me. For the first time, I feel ashamed of what I've become, the things I've done under the guise of the greater good. I realised the greater good had nothing to do with good and everything to do with power and money, but by then, it was already too late to get out. I accepted the choices I made and told myself I would get out one day. Well, I'm out now.

I couldn't blame her. It's easy to believe when you have nothing left. But now, as I think of her, how she had thrown herself into every mission, her determination to prove she was worth the chance they gave her, I feel the weight of my failure. I should have warned her that the promises they made were hollow, designed to mould her into a weapon for their own ends?

'You don't have to do this, Lauren,' I call back, my voice steady despite the hammering in my chest.

Silence. Then, there is a faint shuffle. I glimpse her shadow at the mouth of the alley, her silhouette framed by the harsh light. She has company.

'You know I don't have a choice,' she replies, stepping closer. Her face is taut, her eyes hard but glassy, a flicker of conflict buried deep within.

I chuckle more to myself than to her. 'We all have choices.'

She flinches, a split second, but I see it, the slight hesitation, the way her hand wavers near her holster.

'You broke the rules, Sebastian,' she says, her voice sharp but trembling. 'You questioned the mission.'

'I questioned the morality of bringing a woman who is eight months pregnant into this, Lauren. That's not a mission, that's madness.' I step forward, hands outstretched, knowing the risk but desperate to reach her. 'I understand why you wanted this hunt, because of Anna Levesque. Finally, a chance to make her pay for what she did to your father, the chain reaction she set into motion.'

Her eyes flash, and I know I've struck a nerve. She tries to mask it, but I've known her too long. 'This isn't about me,' she snaps. 'Don't make it about me.'

'Then why are your hands shaking?' I ask, taking another step. 'Why does this feel like it's killing you as much as it's meant to kill me?'

For a moment, she's silent. Her eyes bore into mine. The others hold back. I know why. Her loyalty is being tested too. If she lets me escape, then there will always be questions about whether she still has what it takes, and if there's any question of doubt, she'll soon be standing where I am.

Her hand trembles as she raises the gun, her knuckles white against the grip. 'Stop talking, Sebastian. Just stop.'

I don't move, don't blink. 'I trained you to be better than this. To trust your instincts, your humanity. What happened to that Lauren?'

Her breath hitches, her finger hovering over the trigger. The others are watching, waiting for her to act. I see it in their shadows, feel it in the charged air.

'I--' Her voice cracks, and for a moment, I think she'll lower the gun. But then her jaw sets, her gaze hardening into something unrecognisable.

'You taught me to finish what I start,' she says, her voice hollow. And then the world erupts in a flash of light and sound.

Pain blossoms in my chest, hot and searing. My legs buckle, and I hit the ground hard, the impact rattling through me. Above, her face looms, pale and stricken, the gun still trembling in her hand.

As darkness creeps in, I see her, the girl she used to be underneath the soldier she's become. 'Lauren,' I choke out, blood pooling in my mouth. 'They lied to you.'

Chapter Fifty-One

Anna snatches a few moments' sleep, but it's fitful and in the end, she gives up. Instead, she turns on the laptop and searches for news articles about Thomas Greer. One catches her eye.

LOCAL CEO EXPOSED AS EMBEZZLER PLUNGES INTO MADNESS

The community reels from a string of crimes that have resulted in Thomas Greer, a once-respected CEO and community leader, being committed to the Greenwood Institute for the Criminally Insane. The scandal, which began as an investigative exposé in this very newspaper, has unravelled into a dark tale of corruption, violence and mental collapse.

The reputation of Thomas Greer, 47, took a devastating hit three months ago when this paper published a damning report revealing his embezzlement of over $1.2 billion in public funds from a range of government defence contracts. Investigators later confirmed that shell corporations under Greer's control held the offshore accounts where he siphoned the funds.

With the legal proceedings approaching, Greer's behaviour became erratic. Friends and family described him as paranoid and despondent, frequently claiming he was the victim of a conspiracy. Last week, this paranoia erupted into unspeakable violence.

Authorities were called to the Greer residence after neighbours reported hearing screams. Inside, they discovered someone had stabbed Greer's 45-year-old wife, Margaret, multiple times. Authorities found Greer in the same room, unconscious from a self-inflicted gunshot wound to the chest. A note discovered nearby contained a rambling diatribe about betrayal and revenge.

Margaret Greer, remembered by friends as a kind and dedicated mother, had been urging her husband to cooperate with investigators. Their daughter is serving with the Australian Defence Force and has been recalled from duty.

Greer survived his suicide attempt but was declared incompetent to stand trial after a psychiatric evaluation determined he suffered from severe psychosis and was to be remanded to the Greenwood Institute for treatment and supervision, citing concerns for both his safety and that of the public.

Margaret Greer's funeral is scheduled for later this week, with hundreds expected to attend. The family has requested privacy during this painful time.

Underneath the article is a picture of Margaret Greer hugging her daughter Lauren, dressed in her defence forces uniform. Now she recognises the female hunter.

Anna didn't know who she was at first. Another stranger stepping into the newsroom, angry and out of place. Lauren had a presence about her, though, enough to make every seasoned reporter in the room glance up from their screens. She wasn't dressed for a job interview. Her combat boots scuffed the linoleum, and her eyes, sharp and piercing, scanning the room. When they land on her, Anna feels a shot of adrenaline spike.

'Anna Levesque?' she asks, her voice low but steady, as if testing the weight of her name in her mouth.

Anna stands, heart pounding. 'That's me.'

She closes the distance between them with measured steps. Up close, Anna sees the tension in her jaw, the way her hands flex at her sides as though forcing herself to stay calm. There's something weathered about her, as if life had tried to grind her down and failed, but her demeanour suggests it was a close call.

'I'm Lauren Greer,' she says. 'You wrote a story about my father.'

The room tilts for a moment. Anna had spent weeks poring over court documents, police reports and interviews, piecing together the tragic puzzle of the Greer family. She knew Lauren's name, her face from old photos, her role in the military overseas when her family imploded. But standing in front of her now, she realised how little she knew.

'Lauren,' Anna says, trying to keep her voice steady. 'I didn't think...'

'That I'd show up?' she cut Anna off, her eyes narrowing. 'That I'd want answers? Or that I'd even exist outside of your article?' she reached into her jacket pocket and pulled out a folded newspaper, slapping it onto Anna's desk. 'You didn't think at all.'

Her words hit harder than Anna expected. Anna glances down at the article, the headline staring back at her like: Embezzlement, Tragedy and the Fallout.

'You're thorough, I'll give you that,' Lauren continues. 'You covered it all. How the investigation ruined him, the pressure broke him. How he snapped and murdered my mother. You wrote about his breakdown, his guilt, his failed suicide. Did you even think what dragging all this shit up would do to me, my family?'

'I...,' Anna hesitated; the words caught in her throat. 'I didn't mean to hurt you.'

Anna flinched at Lauren's laugh, a sharp, bitter sound. 'Didn't mean to? You dragged my family's name back into the spotlight, dug up every terrible thing, and plastered it across the front page, again!'

Anna remembers now what Marcus said, *they don't kill you; they destroy you*. She knows the story about Aaron Dupree is fiction. The information about his suicide and she suspects the information discrediting his reputation is too. If the story about Aaron is fiction, and she suspects the story about Victor was also a plant, what if the story about Thomas Greer was fiction too? She had destroyed two careers and the lives of those they love. She can feel her face flush. They had used her, and she had been so blinded by her own ego and ambition that she let them.

She has the address of Aaron's widow. She might help, if for no other reason than to clear Aaron's name. It also dawns on her that his address is not in her devices' no-go zones.

She scribbles down directions in her notebook, and according to the maps, it should take a little over an hour for her to walk there from where she is to the GPS coordinates in Annerley. She shuts down the laptop to conserve the battery, unsure where her next charge will come from.

The city sleeps at this hour. Its streets are quiet, save for the occasional groan of a car engine or the faint clatter of metal cans being kicked. Anna keeps her head down and her steps measured.

Searching for peace, her fingers brush the edge of the pistol in her pocket. Her body aches from a restless night of half-sleep in the alley, but the adrenaline coursing through her veins keeps her moving. She glances over her shoulder, scanning the shadows. The hunters are out there somewhere. She can feel it.

The streets she used to feel so comfortable tramping have taken on a sinister edge, every corner harbouring potential danger. A shadow cast by the flickering streetlight above a pawnshop distorts the graffiti-defaced walls into looming threats.

She reaches an intersection. The muted blare of a distant siren cuts through the stillness. The smell of garbage and petrol mingles in the air, heavy and acrid. Anna turns left, drawn toward the faint glow of a convenience store sign in the distance. Then she sees them.

Two figures emerge from the gloom, their silhouettes unmistakable. Hunters.

Their casual strides betray no urgency, but Anna's gut twists. She recognises them, the same men who had ransacked her storage locker yesterday. Their eyes lock on her. Anna's heart pounds in her chest. Her breath catches. She pivots and bolts down the nearest alley.

Her boots skid on the damp pavement, every slip an invitation for them to catch her. Behind her, their footsteps quickened, echoing. She dares not look back. Instead, she careens around a corner and stumbles into a narrow passageway, wedged between two crumbling brick buildings. The space is tight, reeking of mildew and decay.

A homeless man sits slumped against one wall; his belongings stuffed into a battered shopping cart. His face is a map of weariness, deep lines carving his hollow cheeks.

'Move!' Anna's voice cracks with desperation. He stirs, muttering something unintelligible as if she were a passing shadow.

A sharp voice cuts through the dark behind her. 'Stop right there,' one hunter barks.

The ominous click of a weapon being readied follows, loud as thunder in the enclosed space. Anna spins, her hand already on the grip of her pistol.

'Well, hi there,' the hunter drawls, stepping into the alley, savouring the chase. His partner flanks him, his weapon trained on her.

Anna tightens her grip, her finger brushing the trigger. Her pulse pounds in her ears. 'Stay back,' she warns, though her voice wavers.

The homeless man shifts his gaze, darting between Anna and the hunters, confusion etched on his weathered face. 'Hey, what's going on?'.

'Stay down!' Anna shouts, her focus splitting for a fatal second.

Too late. The second hunter shifts his weapon, aiming it at the man. Time seems to slow as Anna reacts on pure instinct. Her gun fires with a deafening roar, the recoil snapping through her arm. The shot echoes off the walls, drowning out everything around her.

The hunter staggers back, clutching his chest. His weapon slips from his grip, clattering to the ground as he collapses. Blood pours from his wound, dark and thick, pooling beneath him, staining the cracked concrete.

'Dammit!' the second hunter growls, diving for cover. His gunfire erupts, bullets ricocheting off the alley walls. Anna ducks instinctively, but a strangled cry pierces the chaos. She spins around in horror.

The homeless man crumples, a crimson stain blooming across his tattered shirt. He slumps to the ground.

'No!' Anna screams. Her hands tremble as she fires again, her shots going wide. The second hunter curses and retreats, his footsteps pounding into the distance until they are drowned out by sirens.

Anna's ears ring from the gunfire. Her breaths come in ragged gasps, her chest heaving as the scene settles around, a nightmare solidifying into reality.

She drops to her knees beside the homeless man, her hands hovering over his wound. Blood seeps into the cracks of the pavement, glistening under the faint light filtering through the alley. His pained eyes meet hers.

'I'm sorry,' Anna whispers, her voice barely audible. It cracks, raw with guilt. 'I'm so sorry.'

The man's gaze wavers, his breaths shallow and laboured. She bites her lip hard enough to draw blood; tears burn her eyes.

If only she had chosen another alley. If only she had been faster. If only...

His body goes still. The light in his eyes dims. Anna stares, her mind spiralling, replaying the moment over and over in an endless, suffocating loop.

Her stomach churns. She backs away, her hands shaking as she fumbles to shove her pistol back into the pocket of her jeans. The wail of sirens slices through her haze. They're coming.

Her body feels heavy, and every movement is difficult. She forces herself to her feet; every fibre of her being screams at her to flee. But the guilt doesn't let go. It clings to her.

Anna stumbles out of the alley, her legs moving on autopilot. The man's blood is on her hands, figuratively and literally.

Chapter Fifty-Two

She walks past shuttered store fronts conscious of her blood-covered hands tucked into her pockets. Can't risk someone seeing them and raising the alarm.

At the edge of a small park, a squat metal fountain rises from the concrete. She scans the shadows before she crouches down, twists the handle until a thin stream of water sputters out.

It's icy against her fingers. She rubs until her knuckles burn. The water turns pink and then clear. The icy wind stings her raw skin dry.

She pulls her arms tighter around her and sets off again as the sky softens to the grey early light of dawn. She has a goal. She can block out the pain in her back, the craving in her nerves, and now the stinging in her hands when she has something to direct all her focus towards. She puts one foot in front of the other, counting off the steps in her head, telling herself each step is closer to a new ally. Someone who can help.

Anna knocks on the heavy wooden door of the Dupree house, the sound echoing in the crisp morning air. Her eyes dart to the trimmed hedges and expansive driveway, scanning her surroundings. Someone could lurk in the shadows, waiting to report back. A chill runs down her spine.

The door creaks open, revealing a striking woman in her mid-thirties. Her sleek, tailored dress hugs her figure, and her makeup is applied with an artist's precision. Despite the early hour, Anna suspects Aaron's wife, a widow now, is perpetually photo-ready. Anna feels acutely aware of her own appearance: messy hair, scuffed sneakers, and the faint scent of sweat clinging to her. The woman's sharp gaze rakes over Anna, her lips tightening in veiled disgust.

'Can I help you?' the woman asks, her tone icy.

Anna forces herself to meet the woman's gaze. 'Yes, I'm sorry to call on you so early. I'm Anna Levesque.'

Recognition flickers across the woman's face, though her expression remains guarded. 'The reporter,' she states rather than asks.

'Yes,' Anna hesitates, then plunges ahead. 'I know your husband didn't commit suicide, I know he wasn't guilty of all those horrible things he's been accused of, but I need your help to prove it. I'm begging you. Please, let me in.'

Mrs. Dupree stares at Anna, her expression inscrutable, before she steps aside. 'Come in.'

The house is immaculate; every detail is a showcase of wealth and control. Floor-to-ceiling windows offering breathtaking views of the city skyline, and the air carries the perfume of fresh flowers arranged in flawless symmetry. A soft, classical tune drifts from hidden speakers, blending with the faint hum of the air conditioning.

Anna steps inside, aware of how out of place she looks. Her filthy clothes and tangled hair. Her stomach churns, and she fights the urge to shrink into herself.

She follows Mrs Dupree deeper into the house until they come to the door of a room, and she stands aside for Anna to enter. Inside the office, Anna takes in the brag wall. Mounted expensive frames of photographs with Aaron posing with Queensland's elite. Behind the desk, a tall man looks up. His silver hair combed to perfection and his tailored suit hinting at an important day ahead. His presence is as polished and formidable as the surroundings.

'This is Jeremy,' Mrs. Dupree says coolly. 'Aaron's chief of staff.'

Jeremy's sharp eyes flick to Mrs. Dupree, seeking an explanation.

'Jeremy oversees everything for Aaron,' she explains briskly. 'If you have relevant information, you should speak with him.' Without another word, she turns and disappears into the depths of the house.

Jeremy watches Mrs. Dupree retreat before turning his attention to Anna. His expression is neutral, but the tension in his jaw betrays his annoyance. 'How can I help you, Miss Levesque?' His voice is polite, but his tone makes it clear he'd rather be anywhere else.

Anna swallows hard. 'Aaron Dupree didn't kill himself.'

Jeremy arches an eyebrow. 'Really? And how do you know this?'

'Because I was there,' Anna blurts out.

'Excuse me?'

'I saw him die, and it wasn't in this house or by his own hand,' Anna says, her voice trembling with urgency. Jeremy's demeanour changes in an instant. He grabs her arm in a crushing grip, his face inches from hers. 'I don't know what you're playing at, but you'd better leave now. What exactly are you after?'

'I know that Aaron didn't kill himself!' she says again, wondering if he even heard her.

Jeremy's eyes narrow. 'Wait here.'

Jeremy steps out and closes the office door. She slumps into one of the leather chairs on one side of the office. She looks around, taking it all in. Something feels off. She sits straighter as her mind sifts through what she's seeing. Or, more importantly, what she's not.

If Aaron killed himself in this room as reported, why is there absolutely no evidence of a crime scene being established here. She can't imagine that it was cleaned up so quickly. She can hear muffled voices through the walls. Urgent and then, 'She's here, what do you want me to do?'

Anna moves before the last muffled syllable fades through the wall. Instinct takes over. She rises from the leather chair, her gaze sweeping the office again. No tape marks, no furniture shifts, no trace that a man died here. Not even a smudge on the carpet.

She crosses to the door.

Jeremy opens it at the same moment, nearly colliding with her. He startles, recovering too quickly. 'Leaving?' His attempt at a casual tone falls flat. 'I thought you said you had information about Aaron's death.'

'I was mistaken,' she sidesteps him.

He blocks her path, a subtle pivot, a tightening of his jaw he tries to hide. Anna pushes past him anyway, hard enough for him to lose his balance for half a second. It's enough for her to push past him.

She's in the hallway. Jeremy's footsteps snap behind her as she strides toward the foyer. She runs.

'Anna, wait,' Jeremy calls, closer now, breath uneven. She doesn't look back. Doesn't give him the satisfaction.

The front door swings open, cold air slicing through the thick hush of the house. She steps onto the porch. Gravel shifts under her feet as she takes the steps two at a time.

She reaches the gate before he reaches the threshold.

Only then does she glance back. Jeremy stands frozen in the doorway, hands half-lifted, as if unsure whether to follow or retreat.

Chapter Fifty-Three

Anna watches Victor as he approaches the apartment from her hiding spot across the street, her heart pounding hard enough to drown out the traffic. She's wedged into the shadowed recess of a boarded-up doorway, the cold brick pressing between her shoulder blades. From here, she can see everything, the stairwell, the flickering hallway light, the way Victor keeps glancing over his shoulder. He's late. Ten minutes late. And nothing about the street feels right.

She was supposed to meet him at eight. Those lost minutes scrape at her nerves. Maybe he'd been circling the block, trying to smoke her out. Or maybe someone had latched onto him, and he'd had to shake the tail before potentially exposing their plan.

Every movement sets her nerves on edge. The way he slows down to check his watch. The glance he throws over his shoulder, quick, too quick. Anna shifts her weight against the brick wall, forcing herself to stay hidden, scanning the street as he does. Nothing obvious. A jogger with earbuds. A delivery van idling two doors down. A man with a newspaper on the corner bench. Ordinarily forgettable, and yet, she considers, is exactly how they'd look if someone were watching. They would hide among the ordinary, careful not to appear out of place.

Victor reaches the apartment door and knocks. If he's nervous, it doesn't show.

The front door creaks open, and he disappears inside.

Anna watches until the jogger is out of sight and the delivery van drives off. Only when two kids and a dog join the newspaper man and they head towards the park does Anna cross the street.

She scans the street as she goes, her skin prickling with unease. When she slips into the building, the stairwell smells of damp concrete and something sour. She keeps her steps light, her ears straining for any sound out of place. Her pulse quickens as she approaches the apartment door. It's closed but not locked. Victor's way of letting her know it's clear. She pushes it open wide enough to slide inside, and he's already there, waiting.

The door clicks shut behind her. She slides the deadbolt into place. She exhales, finally letting herself take a full breath.

The dim space smells of sweaty socks and old cigarettes; the air is thick and stale. Her nose wrinkles as she scans the cramped room for exits, half expecting an ambush.

Victor sits on a saggy couch, a stained mug of coffee in his hand. The TV on the wall flickers with muted images, the sound drowned out by muffled voices arguing from the apartment next door.

'You're late,' he says, his voice gravelly from too little sleep.

Anna scans around the apartment, clothes strewn across mismatched furniture. Pots piled high in the rust-stained sink, and the flicker of movement in the corner makes her stomach churn. Cockroaches. She shifts with her paranoia prickling at the edge of her nerves. She wonders if Victor's friend is as fucked up as she is, given the similarity to her own apartment.

'I had to make sure I wasn't followed,' she mutters as she crosses her arms tightly over her chest. 'Are you sure this place is safe?' she peeks out from behind the closed blinds to see if anyone's watching.

'Safe enough,' he says as he stands and stretches. With a groan, he gestures towards a room at the back of the apartment. 'In here.'

Anna hesitates. Her fingers twitch at her sides. 'How do I know I can trust him?'

Victor snorts as he grabs his coffee and takes a sip. 'You don't. But I do, and unless you've got a better idea.'

She doesn't trust Victor, let alone a stranger. The memory of her lying about who she is and the role she played in destroying Victor's career still gnaws at her. She can't shake the fear that he will work it out and dare not imagine what he will do then.

She pushes the thought aside and moves toward the room, every step hesitant. A hunched man sits over a battered laptop on a rickety table. His fingers fly across the keyboard. He's younger than she had expected; his dark hair messy and his clothes rumpled. He mutters under his breath. 'This her?' he asks without looking up.

Victor leans against the doorway. 'Yeah, she has this thing in her neck and we wanna see if you can disable it somehow.'

The man looks up and now takes her in. She squirms under his close examination, aware of the stench of desperation and sweat clinging to her.

'I'm Jay, by the way,' he says when it's clear Victor has no intention of making introductions.

'Hi,' she says, but doesn't offer her name. If she tells Jay the truth, then she's exposed to Victor, and she doesn't need another lie to keep track of.

He watches her with unnerving intensity. 'Let's see it then,' he says bluntly.

Anna hesitates, and he chuckles. 'I don't need to touch you, come closer and turn your head.'

After a tense pause, Anna turns and tilts her head to the side and exposes her neck. He pulls out a kind of gizmo you'd more likely see on a science fiction TV show than in a dingy apartment in a Brisbane suburb. He puts it up against her neck. The cold makes her start.

'Stay still,' Jay growls.

The gizmo makes some beeping noises, and she wonders again whether she can trust either of them. He plugs the gizmo into his laptop and watches the screen. Lines of code spring to life, but none of it makes any sense to Anna, and Victor appears equally nonplussed.

'Well,' Victor asks after an age of watching Jay squint at the screen.

Jay talks in a language while English is foreign to Anna.

'Don't bamboozle me with your geek speak. Can you get it out or not?' she snaps.

Jay sits back and pushes up his glasses. 'There's no way I can get that out unless it's been disabled first. There's a claw thing inside it that if it's tampered with while it's active, it will basically starfish and cut anything it's close to, which I'm not sure where the carotid artery is but I'm assuming you don't want to take the risk.'

Jay leans back and steeples his fingers. 'This shit is beyond me, but I have a buddy that knows all about this cutting-edge stuff. Hell, I wouldn't be surprised if Q created it.'

'And you think your friend will help?'

Jay shrugs. 'Thing is I've been trying to reach him since Victor spoke to me last night but he's not answering. He does that sometimes so it's not unusual, but ...'

Then Anna thinks there are few names beginning with the letter Q. 'Is Q short for Quentin?' she asks.

Both look at her strangely, but Jay nods. 'Not that you should ever call him that. So, remember that if I manage to get him to agree to help you.'

'Quentin Thomasson?' she asks. Victor and Jay share a look, then Jay jumps up.

'Who the fuck is she,' Jay asks Victor?

'Why?'

'How do you know his name? Like his real name. You a cop?' he glares at Victor. 'A real cop?'

She shakes her head. Tears threaten as she chokes out. 'When did you last hear from him?'

'I was talking to him Friday morning, he said he was on his way to a funeral and that he'd call later.'

Anna nods.

Victor steps forward. 'What?'

Anna scrolls through the notifications on her smartwatch until she comes to the one from Quentin. She puts the watch in front of Jay and asks. 'Is this him?'

'What the fuck is this?' Jay asks.

'I'm afraid your friend is dead,' she says and chokes as she realises her hopes of getting the device disabled evaporate with the horrified look on Jay's face.

Her heart sinks. 'There's no point,' she cries.

Anna stands off to the side, leaning against the wall, her arms crossed over her chest.

Jay's voice cuts through the room. 'You didn't tell me it was this bad, Victor!' Jay yells, pacing the length of the room. His voice is raw, full of something that's more than anger. 'You told me it was risky. You told me to keep my head down. You didn't tell me my friend would end up dead because of it.'

'Jay, I...,' he starts, but Jay cuts him off with a sharp wave of his hand.

'No!' Jay's pacing quickens, his hands flexing open and closed. 'Don't you dare try to justify this. Don't tell me it's all part of a plan or you didn't know it would go this far. You knew. You knew what kind of people you're dealing with, and you dragged me into this mess anyway.'

Anna winces at the words, though they're not directed at her. The accusation in Jay's voice feels heavy in the room, and Anna can see it pressing on Victor, too. He exhales, running a hand through his hair.

'I didn't have a choice,' Victor says finally, his voice steady but quieter now. 'And neither do you.'

Anna doesn't miss the flicker of rage in Jay's eyes. 'That's bullshit,' he snaps. 'You had a choice when you came to me, Rourke. You had a choice when you showed up at my front door with your threats and insinuations. You could've let me walk away, but no, you had to rope me in, like I owe you something. Well newsflash for you, I don't.'

Victor's jaw tightens, and for a second Anna thinks he's going to fight back. But he doesn't. Instead, he says, 'I came to you because you're the best I know at what you do. Because I thought you would understand. This isn't about you and me, it's about Anna and if you don't help her, she's going to die, like your friend.'

Jay stops pacing, standing there with his hands clenched at his sides, breathing hard. 'I hope whatever you're trying to pull is worth it,' he says finally. 'Because if this goes south, Anna is not going to be the only one paying for it. We all will.' Jay holds up his hand. He takes a couple of deep breaths and then returns to the code on his screen.

Jay grabs her wrist and scrolls through all the options on the smartwatch.

'What are you doing?' she asks.

'There's always a way and if I know Q, he would've programmed in a back door. I have to find it.'

He alternates between scrolling on the watch and looking back at the code. 'We might have to get creative.'

Anna nods as her throat tightens.

Victor steps forward. 'But you can figure it out?'

'Sure,' Jay nods. 'But it's gonna take time.'

'Time is the one thing I don't have,' Anna spins on Victor, her fear and paranoia boiling over. 'Why are you even helping me? Do you even know who I am, what I did to you?'

'I worked it out hours ago, Anna,' he lets her real name hang in the air between them. 'But I also figured they played you like they played me. Now you have more to lose and I figure if I help you, that's my chance to clear my name. As much as I don't like that fact, it's a fact I can't change. So, what do you say?'

Anna stares at him. Her heart pounds. She wants to believe him. 'And if I don't make it?' she asks.

Victor's gaze hardens. 'Then you better damn well make sure you do.'

Anna swallows hard. Her paranoia simmers, but as much as she wants to walk away, she knows she doesn't have a choice. 'Fine,' she says. 'But what do I do now?'

Jay stands and collects his laptop and some other things, including two-way radios, and throws them into a leather satchel. 'Now that's sorted, we need to move.'

'Why?' Anna and Victor ask in unison.

'Because that thing transmits your GPS location every 10 minutes.'

Anna shakes her head. 'That can't be right. Whenever I get close to somewhere on the no-go zones, it goes off straight away.'

'Yep, because it's programmed to increase the frequency the closer you get to a no-go zone.'

'So, it's not transmitting all the time?'

'No,' Jay smiles. 'It's quite clever, really,' he says as he collects more things and puts them in the satchel already fit to burst. 'By limiting the frequency of the transmissions, it preserves the battery life, but that also gives us something to use to our advantage.'

'How?' Anna asks.

'I'll tell you in the car, but first here.' He hands them both a two-way radio each and tunes them all to the same channel. 'We can use these to communicate when we're separated.'

'Why would we be separated?' Anna asks.

'Too many reasons to list, but right now this thing has pinged these coordinates twice. On the third ping it's programmed to automatically do a search for the address, which means,' he looks at Victor, 'thanks to my criminal record, they'll know who I am and what I can do.'

'But the hunters don't get GPS data.'

Victor helps Jay collect what they need as Jay points to each item.

'You think they're going to play by the rules when they know you've got me helping you?' Jay checks his watch, then throws a set of car keys at her.

'What makes you so special?'

Jay stops and looks at her with a smile, then nods at Victor.

Victor nods his head. 'If they know he's helping, trust me, they will want to find you. With enough time and the right equipment, there's not a computer system invented he can't crack.'

Jay nods a mocking thank you, then turns back to her. 'Now you really need to move before that third ping goes off. Downstairs, in the car park, there's an orange Monaro. Drive it around the block which should reset the coordinates and then meet Victor and me out front. If you still have questions, you can ask them in the car when we've put some distance between us and the last ping that thing sent off.'

Chapter Fifty-Four

Anna races down the stairs. She's not a car person, but there's only one orange car in the car park. She races up to it and points the key fob at it. The hazard lights come on for a second to show it's unlocked. She climbs in. There's rubbish everywhere, and she gasps as she sees it's a manual transmission.

'Fuck.'

She learned to drive a manual a lifetime ago. She forces herself to think, puts the key in the ignition, and the car roars to life. She puts her foot on the clutch and puts the car in first, thankful he's parked so all she has to do is drive forward. She applies some gas and releases the clutch. She doesn't move, so she applies more gas, too much, and the engine screams with power.

She pulls her foot off and stalls the car. She looks up at the apartments to see if Victor and Jay are on their way down. They're not. She turns the key again and then remembers the handbrake, disengages it, and creeps the car forward. As she moves, she slips it into second gear. Slowly, she creeps out of the car park and straight into Sunday morning traffic. She crawls her way out, goes around the block and slips back into the car park. Relief floods through her as she sees Jay and Victor waiting for her. Victor pulls open the driver's side door and says, 'I'll drive before you blow up his engine.'

'Thanks,' she breathes as she climbs out and races around the other side of the car.

Jay jumps into the front passenger seat and tells her, 'Back seat and stay low. That way you won't get picked up on traffic cameras.'

She climbs in and pushes clothes and food wrappers along the seat. 'You think they can access traffic cameras?'

'I'd be stunned if they're not,' Jay says.

Victor pulls the car back into traffic.

'Give me your mobile,' Jay asks as he holds out his hand. There's a moment of pause and a look of distrust between the two of them. But then Victor reaches into his pocket and passes his phone to Jay, who disables the location data and hands it back.

'Turn it off for now and only turn it on when you absolutely have to.' Jay looks over his shoulder at Anna. 'And yours?'

'I don't have one with me,' she says.

Jay looks at Victor, questioning her truthfulness. 'She doesn't,' Victor says. Jay looks over at her as if trying to work out if she's lying to them both, but then he turns back, satisfied she's telling the truth. He pulls his laptop out of his satchel and fires it up.

'So, what now?' Anna asks. 'We drive around all day.'

Jay snorts. 'Like I've got fuel money for that. Do you?'

She shakes her head, and they both look at Victor.

'I'm on the bones of my ass too,' he says.

Jay digs out his wallet and pulls out his Go-Card. He leans back and hands it to Anna.

'Take this.'

She looks at him.

'OK,' he says. 'Here's what I'm thinking. We're going to have to split up.'

'No,' Anna cries as panic grips her.

'Let me finish,' Jay says. 'We don't want them to associate our digital trail with yours. With the location data turned off on the mobiles, and if we keep the mobiles turned off until we need them, that should limit how much of a digital footprint we leave behind. This car doesn't have GPS...'

'Or air conditioning,' Victor gripes.

'Beggars and all that,' Jay says. 'Because there's no GPS, they can't track me through this either, other than if I go through traffic camera's so we need to get out of the city and off the main roads as soon as we can. We use two-ways to stay connected.'

Anna nods, relieved. Even though they are splitting up, she doesn't feel so alone in all this anymore.

'In the meantime, I'm going to find somewhere to hold up and see if I can't find Q's back door to this code.'

'And what about us?' Anna asks.

'Stay out of sight, ride the buses and trains, go to shopping centres with free Wi-Fi, but don't stay in one place more than 30 minutes.'

Jay looks at Victor and tells him. 'Head for Roma Street and Anna, when we get close, you get ready to jump out.'

She nods.

'Any joy with that notebook?' Victor asks.

She'd forgotten. She fills them in on what she's discovered about the code and the coordinates.

Jay hands her his phone. 'Take pictures of your notes, the coordinates, and use my phone to hot spot a connection to that chat room.'

'And' she asks.

'Then take as many screen shots as you can of those messages, starting with the latest, and work your way backwards.'

Anna scrambles to do what Jay asks.

'Send pictures to Victor from my phone while I'm trying to get into this code. Victor, you pinpoint where all these locations are and see if you can decipher anymore of that code they're using.'

Jay turns around to Anna. 'You research the people that they've killed already. Wow, there's a sentence I never thought I'd say. Anyway, if we can find out what they all have in common, we might find out who's behind this.'

'But what if they work out what I'm doing?' she asks.

'If you ride the trains all day that will give you free wi-fi and some of the newer trains have USB ports you can use to charge the laptop.' He grabs Victor's laptop and checks the connection type, then rummages in his satchel for one that will do the job. 'It also means you'll be out of the heat and if you keep moving all day it will be harder for them to track you. Change trains and lines as often as you can so if they do work out what you are doing, it will be harder for them to predict which station to try and ambush you at.'

She nods, agreeing with the plan and relieved she now has one, for the time being at least. Jay looks around. Getting his bearings. 'We're coming up to Roma Street now.'

Victor slows as they come up to the passenger drop-off zone. Anna grabs her backpack and her notebook from Jay.

'Check in regularly,' Victor says, waving his two-way radio at her as she opens the passenger door. 'And stay alive.'

Chapter Fifty-Five

Havoc doesn't bother knocking. He shoulders the apartment door open with enough force that it bangs against the wall. The place is small, studio-style, cluttered, with every surface covered in the organised chaos only a coder finds comforting. Monitors glow in sleep mode. A bowl of half-eaten cereal has cemented itself to the counter. A hoodie lies draped over the back of a chair. But no Jay.

Havoc steps inside, scanning. Nothing looks overturned. No sign of a fight. No sign of movement at all.

'Jay?' he calls out, more out of formality than hope. His voice bounces off the narrow walls.

Silence.

He exhales through his nose, pulls out his phone, and hits Dingo's number. He taps the speaker and sets the phone on the desk beside the dark keyboard.

Dingo answers mid-sentence, probably barking orders at someone. 'You got him?'

'No one's here,' Havoc says. 'Place is empty. The place is a mess but not the kinda mess that says someone took him.'

Static crackles faintly on the line. Then Tristan's voice filters through from Dingo's end, quieter but tense. 'Check his workstation?'

Havoc taps a key. All three monitors blink awake, flooding the room with cold white light.

'Everything's locked,' Havoc says. 'No forced entry. No sign he left in a hurry either.'

Tristan exhales hard, the sound sharp through the speaker. 'Damn it.'

'He not answering you?' Havoc asks.

'No,' Tristan says. 'But I've got … other ways of reaching him.' A pause. 'We just have to hope he checks his messages before it's too late.'

Havoc turns toward the windows. The blinds are half-drawn, city lights slicing through them. Anyone could've been watching this place for days.

'Level with me,' Havoc says. 'Any chance the Watcher's people already found him?'

There's another beat of silence, this one longer, heavier. When Tristan speaks again, his voice is flat.

'It's possible.'

Dingo mutters something under his breath on the other end, something sharp and not fit for polite company. 'Can this guy even be trusted?'

Tristan hesitates. The pause is telling. 'I don't know.'

Havoc's jaw tightens. 'That's not a great start.'

'He was Quentin's friend,' Tristan says. 'Closest thing Quentin had to one. And Quentin trusted him with his life.'

'That ain't the same as trusting him with yours,' Havoc replies quietly.

Chapter Fifty-Six

The train is stifling, but it offers ample seating once it leaves the city. She fires up the laptop and connects to the free Wi-Fi.

She moves on to her research, and she notices Marcy was the recipient of a Thorncroft scholarship and then her job with SkyForge, another one of Thorncroft's companies. She does another search and discovers Quentin also was the recipient of a scholarship a few years later, and she wonders, as alumni of the program, whether they could have known each other.

She looks for social media accounts for both of them, but, other than LinkedIn, neither of them has any kind of social media presence; however, but LinkedIn has them as connections.

She's frustrated and getting into her research groove when she realises she has to change trains as she's reached the end of the line. At least with her movements planned for the day when she gets on the next train, she can get straight into what she needs to do. The more Anna thinks about it, the more her instincts tell her to start with Marcy. After all, the fact Watcher couldn't wait to eliminate her before she gave birth to her child suggests Marcy was a loose end they needed to tie up and quickly. But Marcy didn't seem to know anything; if she did, she didn't share it with Anna. Marcy's husband though, perhaps he got too close to something, and they assumed he shared it with Marcy.

She lets Jay and Victor know using the two-way what train she's on. Being on the move all day eases her mind a little. At each station, she uses the fountains to grab a drink and stay hydrated, but her stomach groans at her, reminding her she hasn't eaten, and the pain in her back gets worse as the day goes on.

Jay and Victor contact her later in the afternoon. They tell her they're going to pick her up at Runcorn, which is the next stop on the train she is on. She hopes this means they have worked out a way to disable the watch and the device. She waits and looks out for the orange car, and she starts when a black car pulls up beside her.

'Hey,' Victor calls out, and she races to the car and jumps into the back.

'What happened to the car?' she asks.

'Borrowed this one from a mate,' Jay says. 'The Monaro was too conspicuous.'

So now there's someone else who knows. The list of people knowing what's going on grows and grows, and so does Anna's anxiety that word will get out back to the Watcher and someone will betray her.

'So, what now? Were you able to hack this thing?' she points to her neck.

Jay shakes his head. 'Nah. Q managed to bury his back door really well, or didn't build one in.'

'So, what now?' she asks as her voice hitches.

'Now we consolidate what we know and get you out of cell service range.'

'How is that possible?'

'There's black spots,' Jay says. 'And we found one about thirty minutes away.'

'Then why the fuck have I been running all over the city all day?' she cries.

'Because no service means no Internet,' Jay replies sharply. 'You have to understand the thing in your neck is like a phone. You go out of service and it's like putting your phone in aeroplane mode. All the messages bank up. What that means,' Jay says, 'is that while you stay out of service range the watch won't talk to the device, but the minute you step back into range, all those messages are going to hit the device all at once and there won't be a damn thing we can do to stop them.'

She slumps back in the seat. 'So, what now?' she asks.

'We drive,' Victor says.

After a few moments' silence, Anna asks. 'What did you find out about the coordinates?'

Victor clears his throat. 'Some are private residences, but that tracks with what you thought about the locations of the people they took. Others are businesses.' He reaches into his pocket and pulls out some sheets of paper. 'Have a look through those, see if anything seems familiar.'

Anna takes the paper and reads the list. 'Nothing,' she says finally, weary from getting nowhere and having put two, maybe three, more people in the Watcher's crosshairs.

Chapter Fifty-Seven

The engine hums beneath the cracked dashboard. Anna focuses on what she's been able to learn so far and shares with Jay and Victor as they drive.

'Quentin Thomasson was a technology genius. His specialisation was covert surveillance and communications. His degree was paid for by a Thorncroft scholarship, and he went straight from uni to work for Aegis Defence Systems.'

'I could have told you that,' Jay says.

'I believe in being thorough,' she snaps back.

'Shame that didn't help me any,' Victor quips, and there's something in his tone that sets her on edge, but she ignores it.

'Marcy Lynch was an engineer. Drone technology, mainly. Again, big defence contractor with government contracts.'

'So, she may have known Q?' Jay asks.

Anna thinks back to when they were all together at the warehouse. She can't recall any sign anyone knew anyone else, except for Q and the T-dot, who she still doesn't know a name.

'I think it's someone high up in Aegis Defence Systems or SkyForge. Maybe more than one and maybe working together. I think if we could get to Thorncroft and tell him what's going on, maybe he can help. Maybe that's why I've got his name all through my notebooks.'

'Hold up,' Jay says. 'We've got activity on the chat board. SCARAB: The focus shifting fast, too quick to be walking and not on the rails. She must have found wheels.'

'Oh God,' Anna cries. 'They're talking about me.'

'ORACLE: Agreed, either she's got help or she stole a vehicle.'

Victor smirks. 'That's not gonna help them.' Then he looks at Jay. 'Your mate knows you've got his car, right?'

'Technically.'

'What the fuck does that mean?' Victor yells.

'It means he's out of the country and I have access to his keys.'

Victor lets out a long breath. 'But he's out of the country, so he's not likely to find out his car is missing.'

'Yeah, he's not due back until later tonight,' Jay shrugs.

'And if he catches an earlier flight?' Anna asks.

'Then we need to get off the grid before he activates the lo Jack.'

'For fucks sake,' Victor cries.

'What do the other messages say?' Anna asks, wanting to focus on what she can control, but her mind is a fog with rage.

'LIGHTHOUSE: Rook pull the logs. ROOK: On it. ROOK: Two hits that might fit. Late model sedan and a delivery truck. I'll get the GPS group to locate them. LIGHTHOUSE: then match it with the fog. SCARAB: I can get eyes on the ground. ROOK: she's not in either of them.'

Anna sees a sign for a truck stop. 'Can we stop and get some food?'

'We should keep moving,' Victor says.

'From the guy that probably had breakfast and lunch.'

'You know the human body can survive days without food,' he snaps.

'Well, if you want this body to stay alive long enough to clear your name, I suggest we stop.'

Victor swerves onto the off-ramp, cutting someone off in the process and receiving a blast from the other driver's horn. He pulls up and looks behind her.

'I need money, cash preferably,' she says as she holds out her hand.

Jay and Victor search their pockets, and between them, they cobble together $12.00.

Inside the service station, Anna goes straight for the medications. She can't get what she needs, but Panadol should at least take the edge off. She grabs the cheapest bottle of water she can find and a bag of chips, calculating she has maybe $0.10 to spare.

As she climbs back into the car, Jay says. 'There's been more messages.'

Victor peels the car out of the car park before she can even get her seat belt on.

'Hey,' she complains.

'Read her the message,' Victor growls at Jay.

'SCARAB: I can get eyes on the ground. LIGHTHOUSE: Give coordinates to the hunters and if she's got help, the hunters can deal with them. But I want her breathing. I need the cypher.'

'What cypher?' she says. 'I don't have any cypher. What the hell is the cypher?'

'We think it's code for information,' Jay says.

'Fuck,' Anna cringes.

'What?' Victor asks.

Anna tells him about Aaron's chief of staff and what happened when she spoke to him this morning.

'What the fuck, Anna? And you were worried we'd say the wrong thing to the wrong person.'

'I'm sorry, I didn't think, I never thought he...'

'Damn straight you didn't think.' Victor's hands grip the steering wheel tighter.

'Was his boss dirty?' Jay asks.

Anna takes a deep breath. 'Well, if you ignore what they're saying about him now...'

'Because that's probably the same brand of bullshit they used on me.' Victor snaps.

'Yes, probably,' Anna says. Victor's surliness is wearing her down. 'But before, he was spruiking changes to the CCC and police powers to fight corruption and gaining momentum. It looked like his Bill might pass.'

'So, he was a thorn in their side,' Jay says, then looks back at the laptop. 'We got another message. VANGUARD: understood. Hunters take out the weeds. But keep the garden intact. SCARAB: copy that. LIGHTHOUSE: And find me that missing package.'

'How far away are we from the dead zone?' she asks.

'Far enough,' Victor says as he plants his foot more firmly on the gas pedal.

'Don't speed, we don't want to get pulled over,' Anna warns.

Victor lets off the gas. Then, Anna says, 'Wait, if packages are the prey and he has GPS coordinates in these devices.' She taps the smartwatch. 'Why is one of them missing?'

Jay spins in his seat and looks at Anna. 'They found a way to disable the device.'

Victor watches her in the mirror. 'Who's left apart from you?'

'Marcus. Him I know, but I can't see Marcus having the skills to disable it.'

'How do you know him?' Victor asks.

'He was a source on a story about patient treatment in the Greenwood Mental health Institute.'

'Is that all?' Victor asks.

'What do you mean?' Anna asks.

Victor squirms for a second, then says, 'doesn't seem like the kinda story people get killed over or brakes cut.'

A thought slithers into Anna's mind. Had she told Victor about her brakes having been cut all those years ago? She replays her conversations over the last day with him. Nothing surfaces. She's sure she didn't tell him, so how would he know? Uncertainty coils in her chest. She forces it down. She thought she had been careful about what she shared with him. Besides, she tells herself, he might know from his cop days. She pushes the thought down; he's helping her now, and she can use all the help she can get.

'And the other?' Jay asks, redirecting the conversation.

'I only know his initial.'

'And that was?' Jay prompts impatiently.

'T.'

'Yes,' Jay punches the air.

'How does that help?' Victor asks.

'Did T look like he knew Q?' Jay asks Anna.

'Well, yes, actually they were trying to fashion weapons at the beginning. Working together.'

'Tristan.'

Victor looks across at Jay. 'So, this Tristan bloke has worked out how to disable the device.'

'If anyone can, it's Tris. He and Q went through uni together; they got this sweet deal on their fees and straight into a job. Tris knows Q's code better than anyone.'

'A Thorncroft Scholarship.' Anna asks.

Jay nods.

'But if no one can find him?' Anna says, confused about how this helps other than it's another link with Marcy.

'True, but it means it can be done and Tristan's worked out how.'

Jay pulls out his laptop and reexamines the code. The buzzing of Anna's smartwatch shatters the quiet of the car. Anna flinches, her fingers tremble as she glances at the screen. The message is brief and to the point.

I have Marcus pull over and surrender, and I'll spare him.

Her breath catches in her throat. The words blur before her eyes.

'What?' Victor asks.

'They have Marcus.'

'I'm so sorry,' Victor says as he watches her through the rear-view mirror.

'No, he's not dead.' she reads the message. 'They say they'll spare him if I pull over right now and surrender.'

She remembers the promise she made to Marcus to stay alive and expose the Watcher and the people behind him. Victor's grip tightens on the steering wheel and Anna's gaze flicks at him. She doesn't know who she can trust. She can't shake the feeling that something doesn't feel right.

Victor's voice breaks through. 'They're playing you, Anna,' he breathes. 'If you give them what they want, we'll all be dead.'

Anna can't respond. Her mouth feels dry. Her jumbled thoughts prevent her from forming anything coherent. Instead, she fumbles with the smartwatch. The trembling of her hands betrays her as she thinks about her reply. She navigates to the Let's Make a Deal button Marcy had shown her. But Marcy had made a deal and still ended up dead.

Perhaps she could make a deal to save all of them. Marcus, Victor and Jay. There is no right answer, no safe choice.

Jay watches her over his shoulder as Victor's eyes stay focused on the road ahead.

Marcus's face flashes in her mind. It's all her fault, and yet she has the chance to save him, and she's second-guessing herself. Can she let him die to expose them? But how many have already died because when she first had the chance to expose them, she didn't? She chose the easy way out then. What if his death means they get one step closer to ending the Watcher's reign of terror? It's what he said he wanted, to do whatever it takes to stop them, but did he really mean dying for it? And what about his wife? How could Anna possibly look Lucy in the eye knowing she had a chance to save him and didn't take it?

The smartwatch vibrates, and this time she can see masked men in an elegant office and Marcus, beaten and bloody but very much alive, bound to a chair near the floor to ceiling windows, the Brisbane skyline off in the distance.

A sharp gasp as she sees him, but she's not sure if they can see her, so she keeps her watch close so they can't, and more importantly? They can't see Jay or Victor.

'Choose quickly,' the man at the centre of the room says. 'And choose wisely. I'm running out of patience.'

She squeezes her eyes shut. She presses the fingers of her other hand against the cold glass of the window.

'Come on, Victor,' the man says. 'Talk some sense into her.'

Victor jolts and the car veers for a second. Before he rights its course.

'You think I hadn't worked out who was helping you?' the masked man says.

Victor reaches his hand behind her and sets it on her knee. 'Whatever you choose,' he whispers. 'I'll be with you.'

Marcus springs to his feet. He charges backward toward the window, and before any of the masked man can reach him, the glass of the window shatters. He screams, 'Thorncroft.' Those closest cower from the shower of glass as Marcus disappears from sight.

Anna screams.

'Turn that off,' the masked man screams, 'and someone contain the scene.'

The screen goes dark. Tears sting her eyes, but she blinks them back.

'What?' Victor and Jay both cry.

'He threw himself out the window. Marcus threw himself out of the window,' Anna sobs. The guilt floods through her, suffocating and bitter.

Victor's eyes catch hers in the mirror; the understanding is almost too much to bear. He doesn't speak. There's nothing more to say. Jay taps away on his phone, and Anna sits in the back seat.

'Christ,' Victor complains. 'Don't you know anyone whose car has air conditioning?' Anna sees his tattoo when he pushes up his sleeve. A blue flame. In some countries, people refer to the will-o'-the-wisp as the Whisperer. Anna looks down at her notes, the code names for the users. One of the code names on the message boards was Whisper.

She's sure it's her paranoia playing tricks on her, but at this stage, she can't risk it. If he is innocent and finds somewhere to hide, he can survive. If she keeps him with her and he's working with them, then he could expose everything they're trying to do.

'You have to pull over,' Anna cries.

'We can't,' Victor says. 'We don't have time.'

'I'm gonna throw up,' Anna says.

'She can't throw up in this car mate. Pull over,' Jay cries.

They pull over to the side of the road. Anna rushes out and finds her way into the bush and throws up. She takes deep breaths for a few minutes, as the thought that Victor might be one of the Hunters, or at the very least, working to help them, is more than she can bear. But if he is, the longer he's with her and Jay, the more he's going to learn and the more compromised they will get. But Victor introduced her to Jay, so is Jay compromised too? She recalls Jay's reaction to being dragged into this, and his anger and surprise seemed real, but what would she know. Her instincts have been off for a long time, and she's been running on fumes for the last few days.

'Well, I may as well take a piss then,' Victor says as he walks into the bush.

She watches the space where he walked into the bush, listening for him, for voices. For anything to give her a clue of what's going on. She thinks about Jay, but there has been a tension between Victor and Jay she can't put her finger on. If she has to choose between Victor or Jay, which she thinks she needs to, then Jay is better placed to help her with the technology. She walks around to the driver's side of the car and climbs in. Jay looks at her but says nothing. As Victor emerges from the bush, she starts the car and shouts through Jay's open window. 'Victor. You need to leave. You need to find safety until we can sort this out.'

'I'm not leaving you,' he says.

'I'm not giving you a choice. I've already bought too many people into this mess. They killed Marcus because of me; I couldn't stand it if they killed you too. And besides, this is Jays friend's car so he's going to need to get it back to him. I'm going to go to the dead zone and then I'm going to wait it out.'

Before Victor argues, she's pulling away. He races after her but is lost in a cloud of dust.

'You wanna tell me what that was about?' Jay asks.

'He's already in danger because of me. If they think I don't have help. If they don't know about you. Then maybe I have a chance.'

'So, kicking him out in the middle of nowhere was an idea?'

'Probably not one of my best if I'm honest.'

Anna squeezes the steering wheel tighter. 'I hope you know where this dead spot is.'

Jay nods, and they drive on in silence for a few moments. Then he chuckles. 'I'm actually a little bit pleased you chucked him out in the middle of nowhere. He's a prick. He didn't give me a choice about helping you. It was help you or he was gonna dob me in to the cops.'

'I'm sorry he did that to you, and I'm sorry I haven't cut you lose before they find out about you but, if I'm honest, I need you and as long as they don't know about you, then maybe you'll be OK. But if you want me to pull over and get out, I'll figure something out.'

Jay looks out the window, and Anna wonders what he's going to choose, and she hopes he agrees to stay with her a little longer.

'Can I have the list of those buildings?' Jay holds his hand out to Anna. She retrieves the scrap of paper. He compares the listing and counts the number of coordinates and buildings. 'We're one short,' he says.

'How?' She's thinking the why is not really relevant. 'Victor held one location back so it must be something important.' Jay taps on his keyboard, then after a few minutes' turns to Anna.

'Anna,' he says, 'Don't give up. Not yet. We still have options.'

'What options?'

'Because now we know where they hide. The one building Victor didn't include in his list matches the location where an ambulance has been dispatched for a guy falling from a window.'

Anna looks at the building.

'That's the Aegis Global Group headquarters. Have you any idea how many people work in that building?' she asks.

'A lot,' Jay smiles, seeming not to comprehend how a building with thirty-plus floors doesn't narrow it down. 'Unless they're going to go around and knock out more windows, there should only be one shattered or boarded up. I need you to find the nearest place that's open and has wi-fi and then you need to let me out. I have a few ideas on how to reach out to Tristan, but I can't do any of that from a dead zone, and if this works, I won't need the ride until later.'

Marcus

The cold leather of the chair presses into my back, but it's nothing compared to the cuffs. They bite into my wrists until my hands are numb. Thorncroft doesn't pace, doesn't fidget; he doesn't need to. He stands there, still as stone; his calm is more frightening than his fury.

'You went to Dupree,' he says, 'you lit this fire, don't think I don't know.'

Aaron Dupree. I can still see him. Outside the police station. On the steps. The air is thick and bitter. The device locked around Aaron's throat, and him clawing desperately as he tried to get it off. To breathe. Anna beside me. Frozen in horror as his body spasmed. The cleanup crew was on the scene in seconds.

Then, hours later, the news about how Aaron had committed suicide. Found in his office miles from where it actually happened. A neat lie tied with a bow. Another obstacle removed.

The chill running through me is deeper than fear. Anna wasn't the only one digging into this. Aaron had known too much or threatened too much. He had to be silenced. If Thorncroft can erase a man like Dupree, a sitting politician, what chance do they have, any of them?

For the first time, I wonder if I'm looking at the man who ordered my brother's murder. I had thought they were aiming for Anna, but what if the idea was to shut her up without drawing too much attention to the stories she was working on? What if they thought he was me?' It's not the first time I've wondered if I was the actual target but now I'm sure.

I force myself to swallow, to answer; my throat feels lined with sand. 'Five years ago,' I rasp, 'I spoke to Anna about Greenwood patient care. She dropped the story. That was it. I hadn't heard from her until a couple of days ago, when she reached out to me.'

I don't mention Greer. Better Thorncroft thinks I'm clinging onto old ghosts. Better not to let on how Anna might be a lot closer to the truth than he thinks.

He studies me in silence. He slips on a smooth porcelain mask with nothing on it but a painted smile. He pulls out a phone, not the one from his desk, so I'm assuming it's disposable, something untraceable. He taps out a message and then points it at me. I hear Anna gasp. He must be transmitting to her watch. I wonder if he thinks she hasn't worked it out yet, who he is and what he's been doing all these years, the manipulation, the murders. But what if she hasn't?

'Choose quickly and choose wisely,' Thorncroft says, voice smooth and casual. 'I'm running out of patience.'

He brings the camera closer to me. He's using me to get Anna to surrender. It's not me he's worried about; it's her.

'Come on Victor,' he drawls, mocking, 'talk some sense into her.'

The name slams into me. Victor Rourke. The story Anna did instead of the story I gave her. A cop, but he was chucked off the force. The sort of person he would use to get to Anna. I have to warn her, to tell her what I know, but I'm pretty sure I'll get one, maybe two words out at best, before his goons shut me up.

'You think I hadn't worked out who was helping you?' Thorncroft presses, voice flat, the mask mocking with its painted smile.

He knows because he set it up somehow. He's always three moves ahead. Anna says something, but I can't hear it. But I sense it, fear.

Then I know he's going to use me to get her to surrender, and then we'll both be dead, and he'll have what he wanted all along. She'll think she's saving me, but I already know too much. I've seen his face. I was dead the minute his goons grabbed me.

The thought cracks something inside me. My eyes lock on the window across the room, pale light glinting off the glass.

I'm tied to the kind of chair you might find in a cafeteria, hard plastic. They probably figure it's easier to clean and what damage can I do with a chair, especially when I'm tied to it. Then I realise, it's got four metal legs. If I charge the glass headfirst, I will probably bounce off. But if I go backwards, the four metal legs might break the glass if I hit it with enough force. It's the only thing I can think of to take myself out of the equation. Besides, if I succeed, he can't possibly explain my death away as an accident.

My pulse hammers. I brace my legs, stand and charge backwards with everything I have. His goons watch on stunned.

The chair smashes into the window.

Glass erupts with a deafening crack, shards spinning through the air. I scream his name, 'Thorncroft,' in a final effort to help her.

For a heartbeat, there's only the rush of wind against my skin, the world tipping away beneath me. I think of Lucy.

Chapter Fifty-Nine

The car wheels crunch over the dry gravel road, each shift in the terrain a muted reminder of how far off the beaten path Anna has driven. Despite the surrounding desolation, her smartwatch still clings to a faint signal.

Her mind churns in relentless loops, a distant, hollow gaze fixed on the empty stretch of road winding toward a barren horizon. Then the watch buzzes, jolting her out of the trance.

Marcus Alastair: Deceased. COD: Suicide.

Prey remaining: two. Hunters remaining: four.

Anna's stomach tightens. The occasional rustling of dry grass breaks the oppressive silence of the wasteland against the car's undercarriage and the faint hum of the engine. Outside, the sun-bleached earth stretches endlessly; skeletal trees claw at the sky.

Her fingers clench the steering wheel, white-knuckled, as she steals glances at the watch. The signal flickers and fades as she drives further into the brush, weaving through a maze of twists and turns, making it difficult for anyone to follow her. Finally, the watch shows no service.

The countdown, however, continues.

Her back throbs, the dull ache untouched by the painkillers she's taken.

Her chest feels tight. Is this all for nothing? A cruel joke of hope she's clung to. She believed she could expose them, believed she could fight back. But now, in the road's silence, the weight of her own hubris crushes her.

Her thoughts spiral. Every scenario she conjures ends in failure.

Then, the two-way radio crackles.

'Anna, are you there?' Jay's voice breaks through.

She grabs the receiver, her voice shaky. 'I'm here.'

'They have Victor.'

Anna's breath hitches. She sinks to the ground, clutching the radio. If she's mistaken about Victor, if he isn't working with them, she can't help but wonder whether they will spare him, and if they don't, another life to add to her body count.

'How do you know?'

'It's in the chat room,' Jay says, his voice tight. 'He might not have been working with them after all.'

Anna chokes back a sob. 'Or he's told them we know about the chat room and so we can't trust what's on there anymore. You have to stop. Before they find out about you, assuming he hasn't told them and if he has...'

'I'll worry about that if it happens, what are you going to do?'

She hesitates, staring at the lifeless horizon. 'I'm going to see my parents.'

Jay inhales. 'But...'

'Please,' she interrupts, her voice trembling.

Jay sighs. 'don't come out the way you went in.'

'Thank you,' she whispers.

Chapter Sixty

Jay has been sitting in the corner of the service-centre café for nearly an hour, nursing a cold coffee. The hum of traffic from the attached fuel station, the clatter of plates, the churn of the espresso machine. None of it registers. His focus is locked on the flickering screen of his laptop, using the free Wi-Fi and hoping he can stay under the radar.

He refreshes the board again.

Nothing.

He's about to give up with a new post appears. *Checking in on Katniss.*

'Of course,' Jay thinks. Quentin's favourite books were the Hunger Games series.

Jay's pulse spikes. Jay types a fast response, equally meaningless. *I prefer to call her Mocking jay.*

He sits back and sips his cold coffee and winces at the taste. The café's fluorescent lights buzz overhead. A toddler screams near the pastry case. Tyres crunch on the forecourt.

Then the reply. *How good was the Quarter Quell?*

Jay tunes the two-way to channel 75 because the Quarter Quell in the stories was the 75th games.

Static.

Then. 'Mocking Jay?' Tristan's voice coming through.

Jay exhales shakily. 'Here.'

'Always wished they'd included tributes from district 13,' Tristan says. District 13 served as an underground military base; from there, the rebellion in the books was orchestrated. He's letting him know he's found a safe place to hide.

'I prefer the tribute from District six,' Jay says. District 6 being the district associated with transportation to let Tristan know he's stranded.

'There's a tribute train you can catch, just need to know your district so you can join,' Tristan says.

Jay pulls up maps and gets the coordinates for his location. Then transposing the latitude and longitude, puts the coordinates into the message board.

'Girl on fire,' Tristan says.

'Just waiting for my turn in the parade,' Jay says, letting Tristan know he understands *Girl on Fire* means they are sending a ride and he'll stay put until they arrive.

He changes the channel on the two-way and tries to reach Anna. She's not responding.

Chapter Sixty-One

Anna climbs back into the car, her body heavy with exhaustion but her mind sharper now. She scans the watch. When the network reconnects, she can use the map to find her way home.

As the signal flickers back, she braces for the Watcher's retaliation, expecting the choking sensation signalling her time is up. Instead, the watch emits a sharp beep. Among the messages and warnings, she notices one in particular, *Warning Dose administered*.

Her stomach lurches. She has felt nothing, no constriction, no dizziness. Then another notification appears.

A twenty-four-hour time penalty applied. The hours on the watch drop from thirty-two to six.

'Fuck!' Anna screams, slamming the steering wheel. One more thing they hadn't mentioned. Talk about moving the goalposts. She pulls the car to a stop and jumps out, kicking and screaming, throwing a tantrum a toddler would be proud of. Finally spent, she climbs back into the car and pulls back onto the main road.

She turns the car toward her parents' house, tears blurring her vision. As the kilometres roll by, the ache in her back eases. Her mind races, unravelling the pieces.

And then it hits her.

She's angry with herself she hadn't worked it out sooner. They even informed them of the individual programming of the devices. Aaron was choked because how better to hide it than with a suicide. The details hadn't been clear in what she'd read, but now she realises they will have hung him. She's not sure about the others, but what better way to frame her death than as an overdose? She admits it's perfect, a plausible end for someone struggling with addiction.

'Oh my God,' she whispers, her hands trembling. All this time she'd been desperate for a fix, and it was right there all along.

She snatches up the two-way. 'Jay, are you there?'

When his voice crackles through, she can hear the rumble of a motorbike. 'I'm here.'

'I need you to do something for me,' Anna says, her voice steadying with purpose.

'Name it.'

'Call my parents. Tell them to have the Narcan ready.'

'What?'

'I have an idea,' she sends up a silent prayer her mother hadn't been bluffing when she made a big song and dance about carrying Narcan whenever she visited Anna because she never knew the condition in which she would find her.

'Okay, but I have news too.'

'Meet me at my parents' house and tell me when you get there. You have the address?'

Chapter Sixty-Two

Veronica sits at her desk, her fingers hovering over the keyboard. The weight of each keystroke presses down on her chest. The clock ticks in the background, reminding her that time is running out. The news of Marcus's death is out, and it's spreading. The questions have already surfaced, and Veronica can't afford to let them gain traction. Her phone buzzes, and she puts her earbuds in, all the while considering letting it ring out. But she knows the number. The Watcher. Letting it go to voicemail is not an option. She swallows, steadies herself and answers.

'Veronica,' The voice stops her cold. Not because of the distorter she expects, but because there is no distorter. She recognises his proper voice instantly. She wishes she didn't. Her suspicions weren't paranoia after all. And now she knows the truth, what does that mean for her?

'Yes,' she manages.

'I thought I told you to bury this story?'

'I'm trying,' she replies, forcing her voice to be steady.

'Fix it. I don't care how you do it. Just get it done.'

He hangs up. Nothing but dial tone fills her ears.

Her fingers a blur, crafting one misleading story after another. She glances at the screen as it refreshes, watching with a growing sense of urgency. The story about Marcus is still there, lingering at the top of the feed. She can feel pressure building; too many journalists are asking the right questions. Too many are digging deeper, seeing the strange circumstances of his death.

Veronica's throat tightens as she hits 'send' on yet another story. She floods the news cycle with irrelevant noise. Anything to keep the focus away from Marcus. The algorithms are benefiting her, pushing the story down as more distractions pour in.

But it's not enough. The story about Marcus keeps creeping back up, catching the eye of more journalists. The details don't add up. How did a man end up tied to a chair and thrown out of a window? The questions are becoming louder, harder to ignore. The story refuses to sink into the oblivion of white noise she's throwing at it.

Her fingers hover over the keyboard again, hesitation creeping in. She knows what she's doing, planting fake news, spreading disinformation, but it's necessary. The truth about Marcus's death could unravel everything. The web of lies she's constructed for Thorncroft over the years could come crashing down, and she can't afford it, especially now that she knows who he is. To Thorncroft, failure has only one outcome.

The sound of her fingers tapping on the keyboard fills the room. She pauses, watching the screen as new headlines appear: Fake news about Marcus's death debunked. Conspiracy theories circulate; don't believe the hype. It's all part of the plan, but the nagging feeling in her chest won't go away.

She refreshes the feed and watches the algorithms work to bury the story. More distractions flood in, celebrity gossip, viral videos, pointless debates. Anything to keep the world looking away. But it's not enough; the story about Marcus is still there, lingering at the bottom of the page, refusing to be silenced. Veronica's stomach churns. The truth pushing through the cracks.

She stares at the screen, numb fingers hovering over the keyboard. It's no use. The story has taken on a life of its own. Every time she pushes it down, ten more posts appear, journalists threading connections the Watcher has had her bury or debunk. It's already viral.

She hears Thorncroft's voice in her head. *Fix it. I don't care how you do it. Just get it done.*

But there's no fixing this. Not anymore. Not when she's heard his actual voice. An icy stillness settles over her. She reaches for the bottom drawer of her desk and slides it open. The worn leather passport lies beneath a folder of old press badges.

She grabs her bag, shoving the passport inside. For a moment she hesitates. Keys, wallet and a phone she probably shouldn't take. Speed matters now. Any second he could call again. Worse, he could send someone.

Veronica opens the ride-share app with a shaking thumb. **Destination: Airport. Pickup: Immediately.**

Chapter Sixty-Three

The watch buzzes again, the sharp vibration pulling Anna back into the present moment. Her heart is hammering in her chest, her pulse racing as the countdown ticks down. She knows what's coming. Her mother's voice rings in her ears, the stern warning about the Narcan always ready to be used, and it echoes through her mind now, louder than ever.

I just need to know you're safe, her mother said. There'd been no accusation in her tone, only a quiet, exhausted understanding Anna might slip again.

Anna had scoffed, waving off the fear as if it were smoke she could simply waft away. Rolling her eyes, performing boredom like a shield. *Paranoia,* she'd muttered, grabbing her coat and brushing past the doorway before her mother could reply. But she'd caught the way her mother's shoulders dipped, as if Anna's dismissal had landed exactly where all the others had.

Now, with the weight of the Watcher's actions pressing down on her, the Narcan is the only lifeline she has left.

She glances at the screen of her smartwatch, the words *Proximity alert* flashing before her eyes. Her stomach turns, the knot in her gut tightening with each passing second. The Watcher is getting closer, and once they have the information they want, they'll stop at nothing to silence her. She knows it, feels it deep in her bones. They will administer the lethal dose, no matter what she's done. She can't outrun them. The only thing she can do now is survive long enough to expose them.

The thought of her family, of her parents, and of the risk to their safety weighs on her. What she's about to do will drag them into this world of secrets and danger. If she cannot expose the Watcher, they'll be in even greater danger. The thought of her parents, especially her mother, who has already been through so much, paying the price for her recklessness is almost too much to bear.

Her hands shake as she grips the steering wheel, pressing her foot down harder on the gas. The car speeds down the narrow, winding driveway of their semi-rural property, the familiar sight of the house in the distance doing little to ease her anxiety. She pulls the car to a stop short of the porch; the gravel crunching beneath the tires as she throws it into park.

Her parents are already standing on the porch, both of them watching her with a mix of concern and confusion. Worry etches her mother's face; her hands are clasped in front of her, while her father, standing behind, crosses his arms. Anna's breath catches in her throat as she steps out of the car. The cool air bites at her skin, but it does nothing to cool the fire of fear burning in her chest.

The smartwatch buzzes again, and Anna's breath hitches. *Proximity breach imminent.*

A shudder runs through her, but she ignores it. There's no more time. Her legs move on autopilot as she rushes toward her mother, desperate for the moment of safety her arms offer.

'Mom,' she cries, her voice cracking as she hurls herself into her mother's embrace.

'Oh, Anna,' her mother's voice trembles as she pulls her into a tight hug. The warmth of her mother's body against hers is a fleeting comfort. Anna buries her face in her mother's shoulder, letting the familiar scent of lavender and vanilla soothe her for a moment.

But her mother's grip tightens around her, and Anna hears a shaky breath escape her.

'Anna, what have you done?' Her mother's voice is full of disbelief, tinged with pain, but also with something Anna can't quite place.

Anna pulls back, meeting her mother's gaze. The love and concern in her eyes are almost too much to bear. She wants to tell her the whole truth, to beg for forgiveness, but the words get caught in her throat.

The watch buzzes again, louder this time, and Anna can feel the panic rise within her. She looks down at the small screen, the message flashing: *Proximity breach*.

The Watcher has done exactly what she hoped they would.

The world around her seems to slow down. Her hands tremble, her breath comes in shallow gasps, and she stumbles backward. The last thing she hears is her mother's voice calling her name, her father's concerned shouting close behind.

Her last thought before the darkness takes over is a silent prayer, one she never thought she'd have to make. Please let this work.

Chapter Sixty-Four

The sound of rushing water echoes in the small bathroom as Anna steps under the shower, the heat washing away the grime of the last few days. Her fingers tremble as they work the shampoo into her hair. She smiles as she recalls regaining consciousness and seeing her parents' concerned faces. She had hugged them tight, told them what she could about the Watcher and what she's been through the last few days, and she could see they didn't believe her.

They had taken her inside, and she tried to explain, but the watch was now inactive. Or at least the screen no longer displayed the countdown. It looks the same as any other smartwatch. In the end, she declared she needed a shower, and that she was starving. Her mother's a feeder. Her mother didn't need telling twice as she rushed off to the kitchen.

Her father had huffed but didn't stand in her way.

She doesn't have much time. But there's not much she can do until Jay gets here. She can hear her mother now, clattering around in the kitchen, and her father's raised voice. 'How could she expect them to believe her?' But right now, she needs to feel normal. Especially since the Watcher thinks she's dead. But she still hasn't been able to take the watch off, and she can feel the lump in her neck.

She wipes the condensation off the mirror. Anna looks at her reflection. She swears she can still see a faint glow underneath the surface of her skin.

She emerges from the bathroom; the towel wrapped around her body. She ducks into her parents' bedroom; grateful she and her mother wear the same size. She grabs clean underwear, jeans and a t-shirt. As she closes the sliding wardrobe door, she sees her reflection. It's not the face of a woman hiding in alleyways and cowering in corners. She doesn't recognise herself anymore.

The woman in front of her is a killer. The hunter in the alley, Marcus. She may not have been responsible for his choice to throw himself out of the window, but she was the one responsible for his being there. She takes a deep breath and gets dressed.

She steps into the living room and her mother hands over a plate of steaming penne in a rich tomato sauce. Jasper sits in front of the picture window, and her parents take a seat, all eyes on her. She devours the food and wonders where the hell Jay is. He should have been here by now; and how long Jasper has been here.

Before Anna could even swallow the last bite, her mother snatches her plate away as if it were a potential weapon.

'We need to talk,' her father says.

Her father, already hardened from years of disappointment, stands, his voice low and forceful. 'This paranoia, it's the drugs talking, Anna. You're not seeing things clearly.'

'The drugs, huh?' The words are out before she can hold them back. 'Do you think I don't know the difference between fear and something I put in my body to escape the pain I'm living with every day. Everyone tells me is my addiction and not real and yet I feel it every fucking day. Some days it's so bad I can barely walk or get out of bed.'

She points a shaky finger at Jasper. 'You don't believe me either. I'm nothing but a liability to everyone. I've made a mess of everything and I'm sure you've all had enough.'

Jasper meets her gaze, but there's no warmth. There is only a stony expression. The one where he's heard all the excuses before. Anna's breath catches in her throat, but she presses on. She's angry with her parents for calling him and angrier still at him sitting there judging her. Sure, she's made mistakes. Who hasn't? It doesn't mean she deserves this.

'You remember the story about Greenwood. I know you do. I didn't abandon it because there was nothing to it. I walked away because it was too dangerous. Tell them,' she points at her parents while leaning close to Jasper's face.

Jasper remains tight-lipped.

'I picked it up again because you said if I didn't submit something good, you would fire me.'

Jasper looks down but remains silent as she paces the room.

'And now they're coming after me again, and this time they're not sending threats and cutting my brakes.'

Anna's mother gasps.

'Yeah,' Anna says, nodding toward Jasper. 'He didn't tell you that part, did he? This time they're killing people and I'm running out of time,' she drags a shaky hand through her hair. 'I know you don't believe me, fine! But you're the ones that are gonna have to live with it. Not believing me. Not helping me. With watching me die, right here in front of you because that's exactly how these bastards operate.'

She steps back, breath hitching. 'So, Sophie's choice, help me or don't. But if you don't, I won't see the morning.'

Secretly, she clings to the one thin hope she has left. If Watcher thinks she's dead, maybe he will finally leave her alone. But as long as this thing is in her neck, she will never be safe. The minute he finds out she's alive, he'll kill her. Her life will not be her own.

Anna chokes on her words, the reality of it all pressing down on her.

'Why should we believe you?' Anna's mother's voice cracks as she speaks.

The room falls silent, the tension thick enough to cut through. Anna's mouth goes dry. Her eyes sting with unshed tears, but she holds them back.

'I've done things I can't take back, and I know that. I've lied to you, stolen from you, used you, and taken advantage of your love for me. I know that, and I truly am sorry,' her voice trembles, but she forces herself to keep going.

'I shot a man today and I'm quite sure he's dead, but I didn't stick around to find out. Why would I lie about something like that?'

Her parents don't understand what's at stake; how could they? It's all too fantastic, and she's hardly given them any reason to trust anything she says over the last few years. She can see it in their eyes, the confusion, the disbelief. She's sure they think she's overreacting, the byproduct of a life spent chasing stories and pills.

The sound of a loud beep cuts through the thick air, making Anna jump. Jasper, sitting across from her, pulls out his phone without a second thought, his fingers moving to the notification. His expression shifts. Anna sees the change in his eyes before he even says anything, and it makes her stomach drop. His finger hesitates on the screen for a second too long.

Anna's father, ever the strict, no-nonsense type, glares at Jasper, the sharpness of his gaze enough to make even the most confident person hesitate. But Jasper doesn't look away. Instead, he scrolls, his brow furrowing as he reads whatever's caught his attention.

'What is it?' Anna asks; her voice sounds small and fragile.

Without a word, Jasper stands up, holding out his phone for them all to see. The screen lights up, and there, staring back at them, is a headline: Anna Levesque, 29, dead in suspected overdose.

Anna knew they would do this; how they can make so many murders look like tragic accidents or suicides. They cover up their murders using credible stories, and no one ever looks close enough to question them. Anna's addiction to OxyContin was the perfect narrative, a neat, logical explanation for why she died.

The room freezes. Anna watches her father, his face pale as he reads the article. The shock creeps into his features. Anna's mother doesn't move; her eyes wide, her hand trembling as she grips the edge of the couch.

'Now do you believe me?' Anna asks, the words more desperate than she intended.

Anna's parents exchange a horrified look between them as the reality of everything Anna has told them sinks in.

'Hi,' Jay says from the doorway to the lounge. 'Front door was open,' he says as casually as if he were dropping over to borrow a cup of sugar. 'It worked then.'

'Obviously,' Anna snaps. 'And where the hell have you been?'

'Had to make a couple of stops on the way,' he steps aside as Tristan and Lucy step into the room. 'I bought reinforcements,' he says as the room vibrates from the sound of many motorcycles. He then steps aside and waves for her to look outside the front door. An entire army of motorcycles and their riders fill her parents' front yard.

She looks at Tristan. 'Who are they?'

Lucy smiles, 'Family.'

Chapter Sixty-Five

The cramped living room feels suffocating, as if the very walls are pressing in, reminding Anna of how trapped they all are. Lucy sits beside her, clutching her purse, her hands trembling. She has said little since they began discussing Marcus, but Anna sees it in her eyes, the raw grief she's trying to bury.

Tristan's voice cuts through Anna's thoughts, 'I think this is my fault.'

Anna's mind races as she turns toward him. 'Wait, why?' she says, her voice barely above a whisper. She needs to make sense of this, to figure out how they got here, how things spiralled so far out of control.

'I knew Marcus,' Tristan says. 'I was the best man at his wedding. Thing is... This is my fault. We both knew Greer, Marcus as his carer, me as the person who made sure the thing in his neck didn't malfunction. Problem was, one day it did and for a while Greer was lucid. What he said made sense. We talked about how we could help him. Marcus went to you but then, well, we all know how that ended.'

A wave of nausea hits Anna, but she shakes it off. 'No, it's mine,' she interrupts, her voice tight as she fidgets with the notebook in her lap. Her fingers flip through the pages, scanning the scribbled notes, meaningless now compared to what they've uncovered. 'I should never have reached out to Marcus again.'

Tristan looks at her, his expression softening for a moment, but his words are heavy, as if the burden of everything he's said is too much for him to carry alone. 'I don't think that helped, but I think Jay and I may have figured out what this is really about. And it's not what you think.'

Anna's heart skips a beat. 'What then?' she asks, leaning forward, dread clawing at her throat.

Tristan takes a deep breath, his fingers tapping on the arm of the chair. 'I reached out to Aaron Dupree and told him there was something dodgy going on at Greenwood Institute,' he starts. 'I did it anonymously, but they must have thought it was Marcus.'

Tristan shakes his head, his expression darkening. 'Then Nathaniel started asking questions. Me and Quentin thought he wanted to catch up, but when Marcy wasn't with him, we knew something wasn't right, Nathaniel never met up with us without her, it was their way of keeping each other accountable, of not stepping into the other's space.'

'Nathaniel?' Anna murmurs, trying to keep up.

'Marcy's husband. Well, I hadn't seen Q in years, and you know how it is when you put two geeks together. We love to brag about the shit we're working on and Nathaniel, now I look back, was pushing us in that direction. Asking questions that at the time seemed casual but now I realise they weren't.'

Anna nods, urging him to continue.

'And?' she asks.

'And I thought these devices were for medication. But then Q tells me he's been working on weaponising them.'

She stares at Tristan, unable to comprehend what he's said. 'Wait. The arms thing?' she asks, her voice rising. 'There was a story, I saw it when I was looking into SkyForge,' she scrambles to grab her mother's phone from the table, hands shaking as she searches. She finds the article in seconds and begins reading aloud, her voice steady.

"*Defence giant faces scrutiny over arms deals with controversial regime and technology.*" She pauses, looking up at Tristan, her mind racing. "*Aegis Defence Systems, a leading supplier of advanced military technology, is under investigation for allegedly supplying modified medication delivery devices to a regime accused of human rights violations.*

Tristan nods, his face tight. ' I went to Dupree with this, and he said he'd look into it but Q and I weren't convinced Dupree could help. I just knew I had to do something. Q was working on a back door, a way to get into them without leaving a trace. The plan was to disable it in Greer without it looking like we had. He sent me a number the night we were all grabbed. It took me a while to crack into the software and find the line of code. I think it was supposed to be the back door, but I think Thorncroft found it first because all the line of code Q sent me to said, *nice try*.'

'What did Dupree think he could do?' Anna asks urgently.

'He said he had someone who might shed some light.'

Jay leans forward, his eyes serious. 'We think he was talking about his chief of staff.'

Anna feels a knot form in her stomach. 'But he's...,' she trails off, understanding the inevitable conclusion.

'Yeah, we know,' Tristan says, his voice tense. 'Turns out his chief of staff was the CFO of Aegis Defence when the shit went down with Greer.'

Anna's breath catches. 'Fuck.'

Jay leans in, his tone intense. 'It gets worse. Not long after the shit with Greer, he was promoted. They made him the CEO of VitalCare Biopharma, the same company that manages Greenwood.'

Anna's heart sinks. She grips the edge of the coffee table, knuckles white. 'Oh, crap,' she mutters. She darts her eyes to her notebook, where she'd written Thorncroft's name and the connection to VitalCare.

'I asked Thorncroft to set me up with an interview with Greer,' she whispers. 'A follow-up piece. I thought he could help because VitalCare is part of the Aegis Group.'

Tristan leans forward. 'That might have been what kicked this all off.'

The room spins. Anna's pulse races. 'Because he was worried I would find out,' she murmurs.

Tristan nods. 'Then when Marcus came to you about the patient maltreatment, he had no idea it was so much bigger than that.'

'Jonas?'

'Yeah, well,' Tristan sighs. 'We think the brother was a mistake. They thought he was Marcus.'

Anna swallows hard. 'And they thought I was on to the cover-up about Greer.'

Tristan and Jay exchange a glance. Tristan looks at Anna, his voice grave. 'There's something else.'

Anna steels herself. 'What?'

Jay leans forward, his face serious. 'Victor worked the Greer case.'

Anna exhales, her mind reeling. She straightens, determination flooding through her. 'You're the last man standing, as far as they're concerned, he's going to be throwing everything he's got at finding you, and I think we can use that to our advantage, throw him off his game.'

Chapter Sixty-Six

The silence of the car park wraps around Anna, suffocating the faint hum of distant traffic mixing with the occasional slam of car doors. It feels wrong, too still, as though everything is holding its breath in anticipation. The sharp edge of the evening air brushes against her skin, but it does little to calm the tightening in her chest. The morgue's looming silhouette casts an ominous shadow, sending a shiver down her spine.

'Remind me again why we're sitting in the car park of the morgue?' Anna's voice is clipped, barely masking the anxiety churning in her gut.

Jay glances at her, his jaw tightening with impatience. 'I've already explained this.'

Tristan, ever the calm one, offers a knowing smile. 'Creepy, huh?'

Anna's arms clasp across her chest, a protective gesture. 'We need them to think I'm dead. That part, I get. But it's the rest of it that's making me uneasy.'

Tristan leans forward, his voice lowering to a steady, almost soothing tone. 'Okay, one more time. I created a false record in the QAS system saying your body is being transported here. This buys us time. The device can only be deactivated from the principal computer with access to the system or the equipment, neither of which we have access to right now, so everything we do from here is about getting access to one or both and that starts with me disabling your GPS so they think you're in one of the morgue drawers.'

Anna gasps, trying to keep her composure. 'And then?'

'We need to get to Aegis. Find out whose office has the broken window. I suspect it's Thorncroft, which is why we have Plan B ready.'

Anna's eyebrows knit together. 'And Lucy knows what she's doing?'

'Lucy's got this,' Tristan reassures her with a slight grin. 'She's tougher than she looks. Once we get the laptop or the equipment, we can turn off the devices.'

Jay's voice cuts in, flat and pragmatic. 'Hopefully.'

The words gnaw at Anna's chest. 'And if we can't? If it triggers a fatal dose?'

Jay reaches into his jacket pocket and pulls out a small nasal spray, holding it up like a prize. 'Narcan. I told you I'd come prepared.'

Anna raises an eyebrow, suspicion creeping into her voice. 'How did you even get that?'

Jay's grin widens. 'Borrowed it.'

Anna narrows her eyes. 'Borrowed?'

'Relax,' he says, leaning back, his grin never wavering. 'You should be thanking me.'

Anna's lips press into a thin line. 'Fine. Let's hope we don't need it.'

'Let's hope,' Jay agrees, his voice more serious now.

Tristan checks his watch, the faint glow from the screen casting a cold light over his face. 'Time to go dark,' he announces. With a few clicks on his laptop, the icon for her wrist device flickers on the screen. The GPS symbol disappears, replaced by a line through it. 'Transmission off. Time to move,' he says.

Anna hesitates, her fingers gripping the edge of the car door. She's aware of how every second counts, but the thought of leaving the car park, leaving this moment of relative safety, fills her with dread.

'And Lauren?' Anna's voice softens, uncertainty creeping in as she thinks about Lauren. If anything, Lauren has been deceived more than anyone, but will she believe the truth when they expose it to her, or is she too far gone?

Tristan's jaw tightens, his gaze flickering with something akin to regret. 'She has to believe.'

Anna looks at him, sceptical. 'You really think she'll turn?'

Jay leans forward, his expression grim. 'If she learns what

Thorncroft and Jeremy did to her father, I think she might.'

Anna shakes her head, a troubled frown crossing her face. 'And if she turns you in?'

Tristan rubs the back of his neck. 'Then Plan B comes into play. And I hope to hell Lucy finds what we need before it's too late.'

Anna's gaze hardens as she processes the weight of their situation. 'Lucy's sure she knows where to find the leverage?'

Tristan nods, his face set. 'Yeah. But for the record, this is the part of the plan I'm least comfortable with.'

Her voice softens, but there's no mistaking the firmness in her tone. 'Neither am I. It's his only weak spot. But it's the only way I can think of to make sure they don't kill us all.'

Chapter Sixty-Seven

The Thorncroft estate looms above the Brisbane River, a fortress of glass walls gleaming under floodlights, hedges carved to perfection. To Lucy, it reeks of arrogance. Sensors hum faintly beneath the manicured lawns; guards pace in slow loops; cameras sweep every angle.

Lucy and Jay step out of the way so Dingo can do his thing.

Dingo signals, and the bikies, all close copies of their leader, move into position. A low, mechanical whine rises from the east garden, followed by a flare of light. Two guards pivot toward the distraction, the drone above shifting its path.

Jay crouches by the gate, Dingo watching his back, a compact device already in his hands. His fingers move quick and sure, teeth clenched as he murmurs under his breath. A soft click, then the gate stutters. The security light above it flickers once, twice, then dies. The gate slides open.

Lucy watches Dingo. He's calm, methodical, muscles coiled beneath leather. She and Jay move fast, flanked by the bikies. They sweep ahead. The bark of dogs and she holds her breath. Dingo is prepared. The recon he had sent ahead warned him of what they might face. The dogs go down first. A hiss, a yelp. Lucy gasps. Dingo turns and smiles. 'Tranqs. I heard you when you said no collateral damage.'

She nods. The gate closes behind them.

Inside, the estate is everything she expected and everything she hates. Marble floors reflecting the light, lemon oil clinging to polished wood, paintings heavy with money. No class.

She forces her jaw tight and keeps moving.

As they step into the kitchen, they see Thorncroft's wife bound and gagged. The other bikers having already dispatched the guards, her eyes fearful, no doubt for her daughter. Lucy wants to reassure her that her daughter won't be harmed if they cooperate, but fear is their weapon.

Jay stops as he takes in the security team, rounded up and restrained, pure hatred directed at one in particular. 'Say hi to Victor,' he says.

'I guess that answers that question,' she says.

Jay nods, and they move into the main house. A grand staircase leads to the upper floor, where they know the bedrooms are.

Together they climb the carpeted staircase, one biker in front, two behind, ready to counter anyone not already subdued. The daughter's bedroom is easy to spot. A white door covered in girlish stickers. It stands out from the rest of the house. The only character it's got.

As they approach, her chest tightens. Her throat stings. The kit bag strap cuts into her shoulder. Everything they need to sedate the daughter and monitor her vitals, none of it makes her feel any easier about what she's about to do.

Everyone moves aside for Lucy. Jay whispers, 'we'll cover you, but I doubt they have anyone in her room.'

Lucy nods, unable to speak. Her hand is already on the handle. She pushes, slow, steady, careful not to let the latch click.

The door opens into a young girl's sanctuary. Fairy lights twinkle; books lean against dolls on shelves. Posters of soccer stars adorn the walls. A rabbit night-light casts its soft glow. In the bed, the girl, asleep, thumb curled in her mouth.

Lucy's throat closes completely. She doesn't want this. God, she doesn't want to do this. But what she wants doesn't matter. She knows it's the only way. The child stirs.

Lucy kneels, whispering, 'sweetheart ... shh ... it's okay ...,' her voice trembles despite herself.

The girl blinks, voice foggy with sleep. 'What?'

Lucy forces a smile. 'I'm here to keep you safe. A little pinch, then you are going to have the best dreams.'

Her fingers shake as she uncaps the syringe. The sound of plastic splitting the seal feels deafening. The girl frowns, sensing something, and Lucy's heart lurches. She wants to stop, to throw the syringe across the room, to grab the child and run, but it would be more traumatising for the child, and she had only agreed to this if they minimised the trauma for this innocent little girl.

Jay's voice comes from the hall, clipped and urgent. 'Lucy, get on with it.'

Her breath hitches. She exhales through her nose, presses the needle into the girl's arm, and pushes the plunger slowly and steadily. The girl shifts, tries to move away, but Lucy knows the sedative will in a matter of seconds.

The child whimpers once, then falls back on her pillows, peaceful again.

Lucy brushes her hair back, whispering, 'I'm sorry.'

She tucks the blanket up to her chin, watching the girl's steady breathing makes her chest ache.

She stands, shoulders heavy with shame and resolve. Jays in the doorway, tense. 'We need to move her, they're not far now.'

Upon returning to the landing, Lucy agrees to move the kid. She watches as they gently carry the girl downstairs into Thorncroft's home office. They place her on the couch furthest from the door, and Jay applies a bandage to her neck, then slowly covers her with a blanket, leaving the bandage exposed.

The bikies move the captives, including Victor, into the guest house. Lucy leans into the mother as they walk her past. 'You stay quiet, and your daughter will stay safe. But if you make a sound ... if they' she points to the security guards, 'if they make a sound ...'

The woman nods. Lucy hates herself for the cruelty, but necessity drowns the hate. Thorncroft started all this a long time ago. He's been getting away with murder, and no-one's been able to stop him. No-one's even come close until now. But if they can't, she knows they'll all be dead by the time Thorncroft's done.

She's done her part; she nods to Jay for him to do his part now. She sits on the floor next to the sleeping child and pulls a stethoscope from her kit bag and checks the girl's breathing.

Chapter Sixty-Eight

The crowd outside the high-rise presses thick around Anna, faces tipped skyward toward the blank glass where Marcus fell. Police hold their cordon tight, radios crackling, paramedics crouch over what's left of Marcus beneath a sterile white sheet. Reporters jostle for position, microphones and cameras thrust forward, feeding on the chaos.

Anna slips into the fringe, careful, head down, letting herself be jostled. Her throat prickles where the collar of her jacket brushes the faint lump beneath her skin. She forces her breathing steady.

Through the glass wall above, she catches sight of him. Thorncroft, framed in his office, looking through the window at the scene below. He can't leave without people asking questions. The office Marcus fell from was identified as his. She imagines he's rehearsing his lines for detectives, rehearsing concern without guilt. And then he sees her.

Anna doesn't move at first. She lets him see her, framed against the ambulance lights. People shove past, but she holds her ground until his polished shoes emerge in the foyer. His men close in immediately, muttering into earpieces, but he waves them back with irritation. Too obvious. Too risky, with half of Brisbane's emergency services, journalists and other onlookers with way too many cameras watching. Anna tilts her chin, daring him to step closer. Then she turns, not running, but strolling into the nearest side street.

His jaw tightens. He turns sharply from the glass walls.

Anna feels the shift in the street, the current of attention. She edges closer to the police tape, another face in the crowd, until an officer shoves her back. She doesn't resist. She wants Thorncroft to see her slip sideways, threading herself into the chaos of uniforms and cameras, leaving a trail he can follow.

She keeps moving. Not away, not toward safety. Toward the street, thick with emergency vehicles, sirens wailing overhead. The noise covers her breath. The building's doors hiss open. Thorncroft emerges calm, immaculate, as if nothing had happened in his office. His men tighten formation, shielding him from the throng of journalists, but his eyes stay fixed on her.

Anna dips between ambulance crews, slowing enough for him to catch up, letting him believe he's hunting her. Every step is a dare. She wants to draw him out, wants him to follow her, but she doesn't want him to work out it's a trap.

For a moment, she loses sight of him in the flashing lights and the crowd. She has to allow him not to see her for a minute, to think she's gone, but not lose hope that he can never find her again. Then, the low growl of an engine cuts through the sirens, and there it is, the matte-black Harley on the curb. He's revving so loud someone in Thorncroft's crew has to notice. Havoc, Dingo's Sergeant at Arms, who Anna met less than an hour ago, smiles when he sees her and slips down his visor, although the truth is she knows he's been watching over her since they got here. She swings her leg over the back seat. He guns the throttle once, a warning to anyone close. Anna tugs her jacket tight, leans forward, and as the bike lunges into gridlocked traffic, she glances back, straight at Thorncroft.

Thorncroft's teeth set. He strides to the curb. His driver opens the sedan's rear door, but he ignores it, sliding into the front passenger seat instead. All this Anna watches through the mirror on Havoc's handlebars.

The Harley weaves between ambulances, slipping through gaps cars can't fit. Horns blare, officers shout, but the bike doesn't slow.

The sedan scrapes a bollard with a scream of metal as it pushes forward.

For half a block, Anna loses sight of him, and her chest tightens. She's about to tap Havoc on the shoulder to slow down, but then she catches the flash of his car in the mirrors, pushing hard through the crush of traffic.

The Harley ducks left, sliding past a truck, slipping onto the

Riverside Expressway. Anna turns her head. She wants him to be sure he's following the right bike, but the Harley is hard to miss. Even if you can't see it, you can hear it.

The Harley roars.

She watches Thorncroft in the mirror. He's so close she can see him lean forward in his seat. The chase takes them across the river, through Kangaroo Point and towards the cliffs. The Harley cuts gaps too tight for the sedan, but the sedan catches them. Twice she almost loses him; twice he finds her.

One minute the Harley is roaring through traffic, the next it jolts sideways, metal screaming across asphalt. Anna feels herself thrown, weightless, a blur of headlights and sky, before her shoulder slams into the road and knocks the air from her lungs.

Chapter Sixty-Nine

Tristan waits on the dark street. Jeremy's house sits squat and modern at the end of the cul-de-sac, with clean lines, too much glass, and manicured hedges. The place bought with dirty money, scrubbed to look legitimate.

The bikers fan out around him, five shadows moving with surprising quiet. Two slip through the side gate; one carries bolt cutters, the other a crowbar. A muted snap of metal, a soft grunt and the latch gives.

Tristan advances, keeping low, eyes scanning the darkened street.

A single shoulder slam from a man twice Tristan's weight blows the back door to the kitchen inward, wood splintering, hinges shrieking. Jeremy lurches up from his armchair in the lounge, eyes wide, but another biker is already on him. His knees hit the floor as he's dragged back. Thick hands pin his arms, leather creaking. Jeremy's breath hitches in shallow bursts.

Then Tristan steps in. He doesn't rush; he wants to capitalise on the chaos of the entry. He adjusts his glasses with one finger, laptop bag slung tight to his side, and his eyes lock on Jeremy.

'Good,' he says softly, voice flat, almost clinical. 'Now we can talk.'

'What do you want?' Jeremy pleads.

'Call her,' Tristan grabs the home phone from its cradle and puts in Jeremy's hands.

'Who?'

'Lauren Greer.'

Fear fills every crease of Jeremy's face as he shakes his head.

'You will call her,' Tristan says, voice low and steady.

'What do you want me to say?' Jeremy asks.

'The truth, someone has broken into your house, and you need help.'

'I can't, if I call Lauren, if I bring her here,' his Adam's apple bobs up and down as he swallows hard. 'She'll bring her team.'

'Counting on it.'

'They'll kill me.'

Tristan leans forward. 'And what do you think is going to happen if you don't? You are going to call her. You're going to get her to come over here, and when she walks through that door, you're going to tell her the truth about her father. If you're lucky, she'll kill you quickly, if you don't call her ...,' Tristan looks over to the biker nearest the door. He doesn't blink, cracks his knuckles slowly and deliberate.

Jeremy swallows hard. The biker next to him pushes the phone closer to his face.

Chapter Seventy

Anna's ears ring. The stink of fuel and scorched rubber fills her nose. Havoc is already scrambling up, dragging off his helmet with a curse. The Harley lies sparking against the barrier, wheels still spinning.

Anna forces herself onto her knees, lungs heaving, head whipping, because Thorncroft is already here. He had been closer behind than she had thought.

Doors open. His driver jumps out, scanning. Thorncroft doesn't hurry. He steps forward with the same calm mask he wore in the foyer.

'Stay back!' Anna screams suddenly, raw and panicked, her voice tearing through the night. She staggers toward the strangers who have spilled from nearby parks and cars, tightly clutching phones. 'Don't let him take me! Please.'

A woman in gym clothes reaches out to steady Anna. 'She needs an ambulance.'

Thorncroft is there at once, voice honeyed and authoritative. 'She's concussed. Shock,' his hand rests firm but gently on Anna's arm. 'I'll take her to the hospital myself, faster than waiting for emergency services.'

Anna thrashes against him, nails digging, voice ragged. 'No! Please help me, don't let him, he's lying.'

Two men glance uncertainly at each other. One mutters, 'Maybe we should call an ambulance.'

Thorncroft's smile doesn't falter, but steel threads his tone. 'I'm not waiting around here for every man and their dog to video this poor woman's predicament.'

He pulls Anna towards him. 'Come now,' he says, the model of composure, 'let's get you some help,' he looks over his shoulder. 'We best take her friend too,' he nods towards Havoc, who sits in the gutter with his head in his hands.

The driver hauls open the back door. Thorncroft guides Anna firmly toward it, her heels dragging. She kicks and flails. Her voice hoarse from screaming.

They push her in beside Havoc, who grips his ribs and touches at the blood running down his temple. The door slams shut. Outside, Thorncroft straightens his jacket, nods his thanks to the bewildered onlookers, then slips inside.

The locks click down. The sedan pulls away.

Inside, the silence is thick. Thorncroft adjusts his cuff, voice clipped. 'Too many police and the like hanging around the office, head to the house, use the under-croft entrance.'

Anna presses herself back into the leather seat, heart battering, every nerve screaming to claw at the door.

She turns to Havoc. His knuckles split; the road raked his cheek raw. 'Sorry,' Anna whispers, voice barely audible, 'about the bike.'

Chapter Seventy-One

They arrive fast. A black van crunches over gravel; four shapes in tactical black fatigues spill out. The team is inside the dark house quickly. The bikies melt from the shadows like wolves, and in seconds the kill team is on the ground, weapons kicked away, arms zip-tied, curses spat through clenched teeth. All but Lauren. She's restrained, one man on either side of her. Lauren thrashes, eyes burning. 'What the fuck Jeremy, I don't have time for this shit and who are these ...,' she stops when Tristan steps forward. She knows exactly who he is.

'You disabled the device.'

'I did,' he smiles.

'You know he's going to kill you anyway,' she looks at Jeremy, but all he can do is stare at the carpet.

'Talk' Tristan says.

'I can't,' Jeremy whispers.

Lauren jerks against the two men holding her.

Tristan leans in close, voice like a knife sliding between ribs. 'She thinks he stole billions of dollars. She thinks her father killed her mother. You and I both know that's not true. Tell her or I will.'

Jeremy's eyes flick to Lauren's. There's sweat beading on his forehead, dripping into his eyes. He shakes his head.

Tristan nods to one of the bikers with him. The biker steps forward and places a gun against Jeremy's ribs.

'The only reason you are not dead already is because she won't believe me when I tell her. But that's a chance I'm willing to take,' Tristan says, deadpan. 'If I have to.'

Jeremy's about to break. Tristan can see it in his eyes, pupils darting, skin slick with sweat, hands clawing at his own knees.

'Talk,' Tristan says, voice flat.

Jeremy shakes his head. 'She'll kill me.'

Lauren jerks at the men holding her, fury burning on her expression. 'What are you talking about? Jeremy, what the fuck.'

Her voice makes him flinch. He tries to look anywhere but at her, but her glare drags him back. His mouth opens and closes. Then the words come.

'It wasn't your father,' his voice is hoarse, barely audible. 'Greer didn't steal anything. The embezzlement was me. Me and Thorncroft.'

Lauren's body goes rigid.

Jeremy barrels on, words tripping over each other in his panic. 'We took the money. Billions. Thorncroft pocketed most, but I got a share. I tried to bring Greer in; told him he could profit too. He told me to go to hell. Said he'd report us. By then it was too late. The money was already gone, the trail already burned. Without him, we couldn't bury it, so, so Thorncroft made the call.'

Lauren leans forward as far as she can, but the bikers hold her firm. 'What call?'

The night is heavy with humidity and the faint smell of rain-soaked asphalt. The street is empty. Only the faint hum of distant traffic drifts through the neighbourhood, a lullaby for anyone else. Not for Sebastian.

He crouches behind the low brick wall across from the house, the black van parked a block away, engine off. Rook is beside him, rifle ready, breath steady in the night air. Two more of their team are ghosting through shadows along the side of the house, checking locks, windows and points of entry.

Sebastian glances at the house. Windows dark. Curtains drawn. No movement.

'Looks empty,' he murmurs.

'Doesn't mean shit,' Rook replies, low and clipped. 'Stay sharp.'

The team moves in silently. Doors unlocked, locks bypassed, shadows slipping over walls and through the garden. They fan out once inside, weapons up, eyes scanning. Every creak, every whisper of floorboard makes their pulses spike.

The living room is empty. Furniture in place. Pictures on the wall. A quiet house. Too quiet.

Sebastian signals a sweep upstairs. They climb carefully, boots barely whispering against polished hardwood. Rook leads, rifle poised.

A faint sound, a floorboard groaning under weight. Someone is coming down the staircase.

'Contact!' Rook hisses. He raises the rifle and fires.

The shot echoes through the house. A body collapses at the bottom of the stairs, the sound of impact sharp in the confined space.

Sebastian moves fast, checking the target. The dim light falls across her face, and the team freezes.

Not their target. Not the husband.

It's his wife.

She's staring up at them, wide-eyed, mouth open in shock. Blood is spreading across the carpet from where the bullet struck. Sebastian catches Rook's arm before he can shoot again.

'Wait,' Sebastian says, voice tight.

The woman writhes on the floor, hands pressed against the wound, panic radiating off her in waves. But there's no time. They have to complete the mission.

The husband pulls into the driveway moments later. Tires crunching over gravel. He parks, steps out, unaware of what's waiting inside.

Sebastian signals. A team member moves in with a syringe. One breath, one injection, and the man freezes mid-step. His pupils dilate. Confusion washes over his features. Then a sluggish, incoherent haze overtakes him. LSD. Enough to disorient him completely.

'Move,' Sebastian whispers.

They stage the scene fast. The woman's body positioned at the bottom of the stairs, spent cartridges nearby. The husband seated in the armchair, hands trembling, the weapon used wrapped in his hand. Their work is precise and methodical. Every detail calculated to make it look like he killed her, then tried to turn the gun on himself and failed.

Sebastian steps back, surveying the room. The living room is chaos wrapped in perfection: overturned furniture, the subtle signs of struggle, enough blood to be convincing, but not too much. Rook finishes tying up loose ends, wiping prints and footprints. Sebastian takes one last glance at the scene. His expression doesn't change, doesn't waver. Another job completed.

Outside, the black van hums quietly, ready to vanish into the night. Inside, the husband slumps in the armchair, dazed, incoherent, staring at the body of his wife.

Sebastian and the team slip into the shadows. The night swallows them whole.

Lauren's breath tears out of her in a ragged sound, something between a sob and a snarl.

Jeremy flinches. Tristan kicks him to let him know he's not done yet. 'Greer said he had enough to destroy us. Proof. Said if he died everything would go public. But no matter what he wouldn't tell us where it was, only that it would all come out and there would be nothing we could do about it. That's when Thorncroft came up with the plan.'

'What plan?' Lauren spits.

Jeremy's eyes finally meet hers, watery and full of terror. 'To make it look like he'd gone mad. To break him. They dosed him with LSD, enough to make him incoherent. They staged the scene; made it look like he'd killed his wife. Every photo, every report you saw, it was all bullshit.'

Lauren shakes her head violently. 'No, you're lying.' Her voice cracks, the certainty now a question. 'I saw the evidence, I saw it.'

Jeremy blurts desperately, 'Thorncroft made sure you saw it. He wanted you to hate Greer. Wanted to take advantage of everything you'd learned in the forces. When you came to him, broken and needing answers, he told you your father was a monster. He gave you a new purpose. He gave you a role model in Sebastian. He thought it was funny you should come to depend on the man who was responsible for your mother's death, the leader of the crew sent to silence your father. He wanted you to be his weapon. But you were also his warning to anyone that crossed him. He used you to eliminate any obstacle he faced and by God you're good at it. All that rage towards your father channelled into doing to other families, what he had done to yours.'

Lauren stares at him. Her chest heaving. Tears spill and finally the bikers let her go. Her glare is pure fire.

She steps over to the biker who has the gun on Jeremy. She wipes her eyes and holds out her hand for the gun. The biker is not sure but Tristan nods. 'You wanted the truth Lauren, you wanted it all those years ago and they lied to you, used you. They must have been laughing their asses off at what they turned you into. Question is, what are you going to do about it? But before you answer, I should tell you, I can get you into Greenwood.'

Chapter Seventy-Two

The sedan noses into the dark mouth of the undercroft, headlights flaring off polished concrete. The garage swallows them, the heavy door grinding down behind, cutting off the night and any chance of witnesses. Thorncroft exhales, shoulders loosening for the first time since the chase. Here in his stronghold, he feels safe. Hidden. Free to do whatever he wants.

Behind him, the roar of Havoc's motorbike being ridden by one of Thorncroft's men into the garage.

As Anna climbs out of the car, her pulse pounds so hard she can feel it in her fingertips.

The driver climbs out. Before Havoc can follow, Thorncroft taps the fob. The locks slam down, trapping him inside. The biker hurls himself at the glass, fists pounding, shoulders slamming the door, the whole car rocking under his rage. Thorncroft doesn't even look back.

Thorncroft turns to his driver. 'Fetch three from the team. Straight to my office. And tell my wife to stay out of the way, I don't need her crap right now.'

'Yes, sir.' The footsteps vanish into the service corridor.

Then Thorncroft seizes Anna's wrist, his grip iron. 'Where's the notebooks?' His voice is low, venomous, meant only for her. He drags her hand onto the polished desk, forcing her palm flat.

Before Anna can twist free, he pulls something from a drawer, cold steel flashing in the light. Vice grips. He opens them with a slow squeal of metal and clamps them over her smallest finger.

Through the car window she can see Havoc thrashing inside, his head slamming against the glass, fists pounding until the whole chassis shudders.

'Last chance,' Thorncroft murmurs, and closes the jaws.

Pain detonates. A crack, sharp and obscene. Fire shoots up her arm, and she jerks against his hold. Havoc bellows inside the car, a soundless snarl behind the glass. He kicks the driver's seat forward with such force that the horn blares, but the windows don't break.

'Where are the notebooks?' Thorncroft asks, calm as if reciting a grocery list.

Anna's eyes water. She shakes her head.

Thorncroft exhales through his nose, disappointed. The jaws of the tool open again and crawl to her next finger. Crack.

This time the scream rips out of Anna's throat. Havoc slams his shoulder into the passenger window hard enough to send spiderweb cracks skittering across the glass. He's roaring, every syllable drowned out.

'Where are the notebooks?'

Anna spits blood from biting her own lip. 'Not ... with me.'

He clamps again. Crack. Another finger ruined. Her vision swims, a hot wash of pain blurring the edges of the room. Havoc head-butts the glass until blood smears down the window. His fury shakes the car so violently that it rocks.

Thorncroft leans closer, lips grazing her ear. 'According to Victor, you haven't deciphered them anyway. All this, and you're still in the dark. Maybe I should kill you now and spare myself the trouble.'

Anna lets out a shaky laugh, wild and bitter, bubbling up despite the agony. She turns her head and meets his eyes with a glare. 'You think I was duped by Victor?' Her voice rasps but holds steady. 'Of course I deciphered them. And now anyone can read them.'

For the first time, Thorncroft's mask falters. A flicker, doubt creases his perfect composure. His hand tightens on the grips, then loosens. Anna glances at the window. Havoc is still there, chest heaving, bloodied face pressed to the cracked glass, his eyes blazing.

Every throb of her mangled hand is agony. And every throb is also a victory.

Thorncroft shoves Anna through the internal door and up the stairs, fury snapping at every movement. As they reach the landing, his phone vibrates. He almost ignores it until he sees the ID.

He yanks it to his ear.

'What.'

A panicked voice crackles through. 'Sir, the tracker. The missing package. It just went live again.'

Thorncroft stops dead. His fingers dig into Anna's arm.

'Where?' he hisses.

There's shuffling, frantic typing. 'Right now? It's ... uh ... it's ... sir, it's inside your house.'

Thorncroft steps into his office just as the words hit. His breath punches out of him. His eyes scan the shadows, the corners, the furniture, as though Tristan might be perched on the ceiling.

'In my house?' His voice is a thin, fraying thread. 'You're certain?'

'Yes, sir. The signal's strong, very strong. It's...'

Thorncroft hangs up. His pulse thunders visibly at his throat. For the first time, he looks rattled, not furious, not cruel, but *afraid*.

Which is when a quiet voice drifts from the corner.

'Funny thing about trackers,' Tristan says.

A cough sounds from the far side of the room, soft but deliberate. Thorncroft turns.

Lucy sits in the corner; his daughter's head pillowed against her shoulder. Sleeping, sedated, safe.

Something breaks on his face. Fear.

The doors bang wide. Havoc barrels in with Dingo and the bikies, shoving a first-aid kit at Lucy. 'Her hands,' Havoc growls, pointing at Anna.

Jay's voice is calm and lethal. 'We took the device out of Tristan's neck. And we put it in hers.'

Thorncroft stares at his daughter, his jaw hard, a vein ticking at his temple. For a moment, Anna swears he looks right through her, calculating, measuring. Then he barks a short laugh, brittle as glass.

'You're bluffing.'

The sound makes Anna's skin crawl. He turns his head enough to sneer at Jay, then at Tristan, then back at Lucy. 'You think I don't know how far you'll go? You'd risk a child? My child?' His mouth twists into something cruel. 'You've underestimated me.'

Tristan lifts a brow, shrugging. 'Repurposing. I'm big on

repurposing things.'

His gaze ticks deliberately to the sleeping child, then back to Thorncroft.

Thorncroft blanches. Sweat beads along his hairline.

Tristan continues, voice soft but pointed. 'One reason Nathaniel and I got along, we're environmentalists. We don't waste things. We reuse them. Adapt them. Repurpose them.'

Thorncroft's voice cracks. 'You put it in her?'

'Not me.' Tristan tilts his head toward Lucy. 'She's got steadier hands.'

Thorncroft's horror hardens into brittle rage. 'You're bluffing.'

'Am I?' Tristan gestures lazily at Thorncroft's own wrist. 'Check your device. But you'll need the laptop to make any adjustments. You know ... the one with your override codes.'

Thorncroft's jaw tightens. 'My office.'

Tristan gives him a sympathetic look, cutting deeper than any mockery. 'Yeah, about that. Shame you were in such a rush to leave.'

Panic flashes, real, naked panic.

Thorncroft tries to push past him anyway, but Havoc blocks the door with a single step. Thorncroft hits the wall of muscle and bounces, breath punching from his lungs.

Tristan watches him claw at control he no longer has, his expression unreadable. 'You're running out of time, Thorncroft. And for once, you don't get to decide the outcome.'

Thorncroft's shaking hand lifts to his daughter's bandaged neck. He doesn't touch her; Jay won't let him.

'Please,' he whispers, voice cracking like old plaster. 'Please, she's just a child.'

Lucy's eyes finally meet his, colder than winter stone.

'Then you should've thought of that, before you killed my husband.' she says.

'You think you can get away with this,' his bravado returning. 'I'll hunt you down, all of you. I will wipe you, your families, everyone that's ever known you from the face of the earth.'

Jay chuckles, 'I don't think so.' He points the remote at the television behind him. The television blazes into life, and Jeremy's voice fills the room:

'Thorncroft made sure you saw it. He wanted you to hate Greer. Wanted to take advantage of everything you'd learned in the forces. When you came to him, broken and needing answers, he told you your father was a monster.'

Thorncroft pales.

Jay doesn't answer. He raises the volume. Jeremy's voice cracks, spilling every damning detail.

'He gave you a new purpose. He gave you a role model in Sebastian. He thought it was funny you should come to depend on the man who was responsible for your mother's death, the leader of the crew sent to silence your father. He wanted you to be his weapon. But you were also his warning to anyone that crossed him.'

Jay turns down the volume.

Lucy doesn't flinch. She's crouched by Anna's side, hands steady as she splints what she can of the mangled fingers. Her tone is almost conversational, but there's steel underneath it. 'Are you willing to bet her life on it?' She doesn't look at Thorncroft. Her eyes stay on Anna, gentle but unwavering, while her head inclines toward the couch. 'Because that's exactly what you're doing right now.'

Anna looks at him. 'Think about the lengths you've gone to. To keep your crimes hidden. You think we didn't realise we'd have to stoop to your level to stop you. You think we wouldn't, that we're not capable.' She laughs, 'Please, the whole world knows how fucked up I am, thanks to you. But ask yourself this, if we knew that we'd have to swim in your cesspool of shit to bring you down, and we're all standing here, what do you think we decided?'

'She's a child,' he says, and the words aren't a threat, not even a deflection. They're pleading.

Lucy's hands don't stop moving. She presses a cool compress into Anna's palm, firm enough to make Anna hiss. 'Then save her,' Lucy says, calm as ice. 'The equipment. Where is it?'

Silence stretches. Thorncroft's throat works. He glances once more at his daughter, at the faint flutter of her breath, and for the first time his composure buckles.

Thorncroft's eyes dart between them, then to the child. His breath stutters. 'No. No, no I have the extraction device.'

Dingo's voice rumbles behind him as he enters with Havoc. 'Where?'

Thorncroft spins, eyes wild. 'The car, the boot of the car!'

Dingo nods to one of his men, who bolts out of the office to retrieve it.

Even then, he tries to rally, straightening his shoulders, forcing authority back into his tone. 'But if you let her ...'

Dingo steps closer, his shadow swallowing Thorncroft whole. 'Let her what? This is on you remember. Your device. Your timeline. You set this all in motion years ago when you killed Jonas. It was only when Marcus came to us, we finally worked out who was behind it, but he was never forgotten. That was your mistake. Not Anna, not Greer, Jonas. Fool, you not in charge anymore.'

Anna watches as Thorncroft's mouth opens, then shuts, as though every word he might throw is useless to save his own daughter. For the first time since she's known him, Thorncroft looks cornered.

The biker returns with the equipment; he hands it to Anna, who nods to Lucy. Except for Tristan, she's the only one who knows how to use it. She takes the equipment out, examines it to make sure it's not damaged and then reaches up to Anna and tilts her head to the side so she can get to the device cleanly.

Thorncroft screams, 'No, my daughter first.'

Lucy ignores him, her hands steady as she kneels beside Anna. Thorncroft lunges but Havoc and Dingo pin him, dragging him back.

The numbers bleed down. **01:54**.

Thorncroft thrashes against them. 'Stop wasting time! That's my daughter!' His voice cracks, panic splintering through.

Lucy slides the implant free of Anna's neck. Blood wells, but Anna barely feels it; her eyes are on Thorncroft.

The monitor ticks. **01:09.**

Thorncroft's breath comes fast and ragged. 'Please, please, she's a child! Take it out of her! I'll give you whatever you want!'

00:45.

Sweat beads on his temples. His knees sag, forcing Dingo to hold him upright. His mask, his armour, everything he's built crumbles second by second.

00:20.

His voice breaks into a scream. 'For God's sake!"

Lucy doesn't move. Her eyes are on him, cold and unyielding. 'Do you have any idea what it's like to have what you love the most ripped from you?' He watches her, but he's confused. 'Marcus. He was my husband.'

00:05.

Thorncroft squeezes his eyes shut. His lips move soundlessly. A prayer, maybe.

00:01.

The timer dies. The screen goes blank.

It feels as if the entire room is holding its breath. Lucy reaches the child and carefully removes the bandage from the child's neck. There is no device, no damage to her skin. The girl breathes on. Slow. Steady.

Thorncroft staggers forward, confusion and horror colliding on his face. He realises. They tricked him. He lunges for Anna, but Dingo sweeps his foot and takes Thorncroft's legs from under him. He face plants the floor.

More footsteps in the marble hallway approaching. Tristan enters, wheeling in a man with weary eyes but unbroken resolve. Greer. Alive. And behind them, Lauren.

The television flickers again. Jeremy's confession, already viral, unstoppable. Every news channel features it. Sirens wail faint in the distance.

Jay's voice cuts through the wreckage. 'It's over.'

The office is thick with silence. Thorncroft sags in his chair, hollowed out, staring at his daughter as she stirs faintly on Lucy's shoulder, unaware of how close she came to becoming a victim of his own weapon.

The sirens grow louder. Police drawing near. Jay checks his watch, his voice low: 'We don't have much time.'

Anna's throat aches. She glances at Dingo. 'You and your boys should go. Take anything that ties you here.'

Dingo nods. 'You should too.'

Lucy rises carefully, murmuring, 'I want her back in her bed. To wake up in the morning not knowing what happened. That was the deal.' Havoc scoops the child up gently, and together they slip from the office.

Anna looks at Lauren. 'What are you going to do with him?'

Lauren's jaw tightens. Her gaze never leaves Thorncroft. 'Exactly what he trained me to do.'

Movement at her side. Greer leans forward in his chair, every motion stiff with pain, but his eyes burn with something hard and old. His voice cracks but remains steady. 'No. Me.'

Jay crouches, offering him the pistol. Greer's hands shake violently as he takes it. The weight drags at his arms, years of rage and grief condensed into cold metal.

Lauren kneels beside him, her hand wrapping around his, steadying the trembling barrel. She doesn't say a word. She doesn't need to. Together they lift the gun until it points straight at Thorncroft.

Anna's heart pounds. She can't look away. Thorncroft doesn't beg, doesn't plead. He sits there, breathing shallow, eyes flicking between Greer and Lauren, realizing in these last moments all the control he spent a lifetime hoarding has gone.

Greer's finger hesitates on the trigger. The anguish surges through his face, his wife's death, the lies, the years stolen from his daughter. His jaw clenches. His breath rattles once, twice.

Anna races from the house, the roar of motorbikes dissipating through the night. At the front door, Havoc waits for her. As she swings her legs over the back of Havoc's bike, the crack of the gun reaches her ears.

Epilogue

The cabin stands in the forest's heart, secluded from the world. A secret buried beneath the towering pines. The air is thick with the scent of pine needles, damp earth and the faint sweetness of wildflowers blooming in the fields beyond the porch. The old wooden structure, though weathered and worn, is her sanctuary. Its faded blue exterior blending into the surrounding landscape. The roof slants slightly and sags in places; years of neglect softened the edges of a few cracked windows. But to Anna, this place is hers, carved out of the wilderness, a refuge from the world she once knew.

Greer took the blame for killing Thorncroft, but then everyone knew he was insane, so no story there. The actual story was about those who were under Thorncroft's control. Not only in Australia but across the globe. Politicians, senior government officials and bastions of industry.

The story they could only speculate about was Lauren and Anna. Both off the grid. Anna has already worked out that Lauren is systematically taking out Thorncroft's allies, beginning with those involved in framing her father. Sebastian had trained her well, and she left no discernible trace. But Anna knows. The accidental deaths, the sudden spate of suicides. The victims' names were once written in her notebook while she tried to piece it all together. Their deaths. Their stories she has no intention of exposing.

END

www.ingramcontent.com/pod-product-compliance
Lightning Source LLC
LaVergne TN
LVHW011810060526
838200LV00053B/3719